THE
KILLER
IN ME

An absolutely gripping and unputdownable
psychological thriller

MAX MANNING

Joffe Books, London
www.joffebooks.com

First published in Great Britain in 2022

Cover art by Nick Castle

ISBN: 978-1-80405-603-5

PROLOGUE

The girl wipes her tears with the back of her hand and steps off the pavement. She's in a hurry even though she doesn't have anywhere to go. She just needs to get away. As far away as possible.

Three steps to death. She doesn't see the car, or hear it. She's hurled into the air, arms and legs flailing like a ragdoll. Time slows. She feels as though she's floating.

She hits the road with a sickening crunch and rolls into the gutter. Numb with pain, she tries to get up but her body doesn't work. Her limbs too heavy.

She tries to lift her head, opens her mouth wide, but her scream is silent. Her face is wet. Blood running from her eyes, not tears.

The last thing she hears is a car engine revving. The last thing she sees is the brightest light, then she sinks into the blackest blackness.

CHAPTER 1

Liv

Waiting for bad news is agonizing. Hearing it is even worse. When the words you fear are spoken, you know your life will never be the same again.

The receptionist looks across to where I'm sitting. "The professor will see you now, Miss Miller."

As I stand, she nods, gives a half-hearted smile and returns to flipping casually through the pages of a glossy magazine. Her short dark hair and blue eyes make her a shinier, younger, slightly prettier version of me.

I grip the handle of the office door and glimpse my reflection in the tinted glass. I look confident, a woman in control. Inside, I'm trembling.

Professor Noble doesn't stand when I walk into the room. He greets me with an eyebrow flash, strokes his grey-flecked goatee and flicks his other hand in the direction of the chair on the other side of his desk.

I sit down and nod, my hands pressed against my fluttering stomach. It's only two weeks since I interviewed him for my magazine feature on his groundbreaking work scanning the brains of psychopaths.

It'd been my idea to have my brain scanned too. My editor had laughed when I first suggested it. He said he'd always thought I needed my head examined.

"Thank you for coming so promptly," the professor says.

I'd forgotten how his dark, solemn eyes never stop moving. He's an incredibly clever man but all that knowledge doesn't seem to have made him happy.

I don't know why he's thanking me. I'm only here because he asked me to come. *We need to discuss your brain scan,* his email said. *As soon as possible.*

I shift my position and cross my legs. I'm not normally an anxious person but dread sits heavy in my stomach.

"You asked me to come. Your email said it was urgent."

He rests his elbows on the desk and peers at me over his steepled fingers as if examining an interesting laboratory specimen. Fear tightens my throat, making my breathing shallow and ragged.

Lack of sleep always makes me agitated, and I spent most of last night running through a list of reasons for this meeting. *I'm so sorry to tell you this, but you have an incurable brain disease. You have a tumour in a part of your brain that can't be operated on. I'm afraid you're facing a long, slow death.*

Over the past few months, I've lost a bit of weight without trying and suffered a few dizzy spells, both symptoms I put down to delayed shock and lingering grief. Losing your little sister is going to take its toll, mentally and physically. Until the professor's email dropped into my inbox, I never imagined that I might actually be ill.

A bead of sweat trickles down the nape of my neck. I don't want to hear what I think I'm about to hear because once the words are said, they'll be true. At the same time, I'm desperate for this moment, this uncertainty, to be over.

"Please, professor. I'd appreciate it if you'd cut to the chase and tell me what's going on. The uncertainty is killing me."

Noble takes a deep breath and closes his eyes. They're shut for no more than a second but it feels a lot longer. He's probably finding the situation almost as difficult as I am, and I understand that. He's not a doctor. He's not used to telling people that they're seriously ill. He's an academic, a research scientist. He wears tweed jackets with elbow patches, for God's sake.

"Something unexpected has happened," he says. "I had my reservations, but agreed to scan your brain because you explained that adding a personal element would help readers relate to your article on our study."

He pauses, and I wonder why he's telling me something I already know. Publishing an image of a convicted killer's brain alongside mine would be the perfect way for the magazine to illustrate what the research was about.

Noble pulls at his beard and carries on. "One of my assistants was carrying out a routine check of the 'control' brain scans and came across one that . . . well, let's just say it surprised her."

"I take it that the brain was mine."

He holds up a hand and nods. "That's right, it was yours. Of course, she double-checked to make sure there hadn't been some kind of mix-up, but it was definitely yours."

The fluttering in my gut turns into full-blown, stomach-churning nausea. "It's a tumour, isn't it? Is it brain cancer? Why don't you just tell me what's going on?"

The professor gives me a nervous smile. The sound of my heart drumming fills my ears and I focus on his lips as he speaks because I don't want to see the pity in his eyes.

My mind whirls. I can't think straight. I'm trying to listen carefully but it's a struggle. I pick out certain words and phrases. The scary ones. "Abnormality . . . impaired function . . . grey matter damage . . ." When at last he stops talking, I let out a loud sigh. My mouth is dry and I swallow hard. Now I'm trembling on the outside too.

"I'm sorry, I don't really understand what you're saying. What exactly does this all mean?"

Noble reaches down to his right, pulls out a drawer and picks up a blue cardboard folder. He drops it onto the desk but doesn't open it.

"The images are all in here," he says, prodding the folder with his stubby, slightly ink-stained forefinger. "We wanted to make doubly sure there hadn't been an error before we said anything to you, and there is no doubt. I'm sorry."

I am too shocked to cry. My bones feel like they're melting and I have to fight to stay upright. "Why don't you stop all this bullshit, get on with it and tell me exactly what this means?"

The professor's eyes widen as he shrinks back in his chair. I see him wondering what has happened to the polite, attentive feature writer who doted on his every word.

He picks the folder up and waves it in the air. "Like I said, it's all in there. A selection of images from your scan and information you might find useful."

I open my mouth to speak, but clamp it shut before I can make a sound. Finally, I join the dots and the full picture emerges. Noble sees that I have guessed what's coming and only then does he summon up the courage to tell me everything. The whole truth.

It's not what I'd been expecting to hear and for a moment I'm dizzied by confusion. The room starts to spin and I grasp the edge of the chair with both hands to stop myself sliding off on to the floor.

He explains how damage to the frontal lobe of the brain affects personality and behaviour, but it's impossible for me to take it all in. He asks whether I have any questions and I stare back at him, my mouth hanging open.

I can't speak. I don't know how to react. What can you say when you've just been told that your brain has the structure and functionality of a classic psychopath?

CHAPTER 2

Liv

I feel lightheaded, as if the blood is draining from my body. It's a disturbing but familiar sensation. I had the same reaction when the police told me that Lottie had been killed.

Noble relaxes into his seat, looking relieved that he's broken the news and I haven't collapsed into a blubbering heap. That will probably come later. After the death of my sister, I cried myself to sleep for months. My tears became my best friend, my only source of comfort.

I'm waiting to be told not to worry too much, that everything is going to be all right. I'm desperate to hear that before I go. Besides, I'm not sure my shaking legs will keep me upright if I try to stand.

"Is that it, then? Is that all you have to say? At least tell me what I'm supposed to do now."

Noble tilts his head and shrugs. "I'm sorry. I really am. However, this doesn't have to be catastrophic. Now that you know the situation, it can be addressed."

I'm only half listening. My mind is busy recalling the details of our interview for my feature article. How the professor explained that scans of the brains of killers diagnosed as psychopaths typically show clear characteristics, abnormalities in the prefrontal cortex, especially a part called the amygdala. Both of these are what neuroscientists would describe as the social areas of the brain.

I'm desperate to ask whether this revelation about the structure of my brain means that I am a psychopath, or whether it's more that I have the potential to be one. I feel my stomach tighten at the thought that I have anything in common with the cold-blooded men and women the professor has spent most of his professional life studying. My mouth opens but the words stick in my throat. I can't ask the question because I'm too scared to hear the answer.

I've never claimed to be perfect. Considering everything I had to deal with as a child, I think I turned out to be a better person than even I expected. A woman comfortable in her own skin. Before I lost Lottie, I'd say I was happier than I ever imagined possible. Now this man is telling me that my brain is abnormal and that I share those abnormalities with people who are born evil. This can't be happening to me. I haven't done anything to deserve it.

"What do I do now? What's going to happen to me?" I don't sound like myself. My voice is higher than usual, and whiny.

Noble holds up a hand. "There is no need to be distressed. I had to tell you as soon as possible. I know I'd like to be told if my brain scan looked like that. I know it's a shocking thing to hear but there is no reason to fear the worst."

I raise both hands to my eyes and rub them until they hurt. Of course I fear the worst. I've been told that there's something wrong with my brain. What else am I supposed to think?

Noble sits back in his chair, eyeing me in a way that makes me feel uncomfortable. Like a freak.

"Actually, I don't want to seem insensitive," he says, stroking the point of his goatee. "But I do hope that this isn't going to stop your magazine publishing the feature article on our study. Good publicity helps us get government funding for our work."

I can't believe what I'm hearing. The man must have a heart of stone. There's no doubt that this news would be a great angle for the feature and provide an opportunity for an eye-catching headline. *Brain Scan Reveals I'm a Natural Born Psychopath. How I Found Out I'm a Little Bit Psycho.*

But there is one thing that I'm certain of. I don't want to be the story. Not again. I was persuaded by the police to make a public appeal for information in the press and on television after Lottie's death and I hated the aftermath: the knowing looks, the pity, the social media trolls.

"I definitely don't want this getting out," I say. "This is extremely personal information, personal *medical* information. We definitely won't be using my scan now. But don't worry. I've already written the feature and the magazine will publish it."

I don't bother explaining that if the piece isn't published then I won't get paid for it, and that as a freelancer I can't afford to take that kind of hit.

Noble shrugs. "I know this must be hard for you. It's undoubtedly going to be difficult to come to terms with. I can recommend a specialist if you're interested. I'll email you, shall I?"

I don't answer. I'm overwhelmed by a sudden urge to get away from this place. I stand up, pushing the chair back, a little unsteady on my feet. I'm ready to leave and find the nearest bar. I open my mouth to say thank you but change my mind. I've nothing to be grateful for.

"I'm out of here," I say. "I've had enough of this bullshit."

The professor looks offended. "I didn't mean to upset you. You needed to know what we found."

He gets to his feet, picks the blue folder up off the desk and walks over to me.

"Do take this with you. Please read through it. It might help."

I swing my right hand around to push the folder away. My fingers flap against his wrist and the folder slips out of his grasp. Coloured images of my brain and other printed sheets of paper spill out across the floor. Noble steps back. He tries to speak but manages only a stutter of indignation.

I turn and walk out, praying that my legs don't give way.

CHAPTER 3

Liv

Sitting at a corner table, I lean back and rest my head on the gold velvet wallpaper. Biology isn't destiny, I tell myself. I hope that's true.

I take a sip of white wine. It's colder than I like it and puts my teeth on edge. No matter how hard I try, I'm struggling to get Professor Noble's revelation out of my head. How am I supposed to deal with something like that?

I try to recall the details of the research I'd done on violent psychopaths. Lacking in empathy, narcissistic, promiscuous, risk-takers, socially charming, cruel and sadistic. None of those apply to me. Not really.

Sure, I can be hard-nosed when I'm required to be. In my line of work, you have to be tough to get on. And yes, I'm determined and ambitious, but that doesn't make me a bad person.

I take another, longer sip of wine and toy with the idea of getting drunk. I know that's probably the only way I'll get any sleep when I eventually fall into bed.

London's Canary Wharf is a forest of glass and steel with a shimmering dockside waterfront. The pubs and restaurants are swanky, and busy from lunchtime on.

At the bar, a city boy in a sharp suit gives me the eye, smirks and digs his elbow into his friend's ribs. I frown and look away. I pull my mobile from my jacket pocket and open the photo album. I enlarge one of several pictures of Lottie. My sister smiles at me. My beautiful, dead little sister.

I remember taking the photograph when we went out to a pizza restaurant to celebrate her seventeenth birthday. I'd taken her in when she had nowhere else to go, no one else to turn to. She was mine and she was happy. Then she died. I gulp the wine until the glass is empty. No. Then she was killed.

A large party of men and women enter the pub and mill noisily around the bar. Several of them shout their orders across the room, drawing dirty looks from drinkers who have been waiting patiently to be served. The fresh-faced barman smiles to himself and shakes his head. He's seen it all before.

My head is still spinning. I'm struggling to accept what I've been told. So what if my brain is different? It works the same as everybody else's. I have a quick temper, I admit that, and I can stand up for myself if I need to, but I've never been in trouble with the police. I've never hurt anyone, physically or emotionally. Well, not intentionally. It's not in my nature. Or so I thought.

Since losing Lottie I've had some issues with anger, but that's normal and will pass, so my grief therapist says. Sometimes, after waking in the early hours, I wonder what it would be like to make the man who took my sister's life suffer for what he did. He confessed his crime and they locked him up. A pathetic one-year jail sentence and the prospect of an early release on licence. What a joke.

I get up, nudge my way to the bar and order another wine. Before I get back to the table, I've already drunk half of it. No matter how much I drink, I can't get Noble's description of my brain out of my mind. *The structure shows all the abnormalities I would expect to see in a grade-one psychopath. The difference is that you are not and never have been a violent person and, correct me if I'm wrong, you haven't killed anyone. Violent female psychopaths are quite rare. You've reached your early thirties without getting into trouble with the police and you have a successful career. You really have nothing to worry about.*

My mind is buzzing right now but I don't think it's the alcohol. I can't stop thinking about my Lottie. I'll always believe that the man who left her crushed and broken at the side of the road was let off lightly, despite his remorse, despite the fact that he turned himself in. The prosecution accepted a plea of causing death by careless driving rather than dangerous driving, which means he'll be walking out of prison soon. He gets his life back, while she'll never be more than a fading memory.

The drunken babble around me is giving me a headache. I leave the wine on the table and push my way through the crowd towards the door. I need to think clearly.

Stepping out onto the street, I take a deep breath and start the ten-minute walk to my Docklands home. I've had to accept that the justice system is too soft and that I'm powerless. That there's nothing I can do to take away the pain of losing Lottie.

I'm still the same person I've always been, whatever Professor Noble says.

CHAPTER 4

Sharpe

The Judas slit opens with a metallic click. Narrowed eyes peer into the cell. Daniel Sharpe looks up from where he is sitting on the edge of the bottom bunk. The prison officer stays silent. It's too dark to see whether the eyes are brown or blue, which makes it impossible to guess who's working the late shift.

The peephole slides shut. Sharpe's cellmate is snoring loudly on the top bunk. It's gone midnight but Sharpe is restless. He will have to wait hours, to the point when he's sick with tiredness, before he will have any chance of sleeping.

It's not the snoring that's the problem. It's the other noises that echo along the prison corridors. The shouted threats. The cries for help. The banging on the bars. The new arrival screaming, "I can't breathe," over and over again.

A phrase comes into Sharpe's mind. *A sleepless man is a guilty man.* He'd heard or read that somewhere. If it's true then he has no right to expect to sleep any better when he's back in his own bed.

He drops his head into his hands, closes his eyes and rubs his forehead. Images flash across the blackness like a

13

high-speed slideshow. Burnt rubber on the wet road. The girl as limp as a ragdoll, her bare legs twisted beneath her, half on the pavement and half in the rain-filled gutter.

He squeezes his eyes tighter but the images keep coming. The steps towards the girl, the hesitation, head spinning, stomach churning with fear, sorrow and shame. Checking the street in both directions to make sure he hasn't been seen, climbing back into the car. Driving away.

Sharpe stands up and paces to the wall. The movement disturbs his cellmate, who rolls onto his side. The snoring stops. The cell is eight foot by twelve foot. The cream walls look grey in the darkness. There is one sink, bunk beds and a toilet in the corner. All the furniture is made of steel, every piece bolted to the floor

Sharpe walks to the tiny, barred window and stares out into the impenetrable darkness. He'll be getting out soon. Surprisingly, in one piece. He's always been physically strong but he's learned that, mentally, he's tougher than he thought he was. Head down and mouth shut. Speak only when spoken to, and keep out of other people's business. These are the simple rules that have kept him safe.

Staying out of trouble has other benefits. His sentence has been cut to six months for good behaviour and he's thankful. In all honesty, he agrees with the newspaper reports condemning his early release, and sympathizes with the sister's view that justice hasn't been done. She has every right to feel let down.

He walks back to his bed and sits down. Along the corridor, a prisoner yells a torrent of abuse at a passing guard.

Sharpe clamps his hands over his ears and shuts his eyes. He sees the dead girl's broken body lying on the road. He hears her name, like a whisper, inside his head.

CHAPTER 5

Liv

I treat myself to a cup of coffee from the vending machine before making my way across the magazine's editorial office. It's Swedish-style open plan, with two rows of light oak desks back to back. The design is supposed to encourage collaboration, but I think it has exactly the opposite effect. There are too many distractions, too much noise, and because they have an audience, too many people focus on pretending to look busy.

If you need a private place to speak with a colleague or conduct an interview, you have to book a fifteen-minute slot in one of two glass cubicles. Meeting room one or two.

The features editor is waiting for me, spurning the two available chairs for the edge of the glass table. He keeps his eyes on the screen of his phone, tapping out a text as I enter.

Matt Lamb is tall and angular, with a carefully tangled mop of sandy hair. He's asked me out on dates three times in the ten months I've worked for the magazine and each time I've said no. The third time I almost said yes. He seems kind, and he makes me laugh. Sometimes unintentionally. But it'd be too awkward, wouldn't it? Although I'm freelance, when

I write for his magazine, he's technically my boss. Anyway, with Lottie, and everything else that's going on, a boyfriend would not be a good idea.

I wait for a few seconds while he finishes the message and presses send. "Good morning," he says. "Can we make this quick? I've got a meeting with the editor in ten minutes. She won't be happy if I'm late."

I smile at him but not too broadly. He smiles back, and that's when I know that even if I don't want a relationship with him, I do want something. I'm not sure what. We have a connection. I do feel that.

"I wanted to let you know that I'll have the psycho brains feature ready in a couple of days."

He slips his phone into the back pocket of his jeans. "That's great," he says. "We want it for next month's edition. Something different from all that celebrity froth. I can't wait to read it."

He's holding my gaze, and for a brief moment I want to confide in him, tell him everything. Let him know how frightened I am, how scary it is to find out your brain is abnormal, that you share a condition with serial killers.

"The thing is Matt, I'm going to need some time off and so won't be available to take on any new assignments for a few weeks, maybe longer."

His smile vanishes and he crosses his arms across his chest. "That's a shame. I had you in mind for a couple of great feature commissions. You know I love the way you write. Has someone made you a better offer or something?"

I shake my head, pull one of the chairs away from the table and sit down. Matt follows my lead and sits facing me, waiting for an explanation.

"It's nothing like that. I enjoy working for you, I really do. I just need time off to deal with something. Something personal."

A frown creases his forehead. He pulls his phone from his pocket and checks the time. I know he's weighing up whether he should get involved in the personal business of an employee but I know he won't abandon me. He's too kind. A nice human being.

Like anyone who reads the papers and watches the TV news, he's aware of everything I've been through. Losing Lottie. The stress of the court case.

Leaning forward, he lowers his voice to a whisper. "Is everything all right, Liv? If there's anything I can do, don't hesitate to ask. I know it's been a while, but grief can creep up on you when you least expect it."

"It's not that," I say, dropping my voice to a level that matches his. "It's something else I've got to deal with now. It's a health thing. I don't want to burden you with the details."

Matt sits back and sighs. Apparently relieved that the problem is more straightforward than he'd thought and that he's unqualified to do anything about it.

"Of course," he says. "You can't neglect your health, and I understand if you want to keep the details private. As soon as you're ready to come back, I'll have work for you. There's no need to worry about that."

He checks the time again, impatient to leave for his meeting. I feel a stab of resentment at how easily he has dismissed my problem. Maybe he's not as kindhearted and understanding as I thought. Perhaps he's given up trying to ask me out on a date and doesn't need to pretend anymore.

"Well, actually, I feel that maybe I should tell you what's going on because it is linked, in a way, to the psycho brains feature."

He tilts his head to one side and raises an eyebrow. I carry on before he can start asking questions.

"You remember I had my brain scanned to be part of the study's control group? The images of normal brains?"

Matt nods slowly. "I do. It was a brilliant idea."

I raise my eyes to the ceiling and take a deep breath. "Yesterday, Professor Noble, the neuroscientist running the study, called me in to discuss my scan. They found something, something about my brain, they hadn't expected to see. Something bad."

I stop talking to give Matt time to think about what I am saying. I know the impact will be bigger if he works it out for himself. He stares silently at me for a few seconds, then shakes his head. "No," he says. "Oh God, no."

I press my lips together tightly and nod.

"How bad is it? Is it bad, Liv?"

"It's bad. Pretty bad," I say, a slight tremor in my voice.

"But they can treat you, right? They can sort you out? Surely there are . . ."

He's babbling now, unsure what to say, worried about upsetting me.

I'm not crying but I lift a hand and wipe my cheek any-way. "They told me the tumour is in a part of the brain that makes surgery risky, so there are no plans to operate at this point. But they are hoping that chemo can shrink it."

We both stand up and Matt moves in to hug me. I bury my head into his chest. His body is warm and I can feel his heart thumping. Mine is beating even faster. I've shocked myself. The enormity of the lie I've told both horrifies and thrills me.

Matt steps back. He reaches out, brushing my shoulders gently with his fingers. The tenderness of the gesture almost makes me cry.

"If there's anything I can do just say the word. I'm here for you. I mean it."

I look up at him to show my gratitude. "I'd prefer it if you kept this to yourself. I don't feel comfortable letting other people know right now. It's too early. I need to come to terms with it myself first. I had to tell someone, though, and I know I can trust you."

He swallows hard and blinks. "Oh God, Liv. I'm so sorry."

I've never thought of myself as a particularly loveable person and Matt's reaction almost overwhelms me. I sum-mon a brave smile for him.

"Please don't worry about me. I'm going to fight this thing all the way. I'm determined I'm going to be back writ-ing features for you soon. I know it."

CHAPTER 6

Earl

The chatter level drops and all eyes are on Detective Sergeant Atticus Earl as he walks through the squad room to his desk by the window. Everyone knows the reason for his summons to the boss's office. Bad news spreads faster than a nasty rash.

Earl keeps his expression neutral and his body language relaxed. Inside, his blood is boiling. He slides his chair closer to his computer screen and starts reading his emails, as if nothing has changed. As if the worst thing that has ever happened to him hasn't just happened.

The squad room chatter starts up again as everyone else goes back to what they were doing. Most of his colleagues are feeling sorry for him. All of them are relieved that it's him who got the call. He understands that, but it doesn't make him feel any better.

He's staring out of the window when Detective Constable Blessing Akinola appears at his side, a cup of coffee in each hand.

"I thought you might need one," she says.

Earl isn't in the mood for talking but he doesn't want to be rude. Not to Akinola. She's a dedicated detective, and over the years she's proved herself a decent human being.

He takes one of the cups and grunts his thanks.

"What was that all about?" she asks, nodding in the direction of Detective Chief Inspector Tanner's office.

Earl takes a sip of coffee and shakes his head slowly. "Come on. Don't give me that. I'm out. A casualty of budget cuts. Savings have to be made, apparently."

"Oh shit. I'm sorry. That's not fair. You don't deserve this."

"Life isn't fair. You know that as well as I do. It doesn't take long to work that out doing this job. One of us has to go. I'm the one. Twenty years' service. Three failed marriages. Bye-bye and thanks for nothing."

Akinola grimaces and Earl regrets letting bitterness get the better of him. He doesn't want to go. Catching bad people is his life. He can't imagine doing anything else. But this is nobody's fault. Not even his own. He's a statistic. A number on a spreadsheet.

"How long have we got to arrange a leaving party?" Akinola asks with a smile.

"A few weeks, maybe a month. Whatever I need to tie up the loose ends on my active cases. Get ready to pass them on. Honestly, though, don't bother arranging anything. You'll be wasting everybody's time because I won't be there. Farewells aren't my thing. If I'm going to drown my sorrows, I'd rather do it on my own in the corner of a quiet bar."

"Okay then, maybe you're right, but let's see how you feel in a few days," Akinola says, before walking back to her desk.

Earl downs the dregs of his coffee and opens another email. It's a reminder that the offender in one of his old cases is due to be released from prison and the victim's next of kin needs to be notified. Daniel Sharpe had been a conundrum. In his mid-thirties, running his own business, no criminal record, not a heavy drinker, not a drug user. Yet he'd walked into the station and confessed to a fatal hit-and-run. The boss had been happy to see the case wrapped up so quickly. The press had gone to town on the tragic tale of Lottie Miller. She was seventeen, she was pretty. She'd come to London from Manchester to live with her older sister and five months later ended up dead on the side of the road.

Earl closes the email and sits back in his chair. The sister had called a press conference after the court hearing to condemn the judge for being too soft and criticize the Crown Prosecution Service for not charging Sharpe with manslaughter.

Earl imagines she'll be calling the newspapers again once she hears he's being released early. He'd been the interviewing officer when Sharpe confessed. He remembers Sharpe's hand trembling as he signed his statement. Everything had checked out, but for Earl it was all too simple. Too neat. Too convenient.

He picks up a pen and drums it on the desk. He can't take on new cases, and the thought of doing the paperwork needed to pass on his existing inquiries is depressing. He needs something to focus on, something to take his mind off the fact that his life is a mess and is only going to get messier.

He slips the pen into his jacket pocket and makes a decision. No new cases, his boss said. Nobody said he can't spend his final few weeks as a detective taking a fresh look at an old investigation, even if the offender confessed to the crime and has already served his time.

He'd never been one-hundred-per-cent convinced that Sharpe had told them the whole truth about what had happened that day. Surely, that fits into the category of tying up a loose end?

CHAPTER 7

Fourteen months earlier

"I am Detective Sergeant Atticus Earl and this interview is being recorded. Please state your full name."

"Daniel Sharpe."

Earl pauses. He has conducted hundreds of recorded interviews over the years and knows to take it steady. Sharpe looks on the verge of throwing up. His hands, resting on the desk in front of him, are clasped so tightly his knuckles are white.

"You are here because you want to make a statement about the death of Lottie Miller. Is that right?"

Sharpe sits up straight. "That's correct. I want to tell you what happened. Everything."

"Thank you. Go ahead."

"I was driving the car. Much too fast. I didn't see her until it was too late. I'm so sorry."

Sharpe hangs his head. He dressed up for his visit to the police station. As if looking smart will earn him some credit. A dark grey suit, a pale blue tie and shiny black shoes. Earl wonders if he realizes that his life will never be the same again.

"Can you tell me exactly what happened? From the beginning. Why you were driving at that time. Where you'd been and where you were going."

Sharpe rubs his forehead and groans, as if the memory is painful. "Well, I couldn't sleep at all. Too much on my mind. A lot going on at work, you know? I went out for a drive. It sounds stupid, I know, but I've done it before. I find it calming. At that time in the morning the roads around that part of Canary Wharf are quiet. I didn't go anywhere special. Just drove around a bit. And then . . ."

His voice falters. He hangs his head again. His breathing fast and shallow.

"What happened next?" Earl prompts. "Please go on. You need to tell us everything."

"I decided to head home. It was around 5 a.m., still dark. I'm not sure how I didn't see her but I didn't. It all happened so quickly. I'm not saying it was the girl's fault but I think she ran into the road without looking. All I saw was a shadow in my peripheral vision, then before I could react there was a . . . well, a kind of soft thud and I slammed the brakes on."

"You're saying that you did stop?"

"Yes, I did. I got out of the car and looked back. Like I said, it was still dark. I saw something lying on the side of the road but I didn't go to take a closer look. I didn't want to see. It's hard to explain. My mind was telling me that I'd hit something, but not a person. Not a girl. I think I panicked. I was scared. I didn't want to believe what I'd done. I got back into the car and drove home. I went to work. Tried to carry on as normal, but later, when I saw the photograph of the girl on the TV news, I couldn't lie to myself any longer. I couldn't keep up the pretence. That's why I'm here."

Earl is certain he's not listening to someone with serious mental health issues. The admission hasn't come after hours of interrogation. He should be feeling delighted that the case can be wrapped up but he doesn't, and he can't pinpoint why. Still, his bosses are going to be extremely happy. Nobody witnessed the incident, and the stretch of road where it happened wasn't covered by CCTV. Earl had prepared himself for a long, messy investigation, and the newspapers were already hinting at police incompetence.

"Had you been drinking before going out for a drive? . . . For the benefit of the recording, Mr Sharpe is shaking his head."

"No, I don't think so," Sharpe says.

"You don't think you'd been drinking?"

"Well, I might have had a couple of small whiskeys earlier. That would have been several hours before I went out in the car. I wasn't drink-driving. I was extremely tired."

"Do you live alone? A partner? Children?"

"I'm not married. Not now. But I have a daughter, Emily. She's in her first year at university. I don't see much of her, to be honest. She's lived with her mother since we split up. She won't want to see me at all now, I suppose. Not after this. What I've done, it's shameful."

Sharpe covers his face with his hands. Earl waits until his shoulders stop heaving.

"What car were you driving?"

"A Mercedes E-class saloon."

"Where is the vehicle now?"

Sharpe looks up. "How did this happen to me? I hate what I did. I disgust myself."

Earl doesn't answer. He wants his question answered.

"The car's parked outside my house. I expected there to be more damage. The bumper is cracked and there's a dent in the bodywork near the off-side headlight." Sharpe pauses, bowing his head. "There was blood too. A lot. You'll find the cloth I used to wipe it off in the boot."

Earl switches off the recorder. "That'll do for now. You'll have a chance to read your statement through before you sign it. I suggest you contact a lawyer."

"I did it. I admit that I'm guilty and deserve to be punished. What do I need a lawyer for?"

Earl doesn't reply. The man who has admitted to mowing down a teenage girl and leaving her to die on the side of the road has a point.

CHAPTER 8

Liv

Sitting at the kitchen table, warmed by the early spring sun streaming through the window, I picture myself lying beside a private pool in the south of France, reading a good book and sipping an ice-cold margarita. The image makes me feel good and I promise myself a long holiday somewhere hot.

I take a large bite of toast smothered with strawberry jam, trying not to drop crumbs on the keyboard of my lap-top. Research is vital for a feature writer. It's a part of the job that I love. If I truly have the brain of a typical psychopath, then I want to find out exactly what that means, or might mean. I focus on the screen and start to read.

Psychopathy is traditionally a personality disorder characterized by persistent antisocial behaviour, impaired empathy and remorse, and bold, disinhibited and egotistical traits.

Surely, some of that can apply to most people at certain times in their lives? Nobody is perfect. I certainly know at least two people, both of them journalists, who I'd say tick all of those boxes.

Psychopathy is characterized by superficial charm, high intelli-gence, poor judgement and failure to learn from experience, an incapacity for love, lack of remorse or shame, pathological lying and manipulative behaviour.

While a second slice of bread browns in the toaster, I try to make an honest attempt at assessing whether any of this applies to me. I can be charming when I want or need to be, but not in a superficial way. I don't need to reassure myself that I have the capacity to love. I know that only too well. I experienced the agony of loving a mother who didn't love me back, and the pain of losing Lottie . . . well, it's still raw, and festering like an open wound. I take a deep breath and let out a tremulous sigh. Whatever the shape of my brain, I'm definitely not inhuman. My heart can break like anyone else's.

My mind flips to the day my mother sat me down and told me that I was going to have a sister. I was eleven and I burst into tears. I didn't know how I was supposed to feel, but the way my mother smiled as she caressed her rounded stomach and announced that the baby was a little miracle scared and confused me. I'd always wanted a little sister, and when she arrived I knew right away that she'd love me as much as I loved her. But she was a miracle. She was a treasure and I was worthless. As it turned out, I was right to feel that way.

I push the memory away and am busy making a mental list of the positive things about my personality when the doorbell rings. I walk quickly down the hall, and peer through the glass panel in my front door. Standing on my doorstep is Detective Constable Tracey Bryant, the family liaison officer assigned to me after Lottie's death.

She's a kind soul and spends her working days helping those who have lost loved ones to crime. Gentle and thoughtful, she truly cares about people. She's everything my mother wasn't, and I admire her for that.

As I open the door, she looks up at me from beneath her heavy fringe. She's wearing a dark trouser suit that looks a bit too tight around her hips and shoulders.

"Tracey," I say. "This is a pleasant surprise."

Her smile is friendly but the way her eyelids flicker suggests that she's nervous.

26

"Good morning, Liv," she says. "Sorry to bother you so early, but I wanted to have a word with you about Daniel Sharpe's impending release."

Hearing that name makes every muscle in my body tense. My jaw clenches and I have to force myself to exhale. Tracey shifts her weight nervously from one foot to the other.

"Come inside," I say. "I've a pot of coffee on the go."

I move to let her pass. Without hesitating, she walks through the living area and turns right into the kitchen. I'm impressed that she remembers the layout of the house because it must be at least six months since she last paid me a visit.

Neither of us speak while I pour her drink. She nods her thanks, picks it up and blows on it before taking a sip.

"You always make lovely coffee," she says.

I sit down at the table and she takes the chair opposite me. I'm anxious to hear what she's here to tell me and dispense with small talk.

"Exactly when is he getting out?"

"I know this is hard for you and I'm happy to stay and talk it over if you feel it will help," Tracey says.

I will her to stop worrying about my feelings and get to the point.

"Just tell me when he's getting out."

"He's being released tomorrow morning. I know it must be difficult to understand, but he stayed out of trouble and earned the full sentence reduction."

"How brilliant for him. Be a good boy and you can get away with murder."

"I completely understand what you're going through, but you will get over this. It takes time, that's all. Are you still seeing that grief counsellor I recommended?"

I nod but don't reply because I can't think of anything pleasant to say and don't want to upset her. None of this is her fault. She's doing her job and I know she genuinely cares. But she has no idea what I'm going through, or what I really feel about the man who killed my little sister. If she did, she'd be shocked.

"He's being released on licence, which means he'll have to report regularly to a probation supervisor," she says. "He will, of course, be returning to his home. I know that may be uncomfortably close to here, but there's nothing we can do about that and there's no reason your paths should cross, is there?"

I stay silent and stare blankly across the table at her. I don't tell her that the best thing he can do is keep well away from me. That I dread to think how I'd react if we bumped into each other in the street. After a moment, I stand up and walk down the hall. She has no choice but to follow.

"Thank you for taking the trouble to let me know," I say as I open the door.

She hesitates on the threshold and turns back to me. "I'm so sorry you're having to go through this. I really am. If it's any comfort to you, he may have his freedom but he's lost everything else. If there's anything I can do for you or you want to talk, you have my number."

For a brief moment I consider offering her another cup of coffee, telling her what's happened and confessing that I don't know how I should feel about it other than terrified. Instead, I start to close the door. She takes the hint and goes.

Back in the kitchen, I'm tormented by an image of Daniel Sharpe stepping out of the prison gates, lifting his face to the sun and smiling. My head buzzes and the room spins. I'm struggling to breathe. My legs give way.

I come to, in a heap on the floor, unsure whether I actually blacked out or not. I crawl to the table and haul myself unsteadily to my feet.

I'm weak with despair but know I have to be strong. I can't rely on anyone but myself. The justice system has failed me. Worse still, it has failed my little sister.

CHAPTER 9

Earl

Detective Sergeant Earl washes a mouthful of cheese sandwich down with a swig of black coffee. Across the table,
Akinola grins.

"Where the hell do you put it all?" she asks. "I saw you
demolishing a cooked breakfast in the station canteen less
than an hour ago."

Earl shrugs. He's put on a few pounds in the past year
but he's tall and broad enough to carry it. He considers
explaining that he hates cooking for one and rarely eats when
he's at home but decides the detective constable doesn't need
to know. No one likes a whinger.

"I need to keep my strength up," he says. "My body is
like a high-performance car. It takes a lot of looking after and
needs constant refuelling."

He enjoys the way Akinola's eyes crinkle with amuse-
ment. It's good to know that at least one of his colleagues
will miss him when he's gone.

The bustling coffee shop in Amsterdam Road, a brisk
five-minute walk from the Isle of Dogs police station, is his

favourite mid-morning break destination, especially when he feels the need to sit and think.

"I take it you've dragged me here for a reason," Akinola says, "and I hope you're not planning to propose. Three ex-wives are more than enough for anyone."

Earl rubs a hand across his face. He and Akinola work well together, sharing a dark sense of humour they both use as a coping mechanism. On a night out she's always good company and can match him drink for drink.

They both know romance is off limits. For a start, she's much too young for him. Or maybe he's too old for her. Anyway, since his last divorce, he's sworn off relationships.

"Actually, I want to pick your brains about an old case. The fatal hit-and-run. The victim was Lottie Miller. Over a year ago."

Akinola drums her fingers on the dark wood table and frowns. "I remember it. Pretty straightforward. The driver, Sharpe, a physiotherapist, wasn't he? He did seem genuinely sorry and gave himself up. The whole thing was sorted in a few days."

"That's right. I interviewed him when he made his confession."

"What's this all about?" Akinola asks. "Sharpe was locked up. He's probably out by now."

"He's out tomorrow. You executed the search warrant at his house, I think. Is it right that we never found his mobile?"

Akinola stops drumming her fingers and gives Earl a curious look. "Why the hell are you bringing this up now? The man confessed. He did the crime and served his time. It's done."

"I know that," Earl says, "but the one thing that has always bugged me about the case is that we never got hold of his mobile."

Akinola sighs in exasperation. "He told us he lost it a couple of days before the accident. Left it in a wine bar or something. When he went back the next day there was no sign of it. So what? We didn't need it, did we?"

Earl finishes his coffee. It's lukewarm and bitter. "No, we didn't need the mobile to get the conviction. Sharpe gave us everything we needed. It just bothers me, that's all. I can't stand it when a jigsaw puzzle has a missing piece, even if you don't need it to see the complete picture."

Akinola rolls her eyes. "You're leaving the job in a matter of weeks. Why on earth are you digging around in an old investigation. Nobody is going to thank you for stirring up trouble. You need to stop worrying about a case that's already been solved, keep your head down, start planning your future outside the force and let me organize a big farewell party for you."

Earl isn't convinced but doesn't argue. Akinola is talking sense as usual. That doesn't mean she's right.

She slides her chair back and stands up. "Thanks for the coffee but I have to get back. I've a suspected gang stabbing to investigate."

Earl raises a hand. "You go. I think I'm going to have another coffee."

He stares at her back as she leaves, humiliation slicing through him. He'd normally be assigned as the senior investigating officer on something like a stabbing. He feels the same as he did at thirteen when he was dropped from the school football team. He cried himself to sleep that night but woke up determined to train harder, prove his sports teacher wrong and win back his place. It took him a month.

Earl walks to the counter and orders another coffee. Twenty years as a dedicated detective and he was being cut. Dropped from the team, despite the fact that his experience means he's a valuable asset and second to none when it comes to solving cases.

The fact is, they'll hire a wet-behind-the-ears, fast-tracked graduate to replace him at a much lower salary. Maybe even bring two new bodies in and still save cash. He's aware that it's all down to money but that doesn't make it hurt less.

He takes his coffee back to the table and slides onto a chair. He may be going but he's not going quietly. If proving his boss wrong means stirring up trouble over an old case, then that is exactly what he'll do.

CHAPTER 10

Liv

It's always worse just before a therapy session. The grief. I haven't been able to deal with it properly yet. Even though it's been a while, I'm not healing. Time has let me down. I haven't completed the grieving process, my counsellor says. He tells me I've stalled, pushed my pain away because I don't want to face it, because I'm scared it will consume me.

Even though I know he's correct, I haven't said so. I don't want to feed his superiority complex. Tracey was right about him, he's good at what he does. But he's too smug for my liking.

This is when I'm at my most vulnerable. The moment before I step off the bus, knowing that in a few minutes I'll be sitting in the consulting room talking about Lottie, telling a stranger who already knows more about me than anyone else alive, what my little sister meant to me and how I'm going to move on with my life knowing she's gone forever. This is when the grief swells, a pressure in my chest, a tightening in my throat. I fear it will choke the life out of me if I let it.

I duck my head to shield my face from the stinging rain as I hurry toward the clinic's revolving door.

Inside, the waiting area seats are empty and I guess I'm the first appointment of the day. Behind the reception counter, a woman with a grey-streaked ponytail peers at me over her half-moon glasses as I approach. She must recognize me from my previous visits, although I don't remember seeing her before, because before I reach her, she smiles and gestures with a sweep of a bony hand.

"Mr Walton is waiting for you," she says. "You can go in now."

I respond with a nod, head straight for the corridor and enter the consulting room without knocking.

Clive Walton is sitting in one of two black leather easy chairs facing each other either side of a light-oak coffee table. His right elbow is propped on the arm of the chair, his eyes are half closed and his head is resting on the flat of his hand.

He doesn't react to my sudden arrival, except for a subtle flicker of his eyelids. I perch on the edge of the empty chair, my spine rigid.

"So sorry," I say. "Did I wake you?"

He lifts his head from his hand and straightens up slowly, his lips twitching as he suppresses a grin.

"I wasn't asleep. I was thinking. Trying to decide what we should talk about this morning. Why don't you take your coat off? You'll be more comfortable."

Walton is probably ten years my senior. I'd describe him as good-looking and well-groomed in a casual kind of way. All I know about him is that he's a grief counsellor, and the most chilled person I've ever met. I don't know whether he's single or married, gay or straight. We've had ten sessions, and he knows almost everything about me. Almost. I unzip my coat but leave it on, even though the room is warm.

"I'm fine, thanks."

He shrugs. "Let's get started, then. Is there anything particular you want to talk about this morning?"

I turn my head to watch raindrops race down the windowpane and wonder what he'd say if I told him that I'd recently found out that I have the brain of a psychopath.

Maybe he'd be fascinated to have such a freak in his consulting room. Perhaps he'd conclude that the reason I can't deal with my loss is because I can't process emotion.

"I really don't know what to say. I'm tired of talking. It's not making any difference. It's not helping."

I drag my gaze away from the window and look across at Walton to make sure that he's listening. He uncrosses his legs and sits up a little straighter. He looks slightly on edge, less relaxed than usual. I notice something different in his eyes. A mix of apprehension and excitement.

"I've been thinking," he says.

"I should hope so. That's what you're paid to do, isn't it?"

He shakes his head, smiling condescendingly. "I've thought about this for some time, and because you say you don't feel you're making any progress I believe this is the right way to go. I think we should talk about Daniel Sharpe. I wonder whether it's the way you feel about him that's preventing you from dealing with your grief."

I bite down on my bottom lip to stop myself screaming. My grief fills the room, thick and heavy, pressing down on me, suffocating me. When I reply my voice is like that of a petulant child's.

"What is there to say about him? He's a heartless coward. What else can you say about a man like that?"

He nods thoughtfully. "I wonder," he says. "What he did was abhorrent, of course it was, but have you considered that, in some ways, he's a victim of this tragedy too?"

"You want me to feel sorry for him? Don't go there. Please don't go there."

He shifts to the edge of his seat and angles his body towards me. It's clear he knows he has hit a raw nerve and that knowledge excites him. He wants to keep prodding at it to see how much I can bear. To challenge me.

"I know how you feel about him, but I believe it's this anger that's stopping you come to terms with Lottie's death. You need to address it. Find a way to let it go. Maybe you should try to accept that Daniel Sharpe never meant for any of this to happen. He was weak. He made a mistake, but it was no more than a terrible accident."

I place my hands on my lap, clasp them together and squeeze them until my fingers are bloodless. I open my mouth to speak, then clamp it shut again. I don't want to engage in this conversation. I can't even contemplate forgiveness. It's not a choice for me, especially when I can't even forgive myself.

Walton is frowning now. Trying to understand my silence. I wonder again whether I should tell him about the brain scan. Tell him about the dark, dangerous thoughts that have crowded my head in the two weeks since. Admit that no matter how hard I try, I can't help dreaming up ways that I, personally, can make Sharpe suffer for what he did. If I could be sure that it would make a difference, I'd do it, because I can't go on like this. I know I'm going to need help but I dismiss the idea. I'm not ready to condemn myself, to expose myself to judgement.

Walton gives a shrug of surrender. "Okay, Liv, perhaps we should move on. We can always come back to that subject later. When you are ready, I really feel that it's the one thing that's going to make a difference."

I don't bother telling him that deep in my heart I know for sure that when it comes to forgiving Sharpe I am beyond help.

I stand, zipping up my coat slowly.

"I never want to speak about that man again," I say. "Never. I thought you, of all people, would understand how I feel."

He doesn't move. He gives me a rueful smile and lifts his eyebrows.

"Where are you going? We've only just started. I didn't set out to upset you, you know. I genuinely think your feelings about Sharpe are stopping you making progress, and your reaction kind of proves my point, doesn't it?"

I know he's right, but I also know that learning to forgive the man who took Lottie from me is not the answer.

Not my answer, anyway. Panic flutters in my chest. I have to get out of the room. I need to clear my head before I say something I regret.

I turn quickly and walk out, half expecting to be called me back. Out on the street I keep walking, the wind whipping the rain into my face.

This is the moment it hits me. Nothing is going to change until I come face to face with Sharpe and make him understand the misery he has caused.

CHAPTER 11

Liv

I stand in front of Lottie's grave, staring at the gold lettering on the grey marble headstone. *A beautiful life brought to an end, a shining sister, a loving best friend.* I wrote the inscription myself and it always makes me cry.

I read it again, mouthing the words, but this time the tears won't come. My heart is numb. They say psychopaths live behind a mask of normality, to hide their real nature, to blend in. Maybe, subconsciously, I've been doing that all my life. Is it possible that now I know the truth about myself, the mask is starting to slip?

I drag my gaze away from Lottie's grave and look across the vast expanse of the East London Cemetery, lifting a hand to shield my eyes from the sun. Rows of headstones stretch in every direction, ever more weather-beaten and overgrown as they reach the distant boundary.

Close by on my left, a young woman lays a bouquet of lilies on a fresh mound of reddish earth. Even though the day is warm and windless, she's wearing a dark padded jacket and a woollen beanie hat. I watch as she falls to her knees, puts her hands together and bows her head.

I'm not big on religion, but when Lottie died I found some comfort in prayer. It didn't last. I don't pray now. I don't want to waste my breath. God is supposed to protect good people from evil, I always thought. Where was our all-knowing, all-powerful deity when Lottie, the epitome of a good, innocent young girl, needed saving? If that failure was a deliberate act of neglect, or even plain carelessness, then I never want to speak to him or her ever again. I suspect the truth is simpler.

I turn back to the grave and sit cross-legged on the grass next to the headstone. I won't be praying, but when I come here I always like to talk. Even though I know that wherever Lottie is she can't hear me, it always makes me feel better.

But when I open my mouth to speak, anger grips my throat. I'm forced to stare at the ground and wait in silence until it passes. Sharpe has served his time. He'll have his freedom. He'll have a clean slate. I have my sister's rotting bones.

"I need you to help me," I say, reaching out to touch the headstone, stroking the cold marble with my fingertips. "I know what I want to do. I want Sharpe to feel my pain. Is that what you want too?"

Even as I ask the question, I know I don't need an answer. Lottie was a kindhearted, gentle soul. If she was sitting here and I was lying in that grave, she'd be weeping for me, her heart overflowing with grief but still capable of forgiveness.

"I admit it," I say. I glance over my shoulder to make sure nobody is near enough to hear me. The woman in the beanie hat has gone. "I tell myself that I imagine punishing Sharpe, humiliating him, hurting him, for you. That I want justice for you. The truth is, I also want it for me. Can you allow me that? Is it too much to ask? I want the satisfaction of seeing him suffer. I could do it, Lottie. I'd never have believed I had it in me before, but things have changed. I'm changing. I often find myself thinking about exactly what I could do to him and how I'd do it. I've no doubt I could make him pay and get away with it too. Is that terrible, Lottie? It is terrible, isn't it?"

I look back at the space made empty by the woman in the beanie hat. I'm struck by an impulse to take the flowers she laid on the fresh grave and put them on my sister's. I walk over quickly and grab the bouquet. I do it even though a part of me is horrified. A few weeks ago, the thought of stealing flowers from a grave would never have crossed my mind.

I stand staring at the evidence of how far I have fallen. A butterfly lands on one of the bright yellow blooms. Fascinated, I keep still and watch it close its orange-tipped white wings over its back. The creature's fragile beauty reminds me of Lottie. I bend slowly and put the flowers back where I found them.

I go back to my sister, keeping my eyes on the butterfly. After a while, it unfolds its wings, takes off and zigzags its way towards me, eventually landing precariously on the top of Lottie's headstone. I watch entranced as it basks in the sun before fluttering away and out of sight.

My brain is telling me that the appearance of the butterfly is a random event. I want to believe it's a message. I'd love it to be Lottie's way of letting me know that because she's always by my side I don't have to give in to the darkness inside me. That my world can be beautiful and filled with light again. I so want to believe that.

CHAPTER 12

Earl

Detective Sergeant Earl is up and showered by 5.30 a.m. He dresses quickly to the sound of a twenty-four-hour TV news channel. A sixteen-year-old boy has been stabbed to death in Victoria Park, East London, and the police are appealing for witnesses. It's the ninth fatal knifing in the capital in three months.

Earl walks into the kitchen where three rashers of bacon are burning to a crisp in a blackened frying pan. He places them side by side between two slices of buttered white bread, takes a bite and turns to face the television, where the news-reader is discussing the knife crime epidemic with a sombre Home Office minister.

He listens for a few seconds, and throws his arms up in despair. He reaches for the remote and switches the television off. Budget cuts take thousands of officers off the streets and violent crime rises. Who'd have thought it?

Five minutes later, he leaves his flat. Stepping out onto the street, he runs to his car, pulling up the collar of his coat. Big fat raindrops are falling in the darkness, battering the windscreen and slanting across the beam of his headlights as he drives west along Marsh Wall. He's not due at the station for three hours but wants to visit the spot where Lottie Miller died, at the time when the accident happened.

He'd spent the previous evening studying the case file, painstakingly highlighting points he considered possible inconsistencies. Even as a schoolboy he had an eye for the tiniest detail, never shying away from letting fellow pupils and even teachers know when they'd made a mistake. It didn't make him the most popular kid in class.

An anonymous caller had tipped off the police that he'd driven by what looked like someone lying unconscious on the side of the road. By the time the emergency services arrived, Lottie Miller was already dead.

She'd suffered a serious head injury and several of her ribs were broken or fractured. If the medics had been called earlier, there was a chance they could have saved her.

Earl turns onto Mastmaker Road, pulling up outside a low-rise block of flats. At this time of the morning the street is deserted. No pedestrians. No traffic. He keeps the engine running and the heating on full blast.

It's still dark but the street lights are bright, and if it wasn't for the rain, visibility would be pretty good. He looks out of the passenger window at a black metal litter bin marking the spot where the teenager was found.

He tries to visualize Sharpe jamming on his brakes, climbing out of the car, seeing the dark shape of the teenager's broken body sprawled half in the gutter and half on the pavement, then getting back into the car and driving off.

According to Sharpe's confession, until he saw the TV news reports, he hadn't been one-hundred-per-cent sure that he'd hit someone. He wasn't over the drink-drive limit and hadn't taken drugs. He'd been confused and frightened, and he panicked.

Earl found that part of his story particularly difficult to believe. If Sharpe had stopped and taken a good look, then he would have seen exactly what he'd done. Why would he lie once he'd already decided to confess? What type of person called in an hour after the accident to report a body on the side of the road? Sharpe claimed he'd lost his mobile a few days before the accident. Maybe, when he'd driven home, he'd been overwhelmed by guilt and made the anonymous call. If so, then why would he deny it? And where was his phone?

Earl remembers raising these questions at the time but none of his colleagues had been interested. They had Sharpe, a full confession and the car, which had damage that could be matched to Lottie's injuries. Case closed.

* * *

Earl arrives at the station with an hour to spare before he's on duty. He shuns the lift and takes the stairs to the canteen on the first floor. He's the first to admit that he's let his physical fitness slip over the past few years. He wonders whether if he'd made more of an effort to keep in shape, he might have dodged the redundancy bullet. Maybe, he thinks, it's not too late.

He orders two coffees, one black, one with milk, takes them to a corner table, pulls out his mobile and sends Akinola a text. He knows she's on the early shift and he's hoping she's in the squad room. A few minutes later she arrives in the canteen.

She drags back a chair and slumps down. Her hair is pulled back in a tight ponytail and her smile is strained. Earl thinks she looks tired but he knows her well enough not to say so.

"I thought you might need a break," he says, sliding the milky coffee across the table.

She picks it up and nods her thanks. "It's been a pretty hectic morning. Three arrests and two interviews so far. It doesn't help that we're missing our most experienced detective."

She means this as a compliment, but the reminder that he's no longer part of the investigation team makes Earl's throat tighten and his stomach churn. He gives her a long, wry look but can't think of a witty response, so says nothing.

"I don't suppose you sent me that text because you wanted to sit there and stare at me," Akinola says. "What's up?"

Earl takes a sip of his coffee and checks over his shoulder to make sure he can't be overheard.

"I've been thinking about the Lottie Miller case and it's bugging the hell out of me."

Akinola shakes her head. "You've got to drop this. The man has served his sentence and he's back home. Maybe you're right. Maybe we didn't get to the bottom of what he was doing driving around in the early hours but we do know he ran down that girl. He wanted to be punished for what he did and he was. It's done. You need to leave it."

Earl takes a moment to think. As usual, Akinola is making sense, but he's not prepared to let her know that. Something is nagging at him. A mistake has been made. He wants to prove to Tanner, to the rest of the squad room, including Akinola, that he's good at what he does. That he, of all people, doesn't deserve to be dumped on the scrapheap. More than anything, he wants to prove it to himself.

"I don't think I can leave it," he says.

Akinola shakes her head. Earl can't tell if she's angry with him or embarrassed for him. She drains her coffee and slams the empty cup down on the table.

"I'm worried about you," she says. "I think you don't want to accept that you're losing your badge and you're grasping at this case because you need an excuse to hold on to the job."

Earl knows there's some truth in what his friend is saying but there's more to it than that. As a detective he always considered himself a seeker of truth, or at least what he perceived to be the truth. He can't let go of the fact that maybe he let the truth slip past him on this occasion.

"I took a look at the Sharpe case file yesterday and noticed that we didn't ask his mobile service provider to track his missing phone's whereabouts around the time of the hit-and run."

Akinola looks pointedly at her wristwatch and sighs. "I know you suggested I put in a request, but DCI Tanner thought it unnecessary, remember? The confession was more than enough to get a conviction and I was assigned to a nasty domestic assault case."

Earl does remember. Tanner called him into his office and told him that his obsessive double-checking was a waste of valuable time and scarce resources.

"I'm thinking of putting in a tracking request now," he says. "I know the phone companies are not supposed to keep the records for longer than twelve months, but I think it's worth a try."

Akinola sits back, holding both hands up. "I didn't hear that. I don't want to know, all right? My advice is to forget it and start thinking about what you're going to do next. Tanner isn't going to take kindly to you stirring up doubts around a closed case."

Earl flashes her a smile. "What's he going to do? Sack me?"

Akinola stands up. "I have to go," she says. "Please don't do anything stupid."

Earl watches her walk to the exit and head back to the squad room. He probably trusts her more than anyone he knows and she's got a point. But he's made his mind up.

His mobile rings and he checks his screen. It's ex-wife number three. The only one who still talks to him. He'd hoped the fact that she was also a detective meant the relationship had a chance. It didn't.

"Good morning, Laura," he says, making an effort to sound more optimistic than he feels. He knows why she's calling and he doesn't want or need sympathy.

"Hi, how are you coping?"

She knows, all right. Someone has made a point of telling her. He suspects it was Akinola. The thought of the two women sharing their concerns about his situation annoys the crap out of him.

"I take it you've been fully briefed, then?"

Laura sighs. "It simply doesn't make sense. If you have to lose someone, if you're going to have to tackle the same workload with fewer officers, why on earth would you get rid of your best detective?"

Despite himself, Earl smiles. Unlike him, Laura always knows the right thing to say in awkward situations.

"Yeah, well, what can I do? Seems like it's going ahead." He's trying to sound flippant, but inside he's not ready to accept that this is really happening and he's pretty sure that Laura knows him well enough to see through his bluster.

"It's not necessarily the end of the world," she says. "Look at it as a chance to embrace a new way of life. There are lots of opportunities for people with your experience and skills out there."

He doesn't reply because he doesn't want to even think about starting a new life.

Laura breaks the silence with another question. "How long have you got?"

"A couple of weeks. No new cases. Just a load of admin crap."

"Your worst nightmare. Shuffling around paperwork."

Earl says nothing again and she gets the hint.

"If you need anything or want to talk, you can call me any time, but I suppose I'd better let you get on with that admin."

"Yeah. Thanks, Laura."

He slips his mobile back into his pocket, feeling guilty about not showing more gratitude for her concern. Their marriage had lasted three years and the breakup had been amicable. Of his three marriages, his failure to make his relationship with Laura work was his biggest regret.

Even though she was also a detective sergeant, and a top-rate one at that, in the end it had been the same old story. Working long hours, unable to sleep when he finally arrived home, an inability to talk about or focus on anything else until a case was solved.

Laura is living proof that you can be a dedicated and successful police officer and still enjoy a life outside work. He doesn't disagree that it's possible. He simply can't do it.

If he truly has only a few weeks left as a detective, then there's no way he's going to waste it on meaningless paperwork. He needs something important to keep his mind busy, to stop himself thinking about the future. He's not ready to consider life outside the force. It's a concept he's unable to grasp.

CHAPTER 13

Liv

It's the look on Lottie's face that I can't get out of my head. Anger and contempt are unpleasant, hurtful emotions, and teenage girls are so good at both of them. I suppose you could call it an argument. Teenage girls can be cruel, they're at the mercy of their emotions, but in the end, she pushed me too far. I should never have said what I did. I wanted to hurt her back and I succeeded. I regretted it as soon as the words were out of my mouth. She stormed out of the house and an hour later she was dead.

I've always been a morning person. It's when my brain is at its sharpest. I take a deep breath. The air is cool and smells of rain. I tug the fake fur-lined hood of my jacket further down to hide my face. Beside me in the bus shelter is a gaunt, white-haired man, his back bent with age beneath an ill-fitting raincoat.

From where I'm standing, I have a clear view of Sharpe's home. The man has been in prison for six months and I'd have expected him to want to make the most of his second full day of freedom. He's at liberty to walk the city's streets, but no, it seems he prefers to stay locked up inside his home.

He's probably enjoying the luxury of a lie-in or cooking himself brunch. The thought makes my eyes prickle. The man who took Lottie from me is across the road, living his life, laughing at his luck. How can I expect to be happy knowing that he has the chance of happiness? All the grief counselling in the world won't help me. I know that now. I have to help myself.

I'm trying to think what Lottie would want me to do when Sharpe's front door swings open and he steps out on to the pavement. He turns to lock up and starts walking west along Cuba Street towards Westferry Road. I dodge between the crawling traffic and follow.

He's wearing trainers, jeans and a dark, three-quarter-length jacket. His hands are tucked into his pockets, his shoulders hunched, his head bowed. I wonder if he fears being recognized. It's so pathetic I almost laugh. Nobody is interested. A teenage girl is dead. He has been punished. Everyone gets on with their lives. Everyone, except Lottie. Nobody gives a damn. No one, except me.

He stops outside a café. I slow down and watch him peer through the window. He decides he doesn't like the look of the place and carries on.

At the junction with Westferry Road he turns left. The streets are busy and there's little chance of being spotted, but I keep a safe distance and plenty of bodies between us. I've never followed anybody before, I've never even thought about it, and I'm surprised how weirdly satisfying it is. Watching him without his knowledge gives me a sense of control, as if I'm stealing a little bit of his freedom, and that feels good.

He stops outside another coffee shop, forcing me to feign interest in the flats and houses on display in an estate agency window. After a moment, I risk glancing sideways but he has disappeared.

Heart hammering, I hurry to the door of the coffee shop and peer through the glass. He's standing near the till, talking to a young man with a bushy beard behind the counter. I step back and take a deep breath.

Everything hangs on this moment. I can be who I've always been and walk away, or I can embrace what I now know I am and make my move. Part of me is terrified by the thought of what I am about to do. The other part, the secret me, is buzzing with excitement.

I'm on the edge of the cliff now, ready to step off. The power of change flows through me like an electric charge and it makes me smile. I lift my chin, push the door open and walk inside. Sharpe is sitting alone at a table for two in a corner away from the window.

While standing at the counter waiting for my latte, I pull my hood down and undo the buttons on my coat. I pay for my coffee and take it to a vacant table next to where Sharpe is staring into a mug of milky tea.

As I sit down, he glances across. I don't look at him but I sense his body tense. I sip my coffee, pull my mobile out of my pocket and pretend to read something interesting. I hear him gulp down his drink, followed by a screech as he pushes his chair back.

"You don't need to leave because of me," I say.

I turn to face him, keeping my expression neutral. I don't want to alarm him and I don't want to be too friendly. He looks back at me, blinking hard, a flash of panic in his eyes. His brown hair is shorter than when he stood, shame-faced, in the dock. The vertical lines on his cheeks are deeper, his skin washed out.

"I mean it," I say. "Actually, I'd prefer it if you didn't go."

Sharpe raises a hand and massages the back of his neck. "I think it's best for both us if I do. I'm sorry but I really don't think this is a good idea."

His voice is pleasantly soft, his tone apologetic. I realize I need to make it clear that I'm not hostile, that I'm not going to make a scene.

"I know you must be feeling uncomfortable right now. I said a lot of nasty things about you before and after you were sentenced. I understand you've served your time and I'm trying my best not to hate you anymore. For my own sake. I don't want this hate to taint the rest of my life, but it's hard."

I bow my head, cover my eyes with my hands and wait. He shifts uncomfortably in his seat. I hold my breath. The last thing I want him to do is get up and walk out. He has to stay if this is going to work. I need him to say something that's going to help. An antidote to the poison in my veins.

His chair scrapes the wooden floor again as he turns to face me. "I am truly sorry for what happened," he says. "I've said it so many times and I promise you I mean it. Believe me, if I could undo what I did I'd do it in a flash, but I can't."

Excitement quickens in my chest. He sounds genuinely sorry. A broken man. If that's true, is it enough? God, I hope so.

I lift my head and sigh. "I know you're sorry. I do believe you. That won't bring her back though and it won't help me forget what happened to her. I sometimes wish it had been me crossing that road instead of Lottie."

He pauses and his eyes narrow suspiciously. "What are you doing here? Did you follow me? This isn't right. I'm ashamed of what happened but I can't bring her back for you. I'm sorry."

There he goes again. He says he's sorry but he can't even bring himself to say her name. I guess it's easier for him not to speak of her, not to think about her.

I shake my head. "Of course I didn't follow you. What sort of person do you think I am? I don't live far from here. You know that. I was walking to the Tube station at Canary Wharf and saw you standing outside this place. I wasn't sure it was you at first. I had no idea you were out of prison. When you went inside, I thought, maybe it would be a good idea if . . . well, I'm not sure what I thought."

I know from personal experience that sometimes the truth can hurt you more than a lie. But I don't want to harm Sharpe. Not right now. I want him to feel sorry for me, pity me even, and I know if I'm going to lie, I need to go big.

"I've been struggling with my grief and have been seeing a therapist for the past few months. He thinks that talking to you might help me sort things out. I never thought I'd get this close to you without wanting to claw your eyes out for what you did, but I can't live like this any longer. The hatred is poisoning me."

Sharpe zips up his jacket and slides his chair back. "I don't think talking about this is a sensible idea," he says. "I truly hope you can sort yourself out but I don't think there is anything we can say to each other that is going to help either one of us."

I tilt my head to the side, look him directly in the eye and for a moment consider bursting into tears and telling him I'm suicidal. Cripple him with guilt. I lift a hand to my forehead and push back a stray lock of hair. I sob softly, then stop myself. It doesn't feel right. It's not me. Instead, I close my eyes and bow my head.

"We hadn't seen much of each other for years. I won't bore you with the details but I fell out with our mother, walked out of the family home and came down to London. There was a nine-year age gap between Lottie and me, and we lived very different lives in very different places. Then she came to live with me when she was fifteen."

My words bring back a memory of the day the police knocked on my door to break the news that my mother had been killed in a head-on car crash. They said she'd been drinking. I felt sad, of course I did, but our relationship had died years before. She gave me nothing and took everything. That's when I welcomed Lottie into my life. She wasn't sure at first. I think our mother had turned her against me. In the end her only choice was to live with me or go into care.

Sharpe is staring into the bottom of his empty mug, anguish and uncertainty twisting his insides. I almost feel sorry for him.

"I wish I could help you," he says. "But I can't. I'm not ready to talk about what happened with anybody, let alone you. I've served my sentence and, to be honest, I agree with what you said in the newspapers. I got off lightly. I'll never know whether she, your sister, would have lived if I'd stopped and called an ambulance. I have to live with that."

He stands up and looks down at me, waiting, hoping I'll say something that will help him feel better about what he did to that innocent girl. He still won't speak her name, and that angers me even more than his attempt to make me feel sorry for him. I meet his eyes and feign sorrow while trying to calculate whether to gamble on pushing him a little more. I decide not to risk it.

This is the first time I've seen Sharpe up close. He's unremarkable. A disappointment in many ways. There's nothing about him that suggests he's the cold-hearted monster I've imagined. But I know that doesn't prove anything. Truly evil people know how to hide their horns.

"I want you to understand what you've done," I say. "Lottie was seventeen when she died. She'll always be seventeen, won't she? She shouldn't have been out walking the streets at that time. I was supposed to be looking after her. She had nobody else to care for her. I let her down."

Sharpe steps away from his table and flashes a look at the door. He's desperate to leave. He can't bear to witness my distress because he doesn't want to face up to what he did. But I want him to feel my pain. I want to bring him to his knees.

I blink rapidly and make myself recall what Lottie said, or rather yelled, at me before she left the house, before she stepped into the path of Sharpe's car. The memory makes my left temple throb, the pain spreading quickly behind my eyes.

"I know I've said a lot of hateful things about you," I say, letting him see that I'm fighting hard not to cry, the headache making it easy to look distressed. "I can't apologize for that because what you did was unforgiveable and you know it. But I'm willing to be convinced that you're not a bad person. Not really. That you did what you did because you're weak, not wicked."

Sharpe's breathing is shallow and fast. He can't cope with me almost being nice to him. Tiny beads of sweat break out on his forehead and he wipes them away with the back of a hand.

"I think it best that I go," he says. "I know sorry doesn't cut it, but I am and I always will be. I wish I could . . ."

He stops mid-sentence and heads for the door, weaving between the tables. I watch him step out onto the pavement and walk away without once looking back. I allow myself a small smile of satisfaction. Whether his remorse is genuine or not, I'd say he's definitely struggling to cope with life. That must be hard for a man who's as alone as he is.

After he handed himself into the police, the tabloids spiced up their reports on the case by looking into his personal relationships. It made interesting reading.

According to his ex-wife, he'd cheated on her when she was pregnant with their first and only child. Wracked by guilt he'd admitted everything after the baby was born. She wasn't the forgiving type and left him, taking their daughter with him. The man obviously has a crazy compulsion to confess his sins.

I check my watch and decide I have time to treat myself to another coffee and perhaps even a chocolate muffin. I deserve it.

CHAPTER 14

Liv

I sit at my kitchen table, power up my laptop and search for more sources on symptoms and signs of psychopathology. I want to know exactly what my special brain can help me achieve. That's how I've decided to frame this situation. My brain isn't abnormal: it's special.

Superficial charm, lying pathologically, inflated sense of self-worth, narcissism, manipulative, lack of empathy, remorse and guilt.

Some people might consider these negative qualities, but I can see how they would help you get things done. After half an hour of reading, it becomes clear that most psychopaths are not violent criminals or serial killers, but a high proportion of killers are psychopaths.

One particular paragraph catches my eye. There's a theory that a happy childhood and loving parents can prevent the development of a psychopath's dark side. Physical and mental abuse or a single traumatic event can act as a trigger. I scribble this down in my notebook and find myself laughing out loud.

I skim through few more articles. Over and over, researchers point to the same signs of potential psychopathy in children, including early sexual activity and the torture and even killing of animals. The abuse of family pets, such as dogs or cats, can be seen as experimental, a practice run, a rehearsal before moving on to taking pleasure in harming people.

The sexual activity reference piques my interest. I was barely fourteen when I lost my virginity. The boy was a little older but I knew what I wanted and never regretted it. As far as pets go, we never had one. I begged my mother for a puppy, a kitten, even a fluffy little hamster. If I'd ever been allowed one, I know I'd have treasured and protected it.

Satisfied for the moment, I shut the laptop down. It's obvious that psychopathy is more nuanced than most people think. Questions whirl around in my head. When does self-confidence become narcissism? Doesn't being charming and manipulative simply mean you are gifted with fantastic social skills?

I get up and pour myself a large glass of red wine. I rummage around in the fridge, until I find half a bar of milk chocolate wrapped in foil. I snap off one square, pop it in my mouth and take the rest, and the wine, back to the table.

I sit back in my chair and take a long sip of wine. I'd never describe myself as cruel. I can be manipulative if I feel it's necessary. I can be assertive when required. But can't everyone? Like everybody else I want to be loved and cared for. And I'm capable of love — I really am. I know that much for certain because I have first-hand knowledge of how much it hurts when somebody you love doesn't love you back.

I took my Lottie in when she had nobody else. That was a caring thing to do. I didn't have to. I owed her nothing. Mother made sure that we stayed strangers. But when my estranged sister needed it, I gave her a home and gradually we became close. As close as sisters can be. For the first time I had unconditional love in my life.

My eyes fill with tears. I blink them back. They come from my heart, not my strangely structured brain. I sniff loudly and pop another piece of chocolate into my mouth.

Am I crying for Lottie or for myself? It doesn't matter. The pain is the same.

My internet research has been enlightening. I'm not a monster, but maybe I have it in me to take risks, to do things I'd never previously consider doing. A week ago, I would never have been able to think this way. Am I capable of ignoring my conscience if I feel doing wrong is the right thing to do? Right now, I'm not sure.

My life is more confusing than it's ever been. But, according to Professor Noble, I was born with a brain with faulty connections in the prefrontal cortex and amygdala. The two regions of my brain that regulate emotion and social behaviour do not communicate as they should. I have no say in this. I had no choice over how my brain formed as I lay curled up in my mother's womb.

Like people who are born white or black, gay or straight, smart or stupid, short or tall, I'm at the mercy of my genes. How then can I be held morally or legally responsible for the things I do?

My brain is in the driving seat. Like Daniel Sharpe on the night he snuffed out Lottie's life.

CHAPTER 15

Sharpe

The early March sky is the colour of faded denim. The breeze still carries a hint of winter, and Sharpe's breath curls on the air like smoke as he climbs the concrete stairs to Cabot Square. To the east, the Canada Square skyscraper glistens in the low sunlight.

He crosses the square, weaving between the city suits looking for somewhere to spend their lunch expenses, passes the gurgling fountain and descends the steps. The Tower Physio Clinic is across the road, and she's already waiting with the door propped open. As he approaches, she turns and walks in. He doesn't break stride and follows her into an empty consulting room.

He takes off his jacket and slips it onto the back of one of the chairs next to the treatment table. He wants to reach out and wrap his arms around her, but she can't even bring herself to look at him.

He guesses she's in between clients because she's wearing her uniform, a flared pale-blue tunic with white trim on the sleeves and collar and loose white trousers.

"Thank you for agreeing to see me, Karen," he says, and immediately regrets sounding so subservient.

"I haven't a lot of time," she says, still studying the carpet. "In five minutes, I'm supposed to be sorting out a frozen shoulder."

He stops himself from saying thank you again, interlaces his fingers and rubs his hands together nervously.

"You didn't come, Karen," he says. "Not once. It would have been nice to see you. Prison can be a very lonely place." For the first time, she looks up at him but doesn't offer an excuse. He sees sorrow and regret, and it gives him a tiny sliver of hope.

"I understand it must be hectic trying to run the clinic on your own, but I would have thought, you know, one visit at least. Considering everything."

She smiles thinly and gives a rueful shake of her head. Her light-brown hair brushes her shoulders and her eyes are shrewder and a paler green than he remembered.

"I had to get someone in to take over your clients," she says. "She's a great physio and the customers love her. I think she's going to work out."

"The business hasn't suffered, then?"

"We're surviving, despite everything, but you do know, don't you?"

All hope is gone now. Sharpe does know but he wants to make her say it. He needs to hear the words spoken. Another form of punishment, another layer of humiliation. He deserves to suffer for what he's done.

"Know what, Karen?"

She lifts her chin and looks him in the eye. She stands by her decision and he admires her for it.

"I want you to know that I'll always be grateful. For everything. But you can't come back here, Daniel. It's impossible. The news coverage, your prison sentence, it almost killed the business. We saved it, but it's over as far as you're concerned. I'm sorry."

He wonders why she's apologizing. She hasn't done anything wrong. She's made a positive business decision and he doesn't blame her.

"I'm a good physiotherapist," he says. "I get results. And I own a third of the practice." Before the girl's death, business had been booming. The towers of Canary Wharf are full of deskbound workers hunched over their computers struggling with bad backs or repetitive strain syndrome.

"You have to understand I've no choice," Karen says. "I wish I did. I've instructed a lawyer and he'll be in touch soon. You'll get the full value of your shares in the company and a little extra. I'm sorry, Daniel, but that's the way it has to be. The story was so big I think it's going to be impossible for you to find work as a physio in London. If you move out of the city, who knows? There may be a chance to start over somewhere quiet."

Sharpe takes a deep breath and sighs. None of this is a surprise, but he'd hoped their relationship would count for something. They'd worked together for three years and had been seeing each other for almost six months before his world crashed around him.

"What about us, Karen? Are we over too?"

She flicks a look at the clock on the wall. Her next session is due to start in one minute, but he's not going to let her avoid the question.

"I take it you're washing your hands of me, professionally and personally?"

She closes her eyes for a moment and he braces himself for an onslaught.

"I thought that maybe we had something special," she says. "But you left that girl to die, Daniel. I can forgive a mistake. Everyone makes mistakes."

There's a tremor in her voice now and he can't tell whether it's sorrow or anger. Maybe it's both. "What you did, though, it was cowardly beyond imagination. She might have survived if you hadn't driven off."

His cheeks burn with shame and he steps towards her. She backs away quickly, as if she can't bear the thought of him close to her. He's an outcast. Unclean. Untouchable.

"I know," he says. "I hate myself for it and I have to live with what happened for the rest of my life. I didn't mean to harm her and I didn't want her to die. I panicked. It happened and I can't change it. I'd trade places with that girl if I could. I handed myself in when I came to my senses. That must count for something. I thought we had something special too. I thought if anyone could forgive me, it'd be you."

Karen drops her head, and when she looks up there's a coldness in her eyes he hadn't expected.

"I'd like to think your conscience got the better of you," she says, her voice flat. "It's just that I can't help feeling that you knew you'd be caught eventually and realized that you'd get a shorter prison sentence if you came forward. Is that unfair?"

Sharpe swallows hard but the lump in his throat stays where it is.

If that's what she believes she doesn't know me at all, he thinks. The shame, guilt and humiliation have been hard to deal with. But rejection is worse.

"I'll let you get on with your work, then," he says and leaves the room without looking back.

He strides across Cabot Square and sits down on one of the benches. Nearby, three large grey pigeons pick at the soil of a dormant flowerbed.

Maybe Karen is right. Perhaps he should sell up, leave London and start afresh. He's living in a city of more than eight million people and he's utterly alone.

He takes his mobile from his pocket, opens his contacts and presses call. She answers after three rings.

"Hello, Dad," she says, her voice a whisper.

"Hi, Emily. How's the studying going?"

"Are you out?"

"Yes, I'm back home."

The line falls silent, and for a moment Sharpe has a horrible feeling that the call has been terminated.

"I thought you said that you weren't going to ring me," his daughter says.

"I wasn't, but I needed to hear your voice. I hope you don't mind."

"I'm in the library, Dad, and can't really speak. Is everything all right?"

Sharpe lifts a hand and rubs his forehead hard. "Everything's fine, darling. It's all good."

Silence again, then a rustle of papers. "I have to go now, Dad. Work to do, you know?"

"I do know," he says, and she ends the call without saying goodbye.

He swipes the screen to search for a photograph of her, forgetting that the phone is new.

CHAPTER 16

Earl

Detective Sergeant Earl feels a mixture of emotions as he sits at the desk in the unused office at the end of the corridor. Anger and frustration. Optimism and self-doubt.

The windowless room was previously home to two family liaison officers, but one had been given her marching orders in the first round of budget cuts and the survivor shifted in with the other detectives. It makes a perfect bolt-hole.

Earl rolls up his shirt sleeves and focuses again on the Lottie Miller file. Before Sharpe had walked into the station to confess, the investigation had followed normal protocol.

The call had gone out for all footage from CCTV cameras in the area and the police press office had released a media appeal for anyone who had seen the incident to get in touch.

Earl wipes his brow with the back of his hand and restarts the task of meticulously working through the notes on the thousands of calls made to the witness appeal helpline. He knows nobody called in to say they had actually seen the incident because that would have been flagged up.

He lifts his head at the sound of footsteps in the corridor. They stop right outside the office door. Earl holds his breath as the grubby brass handle turns slowly. The door opens and Akinola enters.

"So, this is where you're hiding," she says.

Earl jabs a finger at her. "Close the door and keep your voice down."

She gives him a stare and says nothing.

"Close the door, please?"

She does as he asks and steps closer to the desk.

"What are you doing lurking in here? You've got a very guilty look on your face."

Earl lounges back in his chair and puts his hands behind his head. "I never lurk anywhere. You know that. I wouldn't know how to lurk even if I wanted to."

Akinola sighs and shakes her head. She puts her hands in her trouser pockets and leans back against the wall.

"Whatever you're doing, I'm willing to bet you probably shouldn't be doing it."

"I'm ploughing through the hit-and-run file, particularly the helpline callers, because I'm pretty sure nobody else would have bothered once Sharpe confessed."

"That's because they had more urgent things to do. DCI Tanner called everybody off the case because he was satisfied that we had it wrapped up."

Earl shakes his head. "In my mind, that's bad policing. Not checking every piece of evidence available to you? That's sloppy."

The desk phone rings and Earl snatches it up, waving at Akinola to be quiet with his other hand.

"Detective Sergeant Earl," he says.

After listening for a few seconds, he nods slowly. "Right, then. Shit," he says. "That's definite, is it? Right. Thanks for nothing."

He slams the phone down so hard it bounces into the air, rolls off the desk and dangles over the side, spinning slowly on its cable.

"I take it the news wasn't good, then."

"Sharpe's mobile phone provider at the time of the hit-and-run. Like you said, they only keep the data for a limited period and it's been wiped. Apparently, they've been a bit behind with their data clearage programme and if I'd asked a few weeks ago they'd still have it."

Akinola walks over to the dangling phone and places it carefully back on the desk. "What do you think Tanner's going to say if he finds out what you're doing?"

"He's not going to find out."

"The way you're behaving, I think he might. You've a couple of weeks at the most to see out. What is there to gain from all this?"

Earl stands up, rolls his sleeves down and buttons them up. "Don't you think, if we find out that we haven't been told the whole truth about what happened to Lottie Miller, then that would be worthwhile?"

"You think Sharpe lied?"

"It's possible. I've always thought something was off about his confession."

"And you have evidence?"

"No. Not yet. That's what I'm looking for now."

Akinola sighs. "I know what you're like when you get an idea in your head. You're always looking for the chance to prove that everyone else is wrong and you are right. Sharpe has already served his prison sentence. He gave us a full and frank confession. It was his car. The bodywork and bumper were damaged and we found a cloth stained with Lottie Miller's blood. He pleaded guilty. He's not really a bad person. I accept that. He wanted to be punished for what he did."

Earl sits down again and rubs his face with his hands. It hurts him more than he'll ever admit to hear his friend accuse him of being a glory hunter.

"I'm not trying to prove that I'm right, I want to make sure that we haven't been manipulated, that's all. If something makes sense, then it's usually true. This case has never made sense to me. Sharpe had never been in trouble before. He's not a drunk. He doesn't take drugs. He says he was driving around Canary Wharf in the early hours because he couldn't sleep. He's never struck me as the type of guy who would drive off and leave a young girl to die."

"Sometimes good people can make terrible mistakes," says Akinola, as she walks towards the door. She grabs the handle and turns back to face Earl. "Good detectives included."

Earl watches the door close behind her and gets back to work. Most of the calls to the helpline are not actual sightings but people suggesting possible suspects. Earl skim-reads them, despairing at the fact that most allegations are made by so-called friends or partners. He's wondering whether Akinola is right after all, when a call log tagline catches his eye. Helmet-cam cyclist.

His pulse quickens as he reads the report. A cyclist called in to report that he had a near miss with a speeding car. He claims he was forced to brake suddenly as he emerged from a side road less than a mile from the spot where Lottie Miller's body was found. The cyclist said he always wore a helmet cam and could provide close-up footage of the car if they thought it important.

CHAPTER 17

Liv

"I didn't expect to see you back here so soon," Walton says, rolling the sleeves of his white linen shirt neatly up to his elbows.

It's something he always does at some point during our sessions. I think he feels that baring his wiry forearms gives the impression that he's working hard, even though he's just sitting back in his comfy chair listening to me drone on.

I called the clinic to make an emergency appointment the morning after my visit to the cemetery. I'd had restless night. I dreamed that Lottie hadn't died at all but had transformed into a butterfly. Everywhere I went the butterfly followed, until in a fit of temper I stamped on it.

"There's no way I could wait until next week's appointment. I need help."

Walton perks up. He's never seen me as frantic as this before.

"Tell me, what's happened?"

"Nothing. It's what's going to happen that's the problem. I need someone to stop me before it's too late."

Walton frowns. "I don't understand."

Nobody will ever understand unless I tell them what's really wrong with me and I can't bring myself to do that. But somehow, I need to force the beast inside me back into its cage.

"I want to talk about Daniel Sharpe."

Walton responds with the smuggest of smiles. "That's great. I'm glad you've come round to my way of thinking." He puffs out his chest and rubs his hands together, impressed with his own wisdom.

"No, you don't get it. I'm not here to talk about forgiveness. I'm here because I'm losing control of my hatred for Sharpe."

"What do you mean?"

"I can't stop thinking about punishing him, humiliating him, destroying him. Sometimes I even fantasize about killing him. Setting him alight and watching him burn. Or knocking him out and dumping him in the Thames to drown."

I pause, waiting for Walton to say something clever, but he gapes at me in shocked silence. Now that I've started, I want to spit it all out. The more I stress how dangerous this situation is the more Walton is likely to help me. To stop me.

"It's an obsession. It's taking me over. When I get these thoughts, I try to push them away, and at first it worked. But they keep coming back and each time it's becoming harder and harder to ignore them. Sometimes they are so bad that I scare myself and I'm frightened of what I might do. I don't know what I—"

Walton holds up a hand to silence me. He's looking less flustered now, and ready to put his years of study and training to good use.

"Do you really believe that, given the opportunity to physically harm this man, you would actually do it?"

I close my eyes and sigh in exasperation. Hasn't he been listening? Can't he see that I'm pouring my heart out to him because he's my only hope? Because I'm teetering on the edge of an abyss and I need him to pull me back. To stop me fall into the void.

"Yes, yes, yes. That's why I'm telling you this now. If I had the chance, and especially if I thought I could get away with it. I've even spent time plotting how it could be done." Shaking with frustration, I clench my hands and rap my skull with my knuckles. "There's something terribly wrong, up here. Something not right with my brain. I don't know what to do."

Walton shifts uncomfortably in his chair, clearly surprised by my outburst. I try to read his expression but it's impossible for me to tell whether he thinks I'm a hysterical fool or completely insane.

"Take some long, deep breaths and try to relax," he says.

I do as he suggests, despite feeling a stab of disappointment at how condescending he sounds. Has he actually been paying attention? Doesn't he understand how desperate I must be to confess this to anyone?

When he's happy that I've calmed down, he gives me a tight smile and a nod of approval.

"I have to admit you surprised me a little. I had no idea you were struggling this badly. But I want to reassure you. What you're feeling is no more than a manifestation of your complex grief. I suggest you make an appointment to see a doctor. You're going to need antidepressants to help you through this phase."

I can't believe what I'm hearing. Despite his arrogance, I always thought that Walton was good at his job.

"Please listen. What I'm feeling, these thoughts, it's more than depression." I can hear my panic rising as my voice gets louder and higher pitched. "It's something else. Something's happening to me and I can't control it. I think I might need to go to hospital. I'm sure it's not depression. It's more like a burning obsession. It's hard to describe, it's like . . . it's like a fire in my head."

Walton holds up a hand again. "Breathe," he urges, "breathe. You'll feel better if you stay calm. Please trust me. This is depression, which is linked to your unresolved grief. Antidepressants will ease your symptoms and help you benefit from these sessions. I can get you through this, don't worry."

I bow my head and stare at the floor. I can't bring myself to look at his face a moment longer. The one person I thought might be able to save me has let me down. I consider suggesting that he needs to see a therapist to work on his superiority complex but bite my tongue. Before I go there's one thing I want to ask.

"I'll take your advice and see a doctor," I lie. "Tell them about my grief and depression. I promise I will. What I've told you today — it's all confidential, right? You can't reveal to anyone what I've said, or they'll strike you off. That's right, isn't it?"

My head is still bowed, so I can't see Walton's face when he answers, but I can tell by his voice that he's wearing his self-righteous smirk again.

"That's almost right but not quite. If I really believed that you posed a threat to a member of the public, that you might do them or yourself real harm, then it would be my duty to report my fears to the authorities. But that isn't the case, is it? You're depressed, your mind is playing tricks on you. These thoughts you're having are fantasies. Nothing more. A course of medication will sort you out and I'm confident you're not a danger to anyone."

I stand up and walk quickly to the door. "Thanks for listening and letting me rant. It feels good to get my worries off my chest. I guess I'll see you in a couple of weeks."

I leave the room knowing that I'll never return.

CHAPTER 18

Earl

Earl stands in the detective chief inspector's office. The harsh strip lighting makes him squint. On the back wall hangs a framed photograph of Tanner, when he was thirty pounds lighter, shaking hands with a former mayor of London.

Tanner fills his throne-like leather chair, his greying hair slicked back and swept behind his ears, his thick arms crossed on his stomach.

"You wanted to see me," Earl says.

Tanner's eyebrows twitch. "No, detective, I didn't want to see you. Far from it. I've got more important things to do before I can even think about going home to see my long-suffering but extremely supportive wife."

Earl has a pretty good idea why his boss has summoned him. He suspects someone has been talking about his interest in the Lottie Miller case. It wouldn't have been Akinola, he's sure of that, but there are a lot of prying eyes in the squad room and a lot of people trying to keep themselves in Tanner's good books.

He shrugs. "Well, I was told that you wanted to see me, sir."

Tanner frowns, lifts a hand and points a fleshy finger at the chair on the other side of his desk.

"For God's sake sit down, man. It's giving me neck ache having to look up at you."

Earl does as his boss suggests. "What am I doing here?" he asks.

Tanner sighs and shakes his head slowly. "You're an excellent detective," he says. "Dedicated and hard-working. We'll miss you in the squad room, you know that. If it was up to me, I'd keep you on."

Earl understands that the sensible thing to do would be to nod gratefully and accept his boss's compliments, but he has never been good at holding his tongue, especially when someone is talking bullshit.

"You could keep me if you really wanted to. We both know that."

Tanners features barely move. His eyes darken. "I'm trying to help you, but you've always been your own worst enemy."

Earl says nothing. In some ways that's true. He's never been interested in office politics, saying the right thing to the right people or chasing promotion for the sake of it. He decided early in his career that surviving on the streets is dangerous enough for a detective, without having to deal with the duplicity of office politics and bureaucracy.

Tanner keeps his voice level but firm. "I understand you've been poking around in an old hit-and-run case without authority. What the hell do you think you're doing? You're supposed to be winding down and preparing the paperwork to hand over your active cases."

For a moment Earl considers denying everything. But he's never mastered the art of lying convincingly.

"I've always felt there was something not right about the Lottie Miller investigation and I wanted to take a last look at it before leaving. You know how much I hate loose ends."

Tanner hammers the desk with his fist. "It was a high-profile case and a big success for the force. I can't see any loose ends. We're being forced to cut staffing levels down to the bone, we're fighting a city-wide rise in violence, especially knife crime, and we're losing. To top it all the press is on our back. We don't need shit being stirred. Do you understand?"

Earl understands all right. He doesn't agree, though. "I know as well as anybody the pressures the force is under, but standards can't be allowed to drop. Don't you think if there are any doubts about a case then it should be reviewed? I'm not suggesting taking detectives off active cases. I can make it my last job before I leave."

Tanner leans forward in his seat. A red flush rises from the top of his tight shirt collar to his cheeks.

"I want you to listen very carefully, because I'm not going to say this again. There are no doubts, do you understand? You are the only one fixated on it. If this is some pathetic attempt to prove what a great detective you are then you are going to end up making yourself look very foolish. I'm telling you to drop it. Now. Get on with your paperwork and start organizing your leaving party. Is that clear?"

Earl stands up. "Crystal clear," he says, and walks out.

Back at his desk in the squad room, he kicks his chair hard, slamming it against the wall. Half a dozen heads turn at the noise. He kicks the chair again to give them a show.

He sits on the edge of his desk, as Akinola walks towards him across the room shaking her head, a faint smile on her face.

"Are you okay?" she asks.

"Nobody ever used to ask me that, now I get to hear it at least once a day."

"Not long now and you'll be out of all this madness."

She's trying to make Earl feel better but she's failing. "I don't want to be out of it," he says. "I like this madness. It's all I've got."

Akinola sits beside him on the desk. "It wasn't me," she says, lowering her voice to make sure their conversation is private.

"I know that."

"What did Tanner say?"

"He wasn't happy."

Akinola grins. "I take it he told you to drop it?"

"He definitely did."

"And are you?"

"I'm definitely not."

CHAPTER 19

Liv

I step out of Bethnal Green Underground station, in the heart of the city's East End, and head north. It's early evening, and the area is bustling with half-drunk, half-stoned people trying to convince themselves that they're having fun.

Walking briskly, it takes me two minutes to reach my destination. Even though it's an unseasonably warm night, I pull the hood of my coat up before turning into Paradise Row, a quaint, narrow back street.

The cobblestoned surface is tricky to negotiate in high heels, and I have to angle my weight onto the balls of my feet to keep balance. To my left, I pass a wall of graffiti. On the right runs a terrace of Georgian houses.

The alleyway is darker than the main road, and I can't make out the features of the solitary, tall figure waiting for me with his back to the railings bordering Paradise Gardens. As I approach, he lifts a hand to raise the peak of the baseball cap enough for me to see his small, round, piggy eyes.

It may be coincidental but the sight of him brings on yet another splitting headache. They plague me every few days now, and I'm having to take so many painkillers I'm starting to rattle.

I step closer, while making sure I still have enough space to back away quickly if required.

"There you are, babe, right on time," he says. "Marty loves a woman who don't keep him waiting."

The only thing that irritates me more than someone referring to themselves in the third person is being called *babe*. Especially by someone I've never met before. I don't know whether his real name is Marty, and I don't want to know. I want to pick up what I need and get away from him as quickly as possible.

Keen not to encourage conversation, I keep it curt. "Do you have the stuff?"

He jams his right hand into the pocket of his puffer jacket and wiggles it about. "Marty's got it, don't worry your pretty head," he says, licking his lips. "What's the hurry, babe? I'm pretty sure you're never gonna need to drug men to get them to sleep with you."

I want to tell him that no self-respecting woman would even contemplate having sex with him, unless they were doped up to the eyeballs. The man has the charisma of a rattlesnake.

Instead, I grit my teeth and, although it pains me, gift him a half-smile. He's an odious creature but he can get me what I need at a reasonable price.

"Well, do you want this, or not?" I ask, taking my hand out of my coat pocket and offering him a wad of cash. He grins, snatches the crisp notes and stuffs them in the pocket of his tracksuit trousers. I keep my hand out, palm up, waiting for him to give me what I want.

"Hope you're not thinking about taking all this juice yourself," he says. "That's not a wise move. It's very easy to overdose if you're careless, you get what I'm saying? Liquid ecstasy, they call it in the clubs. A fucking powerful magic potion, babe."

Patience used to be one of my strong points. But things have changed. I have no intention of spending the evening pitting my intellect against a sleazy drug dealer with a brain the size of a peanut.

I jab my upturned hand at him. "Come on, stop wasting my time. You've got your money. I've got better things to do with my life than hang around here."

With unexpected speed, he grabs my wrist and pulls me close. His grip is surprisingly strong, and I wince. I feel the panic that comes with losing control of a dangerous situation.

"I don't like it when my customers show me disrespect," he snarls. "It's not all about the cash, you know. I provide a proper, professional service. Don't be disrespecting me, babe."

His face is so close, I can smell his sewer breath, and see broken blood vessels in the whites of his eyes. My heart thuds in time with the throbbing in my head. Fear and negativity creep over me, but I draw on an inner strength I didn't know existed and reject them both. The worse thing I can do now is show weakness.

"I have a friend waiting in a car around the corner," I tell him, speaking slowly, as if to a disobedient toddler. "I gave her strict instructions to call the police if I don't return in ten minutes. Time is almost up."

Marty burns the skin on my wrist with a violent twist, smiling at my reaction. "I know you're lying. What kind of fool do you think I am?"

"Well, Marty, or whatever your real name is, I think you're a stupid fool. I knew it the first time I set eyes on your ugly face. Do you really believe I'd arrange to meet a disgusting lowlife like you without making sure I'd be safe?"

I've given up trying to keep him sweet. There's no chance I'll be buying anything off him again.

"Your regular customers might be brain-dead addicts but I'm not like that, and you know it. My friend is almost certainly on the phone right now."

He twists the skin around my wrist again until I cry out, then releases his grip. He produces a small glass bottle full of clear liquid from his jacket pocket, and hands it over. Marty is as dumb as he looks but he's streetwise. He's survived this far by not taking unnecessary risks.

I slip the bottle into my coat pocket, turn around and walk away, taking care not to trip on the cobbles.

Five minutes later, I'm sitting on a packed Central Line Tube train. My sense of triumph is tinged with sadness. The old me would never have walked down an alley to meet a drug dealer. The old me would never have been able to bluff her way out of a situation that dangerous.

This feels like a tipping point. Something tells me there is no turning back. I close my eyes, cover my face with my hands and mourn for the person I used to be.

* * *

Back home by midnight, the first thing I do is pour a large vodka, sit down on the sofa and take a long sip. It has no flavour but leaves a slight, slow burn in my mouth.

I put the glass down on the table beside me, lean back and recall the drug dealer's warning. *It's very easy to overdose if you're careless. A fucking powerful magic potion, babe.* I pull the small bottle from my pocket, unscrew the top and put a drop into my drink. I've no idea how much is too much, but I tip the bottle again and trickle in a little more.

Raising the glass to my lips, I wonder whether I can empty it in one go. I close my eyes tightly and drink. When I put the glass back down on the table, almost half of the liquid has gone. I wait for a while and am surprised at how quickly I feel drowsy. At the same time, I'm more clear-headed than I've been for a long time. My thoughts are slower but they're crisper and make more sense.

I remember reading on the internet that psychopaths rarely kill themselves because they don't suffer emotional pain. And because they love themselves too much. I stare into the oblivion cocktail and feel strangely at peace. This is one way to put an end to my torment. An easy way. But what is it that I truly want? *I want to be the person I thought was, before Professor Noble destroyed everything.*

But that's impossible, I know. So, the next question is: do I let Daniel Sharpe kill me too?

The question alone is oddly comforting, and suddenly, before I can come up with an answer, sleep takes me.

* * *

When I wake, my brain is foggy, my limbs heavy, mouth dry. I think I've been out for an hour or two but the light edging through the window blinds makes me reach for my mobile phone. I'm surprised to see I've been slumped on the sofa, dead to the world, for ten hours. The glass on the table is still half full and, despite everything, I'm content to be alive.

A phrase I used when begging Walton for help jumps into my mind. It's like a fire in my head. The words reveal a hidden truth, and for the first time in weeks I feel calm. I know I have no choice. That fire cannot be extinguished. It must be left to run its course, to rage until it burns itself out.

CHAPTER 20

Liv

I lift the scissors, start behind my right ear and work carefully around the back of my head. It feels awkward, and the metal is cold against my scalp. The blades are sharp, and my hair falls like dark feathers into the sink.

I pause as a cold dread grips me. Do I really want to chop my hair off? No is the answer to that question. It's the last thing I want to do, but it's the first test for the new me. My eyes prickle with tears as I grit my teeth and tell myself to get on with it.

I repeat the process on the other side before switching to the front — quick, short cuts until the whole of the inside of the sink is covered. My head feels lighter and the back of my neck chilly. I scoop up a handful of hair and dump it in the small, stainless steel bin under the sink, turn on the cold tap and swirl the water around until the rest is gone.

Only then do I raise my eyes to the mirror. It's not as bad as I expected it to be. With a bit of imagination, you could call it a rough pixie cut, and it gives me a slightly boyish appearance. It's definitely not my best ever look, but I don't hate it.

I undo my dressing gown, let it slip to the bathroom floor and step into the shower.

Matt had called from his office earlier to ask if he could drop in after work for a chat. I've been away for a week, and he already wants to check on me, show his support. He's a kind man. I don't really like doing this to him, but I can't back down now even if I wanted to. It would be impossible to explain. Why am I doing this to him? Maybe to see how simple it is to switch on the cruel side of my personality. And how hard it is to switch it off.

I dry myself and walk down the hall into my bedroom, where I've laid out a selection of outfits. I choose a loose but stylish pair of dark blue tracksuit trousers with a pale blue top. I kneel by the side of the bed, reach under and pull out a plastic bag. Inside is the cheapest wig I could buy.

I pull it over my newly cropped hair, turn to face the mirrored wardrobe door and can't help but giggle at what I see. I pick up my make-up bag, apply a little mascara, then carefully smudge it to give the impression that I've been crying.

I'm admiring my handiwork when the doorbell rings. I take a deep breath, walk slowly to the door and open it. Matt stands on the doorstep with a lopsided smile holding a small bunch of white roses. He starts to say hello but his mouth seizes up and his eyes widen.

"I know, I know the wig is terrible," I say, smiling in an attempt to put him at ease. "But I feel worse without it at the moment. Though I'm thinking maybe a headscarf would be better."

"Hello, Liv," he stutters, while handing me the flowers and fighting to keep his eyes fixed on my face.

I wave him in and he follows me into the kitchen. "Thanks for the roses. Take a seat. I'm making coffee."

He does as I ask and I feel his eyes on my back as I put two scoops of coffee grounds into the cafetière and add hot water. When I turn around, he's looking more composed.

"I didn't realize the treatment would be starting so quickly," he says.

"Neither did I, but my specialist wanted to get going as soon as possible. I guess he knows what he's doing. The doses are high and the side effects severe. As you can see."

Matt squirms uncomfortably in his chair. "I'm so sorry you're going through this on your own, Liv. I really am. If there's anything I can do for you, know you only need to ask, don't you?"

I wonder if he'd be so easily fooled if he wasn't desperate to date me. Probably not.

Turning away to pour the coffee, to show I'm too emotionally choked to respond to his kindness, I add milk to his cup and sugar to mine. When they're ready, I place them on the kitchen table with a flourish and sit opposite him.

"My mother and I never got on, so even if she was still alive, I don't think she'd be here to support me, and to tell you the truth, I'd hate for Lottie to have to see me like this."

I pick up my coffee, cradle the cup in my hands and offer him a brave smile. He picks up his drink and takes a long sip.

"The coffee's good," he says, taking in his surroundings for the first time since his arrival. "How long have you been here? It's a nice place."

"I like it too. I don't own it, though. It's small, but there is no way I could buy a place like this on what I earn. Not this close to Canary Wharf."

Matt grunts and nods. He has the ability to show understanding without being patronizing.

"It must be difficult," he says. "You're not going to be able to earn until you're well enough to start working again. Are you going to be all right? Because if not, then I can help. I haven't got a lot of spare cash but I have some savings."

I shake my head slowly and smile my eternal gratitude. I do own this house, with a small mortgage, but there is no need for Matt to know that. Lottie was the sole benefactor of our mother's estate and she was happy to take my advice about property investment. It was easy to persuade her to put both our names on the title deeds. When she died, her share of the house came straight to me.

"That's so generous of you to offer," I say. "But as far as finances go, I can manage — for now, at least."

Matt drains his coffee and checks his wristwatch. "I'm sorry but I'm going to have to shoot already. We're close to deadline at the office. You know how it is."

We both stand and I lead him to the door. "It's been so nice," I say. "And thanks for the flowers. It's great to have company, but make sure you give me some warning because I'm going to be at the hospital most of the time."

"I will, Liv," he says, stepping outside. Before I close the door, he turns back, reaches out and cups both of my hands in his.

"I meant what I said. Don't hesitate to call me if you need anything. You know, you are handling this so incredibly well. You're an amazing woman. I think if it was me, I'd be falling apart."

I lower my eyes and try to look pleased and modest at the same time.

"You know what? I think you'd be surprised at what I'm capable of."

As soon as I close the door, I wrench the wig off and throw it onto the floor, where it lies like a small, dead animal. I decide that the next time Matt calls to suggest a visit I'll put him off. I don't want to have to put that thing on again.

It takes me fifteen minutes to walk from my place to Sharpe's house in Strafford Street. I zip my coat up tight, tug the hood down to cover as much as my face as possible and slip on a pair of wraparound sunglasses. Playing around with Matt is a bit of fun, a safe way to test myself. This is serious business.

Standing in the bus shelter again, I think I see movement behind one of the upstairs windows and wonder whether I could walk straight up to Sharpe's house, ring the doorbell and talk my way in.

There is a risk that the sight of me, so soon after our meeting in the café, will freak him out. The last thing I want is for him to call the police and report me for stalking.

I want him punished but I don't yet know what that will involve. I need to think and plan, then think and plan a bit more. If possible, I'd like to have him at my mercy, put him in a position where he is helpless and has no choice but to listen to what I have to say.

I suppose, if he's helpless, then it might even be possible to make him pay the ultimate price. Could I really kill him if I had the opportunity? If I'm honest with myself, the answer has to be no. A true psychopath would say yes, right? That's not me, though. Despite what the brain scan suggests, I know who I am and I don't believe I'm capable of killing, even if I think the person deserves to die.

I'm still considering knocking on the door when it opens and Sharpe steps out. He's wearing a dark jacket, jeans and black trainers. For a moment, his gaze flicks in my direction. I look straight back at him because I know he can't see my face. He twists left and walks away, his hands tucked deep in his pockets, his shoulders slumped. To me he looks a lost and lonely man. It's something but not nearly enough.

I stay on the other side of the street and follow. He's walking so slowly I have to take care not to catch him up. At the end of the road, he turns right and trudges onto Cuba Street. It's then that I guess he's heading for the Thames Path.

A sense of dread engulfs me and I hurry closer. He steps onto the path and looks out across the mud-brown Thames. The water is high, and at this time of the year, still freezing cold. Sharpe rests his hands on the low wall. It would take him seconds to launch himself over the barrier to certain death. My skin is clammy, my heart racing at the prospect of watching a man commit suicide. Even when that man is someone I've imagined killing. Where is that twisted part of my brain that makes me cold and unfeeling when I need it? I'm about to call out to him when he starts walking back towards me.

I keep my head down and move forward. He steps aside to let me pass without looking up. I continue onto the river path, place my hands on the wall as he had and gaze across the water to Rotherhithe. I take a deep breath and instantly regret it. The river stinks of rotting vegetation. I make my way back to the road and am surprised to see Sharpe emerging from the office of one of the Docklands estate agencies. He walks away into the distance, his pace brisker, his head held slightly higher than before.

My head spins at the possibility of Sharpe selling up and moving out of the city. The thought of him being able to start a new life in a place where nobody knows what he has done makes my stomach churn. I can't allow that to happen. Lottie deserves better.

I cross the road, walk up to the window of the estate agency and peer through the glass. I see one employee on the phone at her desk. The other two desks are unoccupied.

An idea surfaces from somewhere in my brain and I'm pretty sure it's from the bad part.

CHAPTER 21

Liv

"This is a great home," the estate agent says, turning the key in the lock and pushing the door open. "If I had the money, I'd buy this place myself."

I laugh politely, knowing that he probably says the same thing about every property he's trying to sell, and follow him in.

"Shall we start downstairs?" he asks. "The owner thought it'd be better if he made himself scarce during the viewing so we have the place to our- selves. This property is so fresh to the market we haven't had time to take photos and print details."

Nathan's brown eyes are warm. His ill-fitting suit is too tight around the shoulders, and he uses far too much styling gel in his hair. I've never liked the wet look. I'd guess that he hasn't been in this line of work for long, but he's trying his best.

"Can we see the kitchen first?" I ask with an enthusiastic smile. "I love a homely kitchen."

Nathan leads me along a short hallway into what he describes as an open-plan kitchen-diner. The space is large and modern, the walls covered with ice-blue units, the work-tops white. The room is spotless. It doesn't look as if anyone has cooked here for a long time.

According to the news articles I found on the internet, Sharpe's wife left him not long after their daughter was born, after he owned up to having an affair. She moved hundreds of miles away and took their child with her. The couple had struggled through four years and five rounds of IVF before Emily arrived.

"This is such a good social space," I say, squinting a little as if trying to imagine my non-existent family sitting around the table enjoying a care-free, nutritious meal. "Very nice indeed."

Nathan beams at me. "Let's move on, then, Ms Hunter."

"Please, call me Alice," I say.

The other room downstairs is a big living area. Again, it looks more like a showroom than a space anyone has actually lived in.

The house is large and close enough to the Thames for the estate agents to describe it as having a "sought-after river-side location". Sharpe is going to be able to start afresh with a lot of cash in his bank account.

Mowing Lottie down, going to jail and being forced to leave the city could turn out to be the best thing that ever happened to him. That can't be fair. Where is the justice in that? On Nathan's suggestion, I go upstairs to check out the bedrooms on my own. I wonder if he's worried that I'll pounce on him, or anxious about being falsely accused of pouncing on me.

In the main bedroom, I search all the drawers and ward-robes. I find nothing of interest and am feeling disappoint-ment when I spot a photograph in a plain silver frame on Sharpe's bedside table.

It's a shot of an attractive girl with fair hair, and I guess it's his daughter. She's a little older than Lottie and is sitting on steps outside what looks like a university building. I take out my mobile and snap a close-up of the photograph.

In the bathroom, I open the wall cupboard and see that keeping Sharpe's electric toothbrush and safety razors company are a woman's lipstick and some eyeshadow. Whoever the woman is, I hope she saw sense and dumped him as soon as he was charged.

Nathan is waiting patiently for me at the bottom of the stairs as I come back down.

"What do you think?" he asks.

I smile broadly at him. "It's lovely up there," I say. "There's such an incredible amount of space. Everywhere you look, you see space."

Nathan's boyish face lights up. "You're right. It is very spacious. It's a fantastic family home."

Outside I shake Nathan's hand, gush about how the property is exactly what I've been looking for and promise to be in touch to arrange a second viewing.

This time, it's only half a lie. I will definitely be visiting the house again.

CHAPTER 22

Sharpe

Sharpe sits at the kitchen table and uses his fork to roll a charred sausage from one side of the plate to the other. When that gets boring, he pricks the poached egg and watches the yolk ooze out onto the toast.

He'd been hungry when he'd starting cooking himself brunch but his appetite has disappeared. He lets the fork fall onto the table and pushes the plate away.

He wonders how his ex-wife spends her Saturday mornings now that their daughter is away at university. Clare has had a few serious relationships since the divorce but none of them had developed into anything long-term. Sharpe would have loved to see her find a new life partner. Maybe it would have distracted her from doing everything possible to stop him having a relationship with Emily.

He recalls the night when he told her that he'd cheated on her. He'd cried and begged for forgiveness. She cried and shouted, swore and screamed so loudly she woke Emily, who was too young to understand what was happening but started crying anyway.

He pours himself a second strong coffee and takes a sip. The estate agent is confident that the house will sell quickly. Sharpe is hopeful that he's not bullshitting, because even though it's not yet officially on the market, there's already been a viewing.

Now that he's made up his mind, he wants to leave as soon as possible. A fresh start is exactly what he needs. He'll have enough money to buy a place of his own but plans to rent at first. He thought about moving to Yorkshire. A quiet, picturesque village, maybe, within easy reach of Leeds and Emily. He knows that's probably not a good idea. Not yet.

As he takes another sip of coffee, the doorbell rings. He's not expecting anyone. Nobody visits him now. The bell rings again and for a moment he considers ignoring it. He walks reluctantly down the hall and opens the door.

His breath catches in his throat and he has to force himself to resume breathing. Liv Miller looks up at him, her eyes wide and intense. She looks pale. The hood of her green coat is down and her dark hair is short and haphazardly cut.

"I know this might seem strange and I'm sorry to bother you, I really am, but I . . ." She falters, her eyes brimming with tears.

He doesn't want to talk with this woman. He doesn't want anything to do with her. She's obviously suffering, he knows that, but so is he. He wants to slam the door in her face but can't bring himself to do it.

"What do you want with me?" he asks. "Are you all right?"

She gives him a rueful smile. "I don't think I'll ever be all right. Thanks to you."

Guilt hits him like a gut punch. She looks frail and a little unstable. His instinct tells him to make it clear they have nothing to talk about and send her away. It would probably be the best thing he could do. For both of them. But he doesn't move and doesn't speak.

"My therapist is away and I desperately need someone to talk to," she says. "I know you might think this is weird but I thought of you."

Sharpe tries to look away but his eyes are drawn to her quivering bottom lip. "I don't think that's a good idea. I'm not the person you need. You must have family who can help."

She blinks several times and a single, fat tear rolls down her left cheek. "I don't have anybody. Not now. After our chat the other day in the café, well, I thought you would . . . To be honest, I'm not coping and I'm worried I'm going to do something stupid."

Sharpe knows what he should say but doesn't know how to say it. He stands perfectly still, his mind a whirl of conflicting thoughts.

This woman has lost her sister, her only living relative. He tries to imagine how he would feel if Emily died but pushes that thought away. He can't bear to go there.

That voice inside his head is back, telling him to shut the door. This woman is clearly troubled, and anything he says is only going to make things worse. She's not his responsibility. He put his hand up and confessed, he's taken his punishment. He owes her nothing. Not even the truth.

He sighs loudly and steps back. "I suppose you can come in for a few minutes," he says.

CHAPTER 23

Liv

I push my shaking hands deep into my coat pockets and follow Sharpe into his house.

He leads me into the living room and invites me to take a seat. I sniff, wipe a non-existent tear from my cheek and park myself right in the middle of the small leather sofa. I try to spread myself out, to discourage him from sitting next to me.

At this point, I don't want him too close. I'm fearful that if I look into his eyes for too long, or notice his chest rise and fall as he breathes, I'll weaken and won't be able to do what I'm planning. I glance around the room, feigning curiosity, pretending I haven't already snooped around under the guise of a potential buyer.

"You really do have a very beautiful home," I say.

He looks embarrassed, and scratches the back of his neck, unsure how to respond. He doesn't tell me that he's decided to move away and that he's put the house up for sale, and I don't let on that I know.

I study him for a moment, trying to guess his weight, measuring his physique with the calculating eye of an executioner. Just under six foot, he looks leaner than when I saw him standing with his head bowed in shame in the dock, while the judge passed sentence. The trousers and sweater he's wearing hang loose on his wiry frame. It appears that the food served up in the prison canteen was not to his taste.

"Can I get you a cup of coffee, or what about tea?" he asks, looking at his wristwatch as if he has an urgent appointment to attend. He doesn't want me in his home but he's much too polite to look me in the eye and say so. A few days ago, I might have appreciated his good manners, but now I understand that people who are strong enough to get what they want don't care what other people think of them.

"A milky coffee would be fantastic, if it's not too much trouble."

I watch him plod to the kitchen. Everything about his body language suggests he's struggling with his mental health. I suppose that's not surprising. It's hard to tell exactly what's going on inside someone's head. The downward spiral of depression is merciless, and he has an awful lot to be depressed about.

I've always considered myself been good at making snap judgements about people, and it's obvious that Sharpe isn't a bad guy. He has no air of menace about him at all. I bet he was born with a brain perfectly equipped for empathy and compassion.

He's being understanding and patient with me, when he doesn't have to be. He feels sorry for me, even though I'm the last person he wants to have to deal with. I'm learning fast that nice, considerate people are always the easiest to control. Kindness can definitely be a weakness, if you come up against the type of person who's prepared to exploit it.

Sharpe comes back into the room carrying two mugs of coffee, and puts one down on a glass-topped table beside the sofa. I reach for it and lift it to my lips. It smells incredible, but I resist the temptation to drink and place it back on the table. I need to string this out.

"I'm afraid I'm meeting someone for lunch in twenty minutes," he says, checking his watch again. "An old friend I haven't seen for years."

I know he's lying. He's clenching his jaw and can't hold my gaze. Anyway, what old friend is going to want to rekindle a relationship and swap stories over lunch with a hit-and-run driver who's just come out of prison?

I squirm in my seat and do my best to look unthreatening, but I'm not going anywhere. "I'm so sorry about turning up like this. I know it must be weird having me, of all people, in your home." I sound so sad and pathetic it catches me by surprise.

Sharpe walks across the room to the window and straightens a fold in the curtains. "It does feel strange and, if I'm honest, extremely uncomfortable," he says. "What exactly are you doing here? I'd have thought I'd be the last person on earth you'd want to see, let alone talk to."

I look down at the floor to give myself time to consider my answer. I have to be careful what I say. Careful and clever. I don't want to alarm him but I need to sound believable. Words can be dangerous weapons if you know how to load them.

"I've come here today because I hate you." I spit the last three words like tiny poison arrows, lifting my face so he can see I mean what I say.

His eyes widen and he steps back unsteadily. He reaches for the wall but grabs the curtain instead. Losing his balance, he stumbles, splashing coffee onto his sweater. He takes a moment to compose himself, puts his mug on the table and sits in the armchair opposite the sofa.

Sharpe shakes his head. "I can't blame you for feeling the way you do. For hating me. How can I? I'd feel exactly the same. Believe me. But I still don't understand what you're doing here in my house, what you want from me."

I drop my left hand into my coat pocket and wrap my fingers around the small glass bottle. It contains everything I need to pull this off, but for the first time I wonder if I can really do it. I want to frighten him, humiliate him. I want him to sit and listen to what I have to say until I have finished. Then I want him to wake up confused, feeling like he's got the worst hangover of his life, not remembering exactly what happened to him but knowing it was bad.

"The truth is," I say, knowing I'm about to tell one of the biggest lies I've told for a long time, "even though hating you feels good, even though I use that hatred to protect myself from pain, to shield me from grief, I don't want to feel it anymore. It's eating me up inside and I know that, in the long run, it will destroy me. I don't want to waste the rest of my life hating you. I want to do my best to live a full life, because I've got to live it for two people now."

Sharpe holds his head in his hands and covers his face. His shoulders tremble slightly and I suspect he's trying hard not to cry. My first instinct is to go to him, give him a hug, but I shut that down quickly. This man doesn't deserve sympathy.

"I thought that if I had the chance to speak to you, maybe even got to know you a little, then perhaps I'd see that you're not the cold-hearted, cowardly bastard I think you are. I'm never, ever going to forgive you. Never in a million years. But that's not the same as hating you so much I want you dead."

Sharpe takes his hands from his face and looks across at me. His eyes are red but they're tearless. I sense he's thinking about opening up. Spilling his guts. I don't want to know how hard things have been for him. How the guilt is gnawing at his soul. I'm relieved when he decides not to go there.

"I really do have to leave soon," is all he can say.

I pick up my coffee and take a sip. "There is one thing I want to ask you. One favour. I read in the newspapers that you have a daughter. Emily, I think her name is."

Sharpe nods, warily. "That's right. She lives with her mother."

He looks like he's about to say something else but stops. I'm guessing he's decided to keep back the fact that his daughter is in her first year at Leeds University. She's studying psychology and — I'm pretty sure Sharpe doesn't know this yet — she's dating a computer studies student. It's amazing what you can find out with a bit of persistent social media stalking.

My Lottie will never have the privilege of going to university. She'll never have a serious boyfriend. I had such high hopes for her. She was as smart as a whip and ambitious with it. She was so like me, and I wanted to give her everything I never had.

"I was wondering if I could see a photograph of Emily," I say.

I don't really want to see it. I have it on my mobile already. She looks a bit of a spoiled brat to me.

"I've thought about this a lot and I think it'll help. My therapist agrees. She's a little bit younger than Lottie, isn't she?"

Sharpe looks at me as if I'm mad. "No, no, that's not a good idea. Definitely not. It's not happening."

I shrink back and look distraught. "Oh, no, of course. I'm sorry. I didn't mean to upset you. I thought that relating to you as a loving parent, a father who loves his child as much as I love . . . as much as I loved Lottie. I thought it might help me come to terms with everything . . . but if you feel that it's not something you want to do. It's only . . . I thought . . ."

He sighs loudly and stands up, defeated by his sympathy for a grieving mother. "I've got one of her upstairs. Give me a minute."

When he's at the top of the stairs, I reach into my coat pocket and pull out the small bottle. An adrenaline rush heats my blood. My breathing is fast and shallow, and my hands are shaking so much I fumble as I try to unscrew the top.

For a moment my resolve falters. Psychopaths don't get nervous. The sound of Sharpe coming back down the stairs forces me to focus. I close my hand around the bottle, sit back and assume a troubled expression. It's not difficult.

Sharpe sits back down in the armchair and I notice that he's empty-handed. I tilt my head and ask the question with my eyes.

He shrugs an apology. "I want to help you, but showing you the photograph doesn't feel right. It'll only remind you of what you've lost, and things must still be so raw. I'm sorry. Please, finish your coffee, but then I need you to leave."

I nod thoughtfully and pick up my mug. "I kind of understand," I say.

He chews hard on his bottom lip. I've exhausted his patience.

He responds by picking up his coffee and taking a large gulp. No turning back now. It's happening. I glance at him cautiously, alert for any reactions, even though I know the drug is tasteless. The research I did last year for a magazine feature on date rape is proving invaluable. Gamma-hydroxybutyric acid, or GHB, is a hypnotic, nervous system depressant.

He's wearing a look of polite impatience. In his mind, the sooner we finish our drinks the sooner his nightmare ends. In my mind, his nightmare is only just beginning.

I offer him a half-smile and blow on my drink, even though it's no more than lukewarm. "This is very nice. What brand of coffee is it?"

He takes another swig. I put my coffee down and stand, my skin flushing with excitement.

"You have to go now. Please leave," he says, with a hint of a slur.

Sharpe already looks pale and sickly. I don't want him to throw up. I estimate that in a couple of minutes he'll be as helpless as a corpse.

He tries to stand, his eyes rolling back in their sockets. I lunge forward and grab his arm to stop him from toppling over. He shrugs me off and flops down in the chair, grunting like a wounded animal. His head drops on to his shoulder, and he starts to drool. He eyes me like a desperate child.

Despite everything, I can't help feeling sorry for him. I kneel beside his chair and put my right ear close to his mouth. His breathing is regular, which is a good sign. He has no choice but to listen now. I can tell him everything. Things

I've never told anybody else. Not even my grief counsellor. What my mother did to me. What I did to Lottie minutes before she died. How my brain is not like his. It'll be a relief to get it off my chest. Cathartic, even. He'll hear it all, then the drug will do what it does best. His short-term memory will be shot to pieces, leaving him unable to recall with any certainty what was done or said to him.

I take my coffee into the kitchen, pour it into the sink and wash the mug thoroughly to erase any fingerprints. I dry it with a sheet of kitchen roll, place it on the draining board and put the damp tissue in my pocket. Back in the living room, I sit opposite Sharpe and give him a smile. His eyes are no more than dark slits now, but he's still looking at me.

I take a deep breath. "If you can hear me, and I think you can, I want tell you that when I said I wanted to stop hating you, I was lying. I hate what you did to Lottie, and to me, and for that you have to pay. That's only fair, isn't it? No one will ever know how special Lottie was to me. It's true, I had nothing to do with her for years, but that wasn't my choice. Our mother decided that I'd be a bad influence. That I didn't deserve to be a big sister. When she died, everything changed and Lottie came back to me. Back to where she belonged. It was perfect. She was perfect. Then you came along and I lost her again."

I've never told anyone about my mother. How everything I did was a disappointment to her, how she blamed me for driving her drunken husband away. She couldn't wait for me to leave home so she could have Lottie all to herself.

Sharpe's eyelids flicker and his head rolls from side to side. I feel a twinge of discomfort in my chest. I may have the brain chemistry of a psychopath, but being merciless doesn't come naturally.

I'm suddenly hit by an overwhelming sense of dread. How have I got myself into this? This isn't me. I'm someone else. I'm scaring myself, but I can't stop. I feel like I've stepped off the edge of a cliff knowing full well that I haven't anywhere near enough time to grow wings.

"When we met the other day in the café, it wasn't an accident. I followed you there, and I'm glad I did. I could see that you were being crushed by the burden of guilt but didn't know how to make amends, how to atone for what you did. I'm here to help you do that, that's all. It may be hard for you to understand, but this is all about atonement. For both of us."

Sharpe lifts his head off his shoulder and looks right at me. Slowly, his eyes close and his head lolls forward. In seconds, he's gone from a trance-like state to total unconsciousness. I slap the arm of my chair in frustration. I have no clue how long it'll be before he stirs. I unzip my coat and take a couple of deep breaths. I'm sweating, and the pain behind my eyes is back with a vengeance.

I climb the stairs and step into Sharpe's bathroom. I pull the sheet of kitchen roll from my pocket and use it to open the cabinet above the sink. There's an unopened packet of painkillers on the top shelf. I take out two pills, dry swallow them and decide to take the packet with me in case I need more later.

I go back downstairs, cursing myself for being so heavy-handed with the GHB. Crossing the living room, I notice Sharpe has slid a little further down the chair. I crouch over him and examine his face. He's motionless and silent. Not even slightest rise and fall or his chest, or the faintest whisper of breath.

It's far too easy to overdose.

My heart is hammering so hard it hurts. I suppress the urge to grab his shoulders and shake him hard. I don't want to touch him.

"Wake up! You need to wake up!" I shout, my mouth inches from his face.

His skin is pale, his mouth slack. I lift my hands to my face to stop myself from screaming.

"Oh my God," I whisper. "What have I done?"

CHAPTER 24

Earl

Earl's memories of his time at university are hazy. Lots of parties, cheap beer, casual relationships and as little actual studying as he could get away with. He doubts things have changed much.

The front of the mid-terraced house is narrow and shabby, the white paintwork stained, cracked and peeling. He stands on the crumbling concrete doorstep and knocks three times. After a minute he knocks again. Harder this time.

Again, there's no response and Earl sighs loudly. He's frustrated but not that surprised. It's Saturday morning. Prime hangover time.

He prepares to knock once more but before his knuckles make contact with the door it swings open. A smartly dressed, fresh-faced young woman looks at him with a faintly quizzical expression.

"Hi there," she says.

Earl flashes his warrant card. "My name is Detective Sergeant Earl. I understand Sam Carter lives here. I need to ask him a few questions."

The woman tilts her head to the side, frowning slightly. "Questions about what, exactly?"

Earl stifles a strong urge to push his way into the house and drag Carter out of his bed. Instead, he shifts his weight from one foot to the other.

"I'm investigating a serious crime and it's important that I speak to Sam as soon as possible. Can you wake him and tell him the police are here?"

The woman waves a hand, turns and leads him inside. The living area is sparsely furnished. One large sofa and several multicoloured cushions scattered around on the carpet. The room looks clean but smells of fried food and sweat.

"Take a seat and I'll get you a tea or something."

"Nothing for me," Earl says. "I'd prefer you to go and tell Sam Carter that I need to speak to him."

She puts her hands on her hips and glares at him. She's only an inch or so shorter than he is, her build athletic.

"You're already speaking to her," she says. "I'm Sam Carter."

Earl holds up a hand by way of an apology. "Right, I get it now. My mistake." The helpline transcript didn't make it clear that the cyclist was female.

Sam grins and sits on the sofa. Earl stays where he is. "I need to talk to you about the call you made in response to an appeal we put out after a girl died in a hit-and-run accident in Canary Wharf. You remember it?"

Sam nods. "Poor girl. That was a terrible thing to happen. But it's all done and dusted, isn't it? I saw on the news that you'd arrested the guy responsible and that he was sent to prison."

"We did get him," Earl says. "But for reasons I can't go into, I'm taking another look at the evidence. I see that you called the information line to say you had a near miss with a vehicle close to the scene of the accident."

"I did call but nobody got back to me. Later, I realized it was because you had a guy locked up and he'd admitted

100

everything. I assumed that what I saw either wasn't important or wasn't connected to the accident."

Earl recalls his uneasiness at shutting down the investigation. He's embarrassed that he caved in so quickly. He knows he should have faced up to Tanner. The right way to run any investigation is to check every piece of evidence, every lead.

"I know it was a while ago, but can you tell me what you were doing in the area at that time in the morning, and exactly what you saw?"

Sam takes a moment to think, running a hand through her long brown hair and flicking it back over her shoulders.

"I'm doing a business management degree at Queen Mary University and work as a part-time bicycle courier. It's great for me because I love cycling. It keeps me fit, and more importantly it helps me pay my fees and rent. I share this place with three other students but it's not cheap. I deliver documents, usually contracts, to various businesses and banks around Canary Wharf, and sometimes to offices in the West End."

Earl licks his lips. His mouth is dry with anticipation. He's regretting not accepting the offer of a cup of tea but he doesn't want to interrupt Sam's flow.

"Go on," he says. "What did you see?"

"I remember that the Canary Wharf office asked if I could do a particularly early delivery for them. It was good money and I was happy to oblige. The roads were quiet because it was so early. I was on my way to pick up the package and it was still dark enough for me to have my lights on. I remember pulling out of Cuba Street onto Manilla Street and this car came out of nowhere, going ridiculously fast. It probably missed my front wheel by no more than twelve inches."

Earl's pulse quickens and he steps forward. "You were close enough to get a look at the driver?"

"The car was going too fast. I had to concentrate on braking sharply enough to avoid getting hit and stopping the bike from toppling over. But, like I said when I called the helpline, I was wearing a helmet-cam and it was running. I always have it on when I'm riding. Cycling in this city can be dangerous, and having a camera is like having my own personal insurance policy."

Earl shakes his head in despair. If they'd followed up the call to the helpline, they'd have video evidence to corroborate Sharpe's statement.

"What about the camera footage? Could you see the driver?"

"I can't afford an expensive camera. The image is blurred but the driver is on there. I've still got the footage. I saved it." Sam shrugs, almost apologetically. "My laptop's in my room if you want to see it."

Earl's heart pounds against his ribs but he keeps his expression neutral. "If you've still got it, then that would be great."

Sam stands up and heads for the stairs. "Obviously, I don't keep everything. That would be impractical. Most of it is boring views of traffic jams. But I do keep any interesting stuff, anything out of the ordinary. Give me a second."

Earl watches her run up the stairs. He sits on the sofa and lets out a long breath. Sloppy police work had led to his team missing an important piece of evidence. At least he had the chance to put that mistake right.

Sam bounces back down the stairs, a laptop tucked under an arm. She sits next to Earl. The screen glows as she opens it up and taps lightly on the keyboard until she finds the relevant file.

"Here we go, then," she says, and clicks play.

Earl holds his breath as the shaky footage shows Sam pulling out onto a seemingly deserted road. The sound of an accelerating engine comes next, then a silver car speeds past the camera in a blur.

"Give me a second and I'll slow the action down," Sam says.

Earl shifts closer to the screen as the car slides into view. He can't be one-hundred-per-cent sure but if he had to bet on it, he'd say it's definitely Sharpe's BMW. When the camera lines up with the passenger window Sam freezes the frame.

"There you are," she says, pointing at the screen. "The image is a little blurry. I'm not sure if the quality would have been considered good enough to stand up in a court of law. But I guess it doesn't matter because the bastard admitted everything, right?"

Earl swallows, blinks and leans even closer. A tingling sensation runs across his scalp, creeps to the back of his neck and slides down his spine. The driver's features are indistinct but the profile, the form, the posture, is familiar. There is no doubt in his mind that the man behind the wheel is Sharpe.

Earl has been wrong before. Mistakes hurt, and he knows that the best way to ease the pain is to own them. This one cuts him to the bone. It feels less like a mistake and more like failure.

* * *

Back at the station, Detective Constable Blessing Akinola leans closer to the screen as she watches the footage from the courier cyclist's helmet-cam for the third time.

Earl stands beside the desk, his shirt sleeves rolled to his elbows.

"What do you think?" he asks. "It's definitely him, isn't it?"

"It's Sharpe. No doubt about it. I take it this means you're going to drop your personal crusade to prove that his confession was bullshit."

Earl gives a brief nod but says nothing. He'd been determined to go out with a bang. Prove to everybody that the squad room's detection rate would plummet without the benefit of his experience.

Akinola sits, swivels her chair to face Earl. "I'm sorry. I know you're disappointed, but at least now you can stop obsessing that we got it wrong. We need to keep this video to ourselves. There's no reason Tanner has to know that you ignored his orders and managed to prove that he was right all along. And for God's sake, cheer up. Even you can't be right all the time."

Earl appreciates her attempt to lift his spirits but he's not in the mood to respond. He's dreading sitting at his desk shuffling paperwork around his desk for the next few weeks, a condemned man waiting for the axe to fall.

Akinola's desk phone rings. She holds it to her ear and listens without speaking. Earl rolls his sleeves down, buttons the cuffs and walks away. Before he's halfway to his desk, Akinola calls him back.

"That was Tanner," she says. "Daniel Sharpe was supposed to report to his probation supervisor this morning. He didn't turn up and he's not answering his phone. It's a breach of his early release licence and could mean him being sent back to prison. Apparently, the supervisor is worried because Sharpe has always been so compliant. Tanner wants me to check it out."

Earl scowls. Sharpe is guilty. He cut an innocent life short. If he's breached the conditions of his early release, then he deserves to go back to jail. It's as simple as that.

"What are you doing right now?" Akinola asks.

Earl eyes her warily. "I've a lot of important admin to get on with. That's what people keep telling me. Why?"

"Important admin? Isn't that an oxymoron? Come on. Let's get going."

Earl can't suppress a smile. "Okay, okay, let me get my jacket."

* * *

The traffic heading west on Marsh Wall is bumper to bumper but rolling at a steady pace.

"Where the hell are all these people driving to on a Saturday afternoon?" Earl moans. "Haven't they got anything better to do than clog up the roads?"

Akinola shoots him an exasperated look. "It might seem strange to you but some people like to enjoy their time off. Go shopping, meet up with friends or loved ones, eat out with friends and family. Surely you remember when you used to do that?"

Earl's face twists into a mock grimace. "Sounds horrific. Can't see the attraction at all."

Akinola laughs. "And you wonder why you've got so many ex-wives."

The traffic slows to a crawl and Earl slaps the steering wheel in frustration. As soon as he gets an opportunity, he turns off the main road onto a side street.

"This way is less direct but we'll get there quicker."

Akinola doesn't reply. She shifts her weight, sits up straight and Earl can almost hear her brain working. He knows there's a question coming and he waits. It doesn't take long.

"Did you know that Sharpe never had a single visitor while he was in prison? His ex-wife, his business partner girlfriend, even his daughter, none of them made the effort to see him. Don't you think that's sad?"

Earl shrugs. "I think the last person he'd want a visit from would be his ex-wife. During the original investigation it became clear that there was no love lost between them. Apparently, she moved up north after they'd split up, to deliberately put as much distance between Sharpe and their daughter as she could. He says she was determined to do everything possible to keep them estranged. 'Poisoned the child against him' was how he put it. He went to court to fight for access but she always made it as difficult as possible for him to develop a meaningful relationship with the girl."

Earl slows down and pulls up outside Sharpe's home. "Here we go, then," he says.

The detectives get of the car and walk up to the front door. Akinola presses the doorbell twice. While they wait, Earl takes a couple of steps back and surveys the front of the house.

"Nice place," he says. "The physiotherapy business must pay pretty well."

Akinola presses the doorbell again and this time holds the button down for a good ten seconds. Earl taps her on the shoulder, gesturing for her to step away from the door and join him. He points to the window downstairs and then the two windows on the first floor.

"Can you see, all the curtains are still drawn? Bit strange this late in the day."

Akinola steps across to the ground-floor window and peers through a narrow gap in the curtains.

"Oh shit."

Earl leans across and presses his face to the window. Through the gap he sees Sharpe slumped motionless in the armchair, his legs splayed, his torso twisted at an unnatural angle.

"We need an ambulance now."

Earl runs back to the front door. It looks solid. He hasn't kicked a door in since he was a uniformed copper patrolling the streets. Taking a deep breath, he rocks back, then lunges forward, launching the sole of his shoe at the plastic panel closest to the lock. The panel splits with a loud crack but the door stays in the frame. He tries again. Another loud crack.

The noise attracts the attention of three passing youths, all of them dressed in jeans and dark hoodies. They stop and start filming him with their mobile phones. He waves and yells at them to move on. They ignore him.

He steps back to launch another kick but Akinola steps forward.

"Hold on, let me have a go," she says. Her point of impact is higher than Earl's, her foot crashing into the panel several inches above the lock. The door splinters, collapsing backwards out of the frame. Her momentum takes her forward and Earl follows.

In the living room, Earl kneels beside Sharpe and places two fingers on his right carotid artery. The skin is cold. A pulse undetectable.

Akinola kneels on the other side of the chair. "Is he still alive?"

"I'm not sure. I think so, but barely. He has no visible wounds. It looks like a drug overdose."

Earl is gripped by a sense of dread. This man is going to die in front of them, right here, right now. He leans across, placing his left cheek close to Sharpe's bloodless lips.

After a few seconds, he looks up at Akinola. "I think he's still breathing, but he won't be for much longer. Where the hell is that ambulance?"

CHAPTER 25

Liv

I lie back, close my eyes, take a breath and slide down the bath until my head is submerged. In my mind, I see Sharpe's lifeless body sprawled in the armchair. I watch him, willing him to stir, until my bursting lungs force me to resurface.

The water is hot but I can't stop shivering. Sharpe is dead, and the fact that I didn't mean for him to die doesn't make me less frightened. I have killed a man.

I know I should be overwhelmed with remorse. I should hate myself for what I've done but I don't. Fear is my over-riding emotion. I'm confused about what this makes me and can't stop thinking that the next time someone knocks on my door it will be the police.

I climb out of the bath, wrap myself in a towel and slide down on the floor, my back against the bathroom door. I try to reassure myself that when the body is found there's no reason for anyone to suspect foul play. Sharpe died because he took too much of a recreational drug. A self-administered overdose. A depressed, lonely jailbird, weighed down by guilt, seeking oblivion in drugs. There's no reason the police should suspect anything different, is there?

I pull the towel tight around my shoulders. I'm still shivering but the feeling of panic deep in my chest is beginning to subside. There's no evidence that I was in Sharpe's house, no reason to link me with his death. Maybe it wasn't even an accidental overdose. He had lost everything. Who could blame him if he wanted out?

I reach for the bottle of wine and the glass I'd placed on the wicker lid of the laundry basket and pour. Perhaps everything is going to work out after all. The wine is a little warm, but I down it quickly and fill the glass again. I take another large gulp and start to feel the buzz of the alcohol in my blood.

The shivering has almost stopped and I lean my head back against the door and sigh. Sharpe's death was unintentional but there is a positive side to it. I set out to make him pay for what he did and that has been achieved. Killing someone, even accidentally, can't be an easy thing to live with. I'm not heartless, I'm not a monster, but I don't have a choice. I have to pull myself together and handle it.

I know I'm not going to be able to sleep. The wine is doing a good job of making me feel better, more optimistic. Maybe I should hit a local bar. I stand up, feeling a little unsteady, dry myself and change into a black, knee-length skirt, a dark green sweater and high heels. My hair is too short to do anything with but I blow dry it anyway.

I lock up the house and walk across the South Quay footbridge to a Canary Wharf bar I once visited with a couple of girlfriends. It's expensive and glitzy. The kind of place where I belong. I sit at the end of the bar and order a glass of white wine and a goat's cheese, avocado and walnut salad. I haven't eaten all day. The food is better than I'd expected and I clear the plate in minutes before treating myself to another glass of wine.

It's early evening and the place is already filling up. Most of the tables are occupied by couples. On stools along the bar, three lone men are nursing their drinks. Most of them are watching a news channel on a large screen suspended on the wall.

A man in a pinstriped suit shoots me sideways glances. He's good-looking, in a clean-cut, conventional way. I ignore him. Psychopaths are supposed to be highly promiscuous but I have way too much on my mind. Willpower and wine are the only things preventing me from collapsing in a hysterical heap on the floor.

I empty my glass and try to attract the barman's attention by waving it. He sees me, gives a nod and fetches me another wine. While I'm waiting, the man in the pinstripe suit makes his move.

"Let me get you that," he says. "My treat."

It's not the best chat-up line I've heard, and close up, he's not that good-looking. His face is flushed, and tiny beads of sweat dot the skin above his upper lip.

"No thanks," I say. "I don't need anybody to treat me." I like confident men, but arrogance is even more unattractive than a slimy upper lip.

I look him directly in the eyes, waiting for his next gambit. He blinks at me, baffled by my response, as if nobody's ever turned him down before. If only he knew I'm doing him a favour. That the last man who spoke to me is dead. We stare at each other blankly for a few seconds before he gives up and retreats to his stool.

As he takes his seat, a younger man sat further along the bar, with cropped hair, dressed in jeans and a check shirt, tips his head and offers me a half-smile. I'm considering smiling back, when my attention is drawn to the TV. A red breaking news bulletin banner slides across the bottom of the screen.

Convicted hit-and-run driver Daniel Sharpe is in intensive care in hospital after suspected drug overdose . . .

My heart flutters in my ribcage like a panicked bird. My breath catches in my throat and I grip the edge of the bar with both hands to steady myself.

A photograph of Sharpe taken outside court before his sentencing appears on the screen. The volume is low and I lean forward, straining to hear the blonde female newsreader.

"*It is believed that he was rushed to hospital earlier today after police officers called at his home. A hospital spokesman described his condition as critical. The police refused to confirm reports that Sharpe, recently released from prison, had attempted to take his own life. More on this story later.*"

I return to my stool and pick up my drink. My hand trembles slightly as I raise the glass to my lips.

The man in the check shirt appears at my side. "Are you feeling all right? You've gone very pale."

Even though he undoubtedly has an ulterior motive, it's kind of him to ask and I reward him with my best brave smile.

"I don't know why but I've suddenly come over a bit dizzy and nauseous. It's not the drink. I haven't had a lot. Honestly."

He frowns and steps a little closer. "Is there something I can do to help? Get you a soft drink, maybe, or a glass of water?"

"I think it's best if I go home and put my feet up," I say. I'm lying, of course, because all I want to do is get back and put on a news channel. Lies are my truth now.

"I could walk you home," he offers. "Make sure you're okay."

I shake my head, push past him and head for the door, weaving through the crowd. I'm not a killer. A strange mixture of relief and disappointment churns deep in the pit of my stomach.

Outside, Canary Wharf's shining towers light up the dark sky. In the distance a siren screams. My knees start to shake as I imagine a fleet of police cars, blue lights flashing, parked the length of my street. I remind myself that the newsreader said Sharpe was in a critical condition. That suggests there's a good chance he won't recover, that death is imminent, doesn't it? As long as he never regains consciousness, then there won't be a problem. I'm struggling to stay calm. Remember, psychopaths don't feel fear, I tell myself, even though I'm not sure it's true.

"I have nothing to worry about," I murmur under my breath. The chances are he won't make it, and it's already being suggested that he deliberately took an overdose. *Stay calm, stay strong*, I tell myself. *Everything is going to be all right.*

As I think it, I don't believe it. I've even started lying to myself now.

CHAPTER 26

Sharpe

He wants to open his mouth and scream but he can't. He's floating in a sea of blackness. Is this death, or a bad dream?

He tries to raise his eyelids but they don't respond. His fogged brain fights to work out where he is, what happened to him and how long he's been suspended in this world of nothingness. But the arrow of time has stopped. Someone has pressed the pause button.

An electronic beep surprises him. Then another, and another. He senses movement close by. He can hear each drawn out, hissing breath. There's another sequence of beeps.

He's in hospital. It's quiet, which means he's in a private room, not on a bustling ward. His vital signs are being monitored. The laboured, mechanical breathing is a ventilator, pumping air in and out of his lungs. Keeping him alive.

A door creaks open. Light footsteps. A thumb presses firmly on his right eye and pushes up the lid. Sharpe catches the scent of a tangy, floral perfume. The doctor, or nurse, moves on to his left eye. He imagines her aiming a small, powerful torch beam at his pupil. Not even a pinprick of light penetrates his darkness.

All this listening is tiring. He feels himself drifting away, sinking, but doesn't want to go. He tries desperately to move his head to one side, to wiggle his fingers, twitch his lips, anything to let this woman know that he still exists, that he's locked inside his shell of a body.

The door opens again and a second person enters the room. The odour of cooked food and coffee wafts in from the corridor. The footsteps are heavier and slower. Sharpe guesses the new arrival is a man. He approaches and stops on the opposite side of the bed to the woman. Without a word he reaches out and runs a damp cloth gently over Sharpe's face, under his chin and behind his ears.

"The patient's name is Daniel, Daniel Sharpe," the woman says.

For the first time, Sharpe feels a flicker of hope. They know who he is and they're going to do their best to fix him.

"An overdose of GHB. We don't know whether it was accidental or deliberate. Had so much pumping around in his bloodstream I am surprised he's still with us. Been in a coma since an ambulance brought him in fifteen hours ago and is showing no signs of coming out of it. There appears to be some brain activity but nothing significant."

The male nurse has moved on to cleaning Sharpe's hands, carefully wiping between his fingers. "Poor bloke must have been in such a bad place to do something like that," he says. "Beats me how someone can sink that low without friends or family noticing."

Sharpe is unsure whether he heard right. Maybe his brain is playing tricks on him. Maybe the doctor has walked into the wrong room, has her patient notes mixed up and is talking about a different person.

He balls his hands into fists, waves them and yells as loud as he can: "*No, no, no, you're making a big mistake. I'm here. I'm still here, for God's sake. You've got it all wrong.*"

Nobody in the room hears him shout, or sees him punch the air in frustration, because his body is silent and still. He doesn't want to die. Not before, and not now. Not like this.

114

Anger triggers a memory. Sharpe sees a woman's face. She's familiar but he can't remember why.

The doctor walks away from the bed to the corner of the room where the monitor is beeping. She mutters something under her breath and scribbles something down on a clipboard.

"You're going to need to check on him, his vital signs, through the night, every two hours," she says. "Make a special note of his blood pressure and temperature, and make sure his airway is clear, of course."

The nurse says nothing. Sharpe gets the impression he doesn't like being talked down to. After a few seconds of silence, the doctor leaves the room. Once the door closes, the nurse walks around the bed and runs his fingers over the breathing tube, pressing down where it touches the corner of Sharpe's mouth.

"That's definitely going to get sore there if we don't lubricate it," he says. "Don't worry, I know what I'm doing. I've done this for years. She's a right stuck-up bitch. Thinks she knows it all, she does. Most of the doctors in this place are the same. Patronizing bastards. Think they're better than the rest of us."

Sharpe isn't sure whether the nurse thinks there's a possibility that he can hear and understand what's being said, or simply likes the sound of his own voice. He wasn't aware that he had a breathing tube in his mouth until the nurse mentioned it, but it makes sense. He can't breathe by himself. Not yet. He needs life support. A basic process. Oxygen in. Carbon dioxide out.

He can smell beer on the man's breath and wonders if he always pops into the pub before working a night shift. The nurse is humming a cheery tune that Sharpe doesn't recognize.

"Lots of other patients to see," the nurse says. "We're always short of staff in this place, especially on the night shift. But don't worry, I won't forget about you. I'll be back."

Thinking is exhausting. Tiredness is dragging Sharpe down further into the blackness. He tries to resist but he hasn't the strength. As he starts to slip away, he recalls what the doctor told the nurse. *There appears to be some brain activity but nothing significant.* This can't be happening. He's sinking into the depths and may never come back up again.

They must have got it wrong about him taking an overdose. He's never done drugs. Not even in prison. They need to know that. The only thing he remembers is the woman. Pale skin, dark hair. Big eyes.

Not knowing what happened is scary. But what frightens Sharpe more than anything is the four-letter word the doctor uttered. Coma. Lost in nowhere land, between the living and the dead.

CHAPTER 27

Earl

Earl closes the door and turns to face his boss. Tanner eyes him from behind his desk like a malign toad.

"Take a seat, detective," he says.

Earl doesn't move. "I'd prefer to stand. I don't suppose this is going to take long." He's never liked being ordered around, especially by senior officers who spend most of their day sitting on their arses.

Tanner rubs the bridge of his fleshy nose and shakes his head. "You never do yourself any favours. You clearly fancy yourself as a bit of a maverick."

"I'll take that as a compliment."

Tanner hunches forward, resting his forearms on the desk. "What's the latest on Sharpe? Is he going to make it?"

Earl shrugs. "He's in a coma. On life support. The doctors are saying there's a slim chance he will regain consciousness, and if he does it's possible that he'll have suffered some permanent damage."

Tanner points to the vacant chair. "Will you sit down? Please."

This time, Earl does as he's asked. The two men look across the desk at each other until Tanner breaks the silence.

"What are we dealing with, then? Accidental overdose?"

Earl shrugs. "Hard to tell. He had so much GHB in his system it's amazing he's still with us."

"A suicide attempt, then?"

Earl hesitates. He'd never have considered Sharpe someone who might take his own life. But nobody really knows what's going on inside another a person's head. He'd thought Sharpe wasn't the type of man to run down a teenager and leave her to die, and he'd been wrong about that.

"It's possible, I suppose. His probation supervisor said he had handled his time in prison well and was looking forward to moving on with his life."

Tanner grunts and rubs his forehead. "Guilt, shame and public humiliation have pushed much stronger people than him over the edge. An accidental overdose or suicide attempt — the newspapers are going to be all over this story, and I don't want any leaks until this is all tied up and handed over to the coroner's office. Is that clear?"

Earl doesn't need to answer. He's always believed that if someone looks stupid, then they probably are stupid. Tanner is the exception that proves the rule. He may be one of the laziest DCIs Earl has worked under, but he's also one of the smartest.

Tanner allows himself a self-satisfied smile. "I have some good news for you. We've had so many fatal stabbings in this part of the city, I've been told to prioritize tackling knife crime. The squad room is already so badly stretched, I've decided that this isn't a good time to lose an experienced detective. I've had a word with human resources and your redundancy is being put on hold, for now."

Earl keeps his expression neutral as he suppresses a strong urge to punch the air. He doesn't trust himself to speak and turns his head to hide his eyes.

"The first thing I want you to do is sort out the Sharpe business. Liaise with forensics, check out the situation at the hospital and speak to his family. It seems like there's a chance he's not going to come out of this coma. If he doesn't pull through, I want you to collect all the evidence relating to the death and pass it on to the coroner for the inquest."

Earl's mind is racing. A rash of fatal knife attacks has given him a lifeline. A chance to prove that the force can't live without him. The truth is — and only he knows it — he can't live without the force.

"I'm on it, no problem. And, er, thanks."

As he stands to leave the room, Tanner holds up a pudgy finger. "I've put myself out to get you a reprieve, you understand?" he says. "Don't let me down."

Earl responds with an almost imperceptible nod. He's thankful to have the chance to get on with proper police work, and more importantly, to be back on the team. He's not going to let anybody down.

CHAPTER 28

Liv

I sit in a coffee shop at a table tucked in the corner, squinting at the screen of my mobile as I swipe my way through the newspaper websites. I only have eyes for one story. The headlines scream at me, mock me. *Hit-and-Run Killer in Coma. Death Driver Driven to Drugs. Lottie Killer in Overdose Mystery.*

Sharpe is clinging on to his miserable life. It feels like a kick in the teeth. I didn't want him dead, but now I don't want him alive. If he comes out of this coma, it's possible he'll remember what happened and the police will come for me. This isn't how it's supposed to be.

According to the news reports, doctors say his chances of survival are slim. If the police had arrived at his home just a few minutes later, he would have died there and then. His good luck. My bad luck.

I sip my vanilla latte and put my mind to working out how best to sort out this mess I'm in. I have no choice other than to be proactive now. I can't sit at home waiting, hoping that Sharpe will die before he can incriminate me. I imagine the police knocking on my door, handcuffs rubbing my wrists raw. The thought terrifies me.

I did my best to avoid leaving fingerprints or traces of DNA in the house, and nobody, as far as I can tell, is suggesting that what happened to Sharpe wasn't self-inflicted. Unfortunately, thanks to those police officers and a hospital ventilator, he's still breathing.

I put my coffee down and walk over to the counter in search of a comforting sugar hit. As I study the cakes and pastries on offer, the barista spots me and gives a slight double-take. I cropped my hair to look ill but some men seem to find it appealing.

"I recommend the chocolate muffins," he says. "They're especially good today."

I respond with a coy smile. "If they taste as good as the coffee, I'm in."

He beams, delighted that someone has at last acknowledged his coffee-making skills, slips a muffin onto a plate and hands it to me. "On the house," he announces. "For the prettiest smile I've seen today."

I want to tell him he's a sexist, patronizing arsehole but hold my tongue and try to look embarrassed yet pleased. I return to my table, smiling. If I'm going to protect myself, I have to be bold. I have to use all my qualities, even the bad ones.

I take a large bite of the cake and the dry, chemical-tasting sponge transports me back to my tenth birthday. It was only me and my so-called mother then. Lottie didn't come along until later. We weren't short of money. Far from it. My mother worked for herself as a tax consultant, drove a big car and had a wardrobe full of designer clothes. She didn't like spending her cash on me, though. I think, by then, she'd already written me off as a disappointment. A faulty child she couldn't take back to the store and exchange for a new one.

Like most days, I'd walked home from school on my own. I could make friends, that wasn't a problem, but for some reason I couldn't keep them for long. Maybe it was because I was always visiting their happy, shiny homes, eating their cookies and drinking their lemonade but never returned the favour.

Still, I was excited by the thought of a home-baked cake and presents, mother smiling at me, clapping her hands while singing happy birthday, even though she was tone deaf. Of course, that day it didn't work out that way. I should have known better. I let myself in the back door. On the kitchen table I found a stale chocolate muffin with a single candle stuck in it, a box of matches, and a note explaining that an important client had requested a meeting.

By then, I was already fully aware that we didn't have that special connection other mothers and daughters had. It was never there. I think I first felt her coldness towards me after my father abandoned us, when I was six. Looking back, I suspect she'd been faking the loving-mother act for his sake.

Things changed for the worse when Lottie arrived. She doted on the new baby with a fierceness that scared me. I became even more irrelevant. An inconvenience. A disappointing waste of space.

I pop the last piece of cake in my mouth and an idea grips me. I'd learned while researching my article on Noble's study that psychopathy has a strong genetic component. If I was born with a psychopath's brain, then I must have inherited it from someone. I grin at the thought that if I traced my family tree back through the generations, I'd find it littered with notorious criminals.

I warm to the notion that the DNA that created my abnormal brain came from one of my parents. It's strangely comforting to see it as a quirky, family trait. If I had to bet, I'd put my money on my mother. My dad was wayward and untrustworthy. He ran off with the divorcee next door. They moved to the west coast of Scotland and had two children. I didn't hate him for long. You'd have to be a saint to stay in a relationship with my mother. He's definitely no saint, but I remember his laugh, his hugs and the warmth in his voice when he sang to me. The best thing mum ever did for me was crash her car and die. It meant I could be with Lottie again. Be part of a proper family again.

The barista is shooting sideways glances at me. I pretend not to notice and decide to leave before he plucks up the courage to ask for my telephone number. I don't trust myself to let him down gently, and I don't want to create a scene.

I stand up and head for the door. He looks crestfallen as I stride past the counter, until I give him a smile and a mischievous wink. His face reddens and he smiles back at me. I'm definitely in line for a freebie the next time I pop in.

A grey blanket of low cloud hangs over East London, the air cold and thick with moisture. Walking back home, I start planning my next move. I have to make sure that, if Sharpe comes out of the coma, he doesn't start talking to the police. How do I shut him up? There has to be a way. This is about self-preservation, and I know now I'm capable of doing whatever it takes.

CHAPTER 29

Sharpe

A sliver of Sharpe's consciousness emerges from the deep. It takes him a few minutes to make sense of the various noises and remember he's in hospital. The drawn out hiss of the ventilator has become a sound he treasures. As long as he can hear it, he knows he's alive.

He visualizes his body on the bed in the centre of a room, shrouded in a crisp white sheet. As lifeless as a corpse on a mortuary slab. His brain is still fogged, his memory blurred. How, why, when did this happen? He can't answer these questions. What he does know, because it's a feeling not a memory, is that he didn't do this to himself. Someone else did it. Someone wants him dead.

A flurry of footsteps. At least two people. They approach the bed together. "Good morning. How are you doing today?" Sharpe recognizes the voice. It's the male nurse who moans about the doctors.

"We need to turn him on his side. It's important to regularly alter his position to stop him developing sores."

Hands grab his shoulders and legs and roll him onto his left side.

"What happened to him?" It's a young woman's voice. Sharpe guesses she's a trainee, and the thought annoys him. Trainee nurses are no good to him. He's hanging on by a thread. As good as dead. He needs experienced doctors, consultants, coma experts, if he's going to be brought back to the land of the living.

"Bloody fool took an overdose. GHB, apparently. It might have been an accident, but I reckon he tried to kill himself."

Sharpe feels pressure around his left wrist and the prick of a needle piercing the skin of his upper arm. He flinches, but externally shows no reaction to the stabbing pain. He doesn't know what drug they're injecting him with but prays it will help bring him out of the coma.

"Do you think he's ever going to wake up?"

"You never know in these coma cases, but it's not looking good. In a couple of days, if he's still not responding to stimulation, they'll probably do a test for brain activity, and if that doesn't go well, they might consider talking to family about switching off the ventilator."

A single phrase echoes in Sharpe's ears. *Switching off the ventilator, switching off the ventilator, switching off . . .* Fleetingly, panic pulls him back down towards the blackness, but as the meaning of those words sink in, he resurfaces. If there's no hope of bringing him back, he'd choose death over the hell of being a living corpse.

One of the nurses is cleaning behind his ears, his neck and his face with a moist cloth. Probably the young woman. The sensation is smoother and gentler than before.

"There you go," she says. "That's better, isn't it? As fresh as a daisy now."

Sharpe wonders again whether they really think he can hear what they're saying. One moment they're wishing him a good morning, the next they're chatting casually about the possibility of switching off his life support machine.

A scribbling sound at the foot of the bed suggests that the male nurse is making notes on a clipboard. "Would you believe we've had the police on the telephone asking when he's likely to be fit enough to be interviewed?" he says with a chuckle. "I don't think they realize he's not even fit enough to take a breath by himself."

Mention of the police sparks something in Sharpe's brain. Images flash in the darkness like a movie trailer. A dead girl on the side of the road. A blood-smeared car bumper. The cold metal bars of a prison cell.

He hears knocking. He opens the door and sees the dead girl looking up at him. She did this to him. Sharpe doesn't know how, but he has no doubt she did it.

He concentrates on trying to move his right forefinger to attract the nurses' attention but nothing happens. No connection between his brain and his hand.

Remembering is hard work. He starts to slip away, his head still swirling with shadowy pictures and faces. He tells himself that if his memory is returning it must be a good sign.

The nurses are talking as they prepare to leave and he tunes into their conversation in an effort to fight the blackness.

"He's got family up north somewhere," the male nurse says. "They've been informed and they're on their way. They've been told he's in a coma, but I think they'll be shocked when they see exactly what that means."

They leave the room, and as the door clicks shut behind them, Sharpe clings on to the mention of family. He sees a young girl's face. Even though her features are indistinct, he knows she's the one who's coming to see him. His daughter. He digs for a name but nothing comes. He doesn't even know his daughter's name.

He puts everything he can into attempting to open his mouth and tries to call out. No sound comes but for a split second his world is filled with dazzling, white light. The darkness returns, and as he slips into nothingness, he understands. In trying to shout, one of his eyelids flickered and lifted a fraction. He moved. Moved when there was nobody to see.

126

CHAPTER 30

Earl

"Has he ever talked about trying to kill himself?" Detective Sergeant Earl asks, tugging at the collar of his shirt. The interview room is warm and windowless.

Emily Sharpe, her eyes bloodshot and puffy, drops her head and sobs into her hands. Her mother, wrapped in a stylish grey raincoat, dyed blonde hair fixed into a carefully coiffed ballerina bun, leans across and puts an arm around her shoulders.

"Emily's father has always been good at feeling sorry for himself," she says. "He likes to blame other people for his problems, usually me. I couldn't truthfully say what's been going on in his head, but serving a jail sentence isn't going to be good for anyone's mental health, is it?" She edges closer to her daughter's chair and hugs her tighter.

Earl has come prepared. He pulls a packet of tissues from his jacket pocket and slides them across the desk. Several tabloid newspapers reported after Sharpe's arrest that he and his wife separated and divorced when Emily was a baby. He'd admitted sleeping with a work colleague during his wife's pregnancy. *What makes this man want to confess everything?* Earl wonders.

Emily takes a couple of the tissues, dabs her eyes and wipes her nose. Her natural ash-blonde hair is shoulder length. She's wearing grey jeans, a shiny, silver padded jacket, and looks younger than her nineteen years.

"When was the last time you saw your father?"

Emily sniffs loudly, shrugs and fiddles with the zip of her jacket, yanking it up to chin and down again. "I don't know exactly. I can't really think straight. We haven't been in contact for a long time, not really. It's been difficult."

"There have been telephone calls and the occasional email but she hasn't seen Daniel for years," her mother interrupts, unbuttoning her coat. "Probably three, maybe even longer. He'd pay us a visit when it suited him. We never knew when he'd turn up, and sometimes he wouldn't show his face for months. In the end we decided that it was all too disruptive and it was better to cut him off completely, didn't we, Emily?"

Emily doesn't answer. She bursts into tears again, takes another tissue from the packet and buries her face in it. Her mother glares at Earl as if he's to blame for her distress.

"I did read in the newspaper at the time of your ex-husband's sentencing that he'd been to the family court several times to try to get and enforce access orders."

Emily's mother's cheeks flush and her eyes narrow. "Don't believe everything you read in the newspapers, Detective. We moved up north because I wanted to get as far away as possible from London, and the distance made everything difficult. I had to get on with building a new life for us. Daniel was adamant that he wanted to be a proper father, but it was all talk. By the time Emily was nine he'd stopped making the effort to see her regularly. Too busy with his career and new girlfriends, probably. A few years ago, we decided Emily needed to concentrate on her schoolwork and exams. It was the right decision, wasn't it, darling? She got top grades and she's at university now studying psychology."

Emily rolls her eyes and cringes. Earl guesses that her mother tells everyone she meets about her daughter's academic achievements.

"I understand that you're planning to visit your father later today?"

Emily nods. "Is he going to die? Or have brain damage or something?"

Earl presses his fingertips hard on the folder on the table in front of him. He read the medical report that morning but decides to leave it to the doctors to explain the details. There's nothing he can say to her that will soften the impact of seeing her father being kept alive by a tangle of tubes and wires.

"I know you've already been told that he's in a coma and I can't say much more than that. The doctors at the hospital will be able to tell you a lot more about his condition and the prognosis. All I will say is that people have been known to recover from comas and go on to live full and normal lives."

Emily looks directly at him across the desk, tears spilling down her face. "Do you think he tried to kill himself? Why would he want to do something like that? It doesn't make sense."

Earl is unsure what to say. Only Sharpe knows whether the overdose was an accident or deliberate. Nobody wants to die, not even people who make the decision to kill them-selves. It's more that they reach a point where they feel they can't go on living. Sharpe had reasons for believing that his life was screwed and he had only himself to blame.

"It's probably everything that went on surrounding the hit-and-run," Emily's mother says. "The poor girl who died, the time he spent in prison. Shame, humiliation and guilt are incredibly hard things for anyone to bear."

She stands abruptly, reaches for Emily's hand and pulls her up. "We'd better be going, if that's all right with you, officer? We have to check into our hotel before we make our way to the hospital."

Earls stays in his seat. "Of course, we're all done here, but there is one thing. I was wondering, did you drive down to London?"

Emily throws her mother a sideways look. "Mum doesn't like driving," she says, her voice still husky from crying. "She finds it stressful. I've passed my test but I'm not confident enough to drive around the city. We came down by train from Manchester this morning."

Earl sits back, drumming his fingers on the arms of his chair. "I was thinking, if you can wait a few minutes, I might be able to arrange for one of our officers to drive you to the hospital."

Emily's mother opens the door and ushers her daughter out. "That's kind of you," she says, "but we're happy to take a taxi, aren't we, darling?"

Once the door closes, Earl pushes his chair back, rests his feet on the edge of the table and lets his mind wander. He tries to imagine what his life would be like if he was a parent. Maybe he'd be a better person. Would that make him a better detective?

His train of thought is interrupted by his mobile ringing. He considers letting it go to voicemail, but when he sees the caller is Becky Andrews, he answers.

"Hi, Becky, anything interesting for me?" He regrets the question as soon as he asks it. Andrews is the best crime scene manager he's ever worked with, and her tongue is as sharp as her brain.

"If I didn't have anything interesting to tell you, why would I waste my time calling? The forensic report isn't complete yet but I wanted to give you a heads up on a couple of things we found at Sharpe's place."

"Sounds intriguing. I'm listening." Earl's pulse quickens. He stands up, paces across the room and back again.

Andrews hears the anticipation in his voice. "Don't get overexcited. These are preliminary findings. Along with Sharpe's fingerprints we found some on the door handles. No matches on the database, but we found some leaflets from local estate agents. I'd check with them to see if they sent someone around recently. We found a cup that still had a small amount of coffee in it, and that contained gamma-hy-droxybutyric acid — that's GHB, or liquid ecstasy, which is popular with nightclubbers across the city, as well as being the weapon of choice of date-rapists."

Earl is aware of the potency of the drug. "It's easy to take too much, isn't it?"

"Extremely easy. The difference between a mellow high and coma can be as little as a few drops. It's a powerful central nervous system depressant. It's clear from the medical report, Sharpe took so much he probably fell unconscious within minutes."

"Right, so he could have been simply trying to get high to forget his troubles and overdid it?"

"That's a pretty accurate assessment. The only way we could know for sure that he tried to kill himself would be if he'd left a suicide note."

Earl groans, wondering when the forensics chief is going to get to the interesting bit.

"But there is something else," Andrews says. "While examining the living room, one of the team found what he initially thought were a couple of dark human hairs on the sofa. Back at the lab he discovered that they were actually the type of fake fur fibres commonly used by manufacturers to line coat or jacket lapels and hoods. We checked the wardrobes in the house and Sharpe doesn't own a garment of that kind."

Earl stops pacing and sits on the edge of his desk. "You're saying someone else might have been in the room shortly before he took the drug, or was even there when he overdosed?"

"It's a possibility worth looking at. I can't say any more than that. It's my job to give you the forensic evidence. I can say for certain that the fake fur fibres were there on the sofa in the house. I can't say how long they were there, or how they got there. It's your job to work that out. You're the detective. Do some detecting."

CHAPTER 31

Sharpe

He resurfaces, and the first thing he remembers is the flash of light. He lifted one of his eyelids. The memory fills him with hope. It may have been only an eyelid, but he moved.

He's lying on his right side and it's uncomfortable. He has no idea how long he's been in that position. The skin on his right hip and shoulder is burning. The nurses need to move him before pressure sores develop. The cannula, inserted in a vein on the back of his right hand, stings and the breathing tube is rubbing his throat raw. Pain is a fresh sensation. He welcomes it. He takes it as a sign he's more alive than dead.

The hinges on the door creak. Raised voices, the rattle of trolley wheels and the clatter of crockery fill the room until someone shuts the door. At last, the nurses have come to adjust his position. He wants to tell them to hurry but his lips won't move. A shuddering intake of breath is followed by a groan. His visitors aren't nurses.

"I know it looks bad, but this is normal for a patient in a coma."

Sharpe recognizes the female doctor's voice. "Your father has been like this for three days now. At the moment he needs a ventilator to keep him breathing. We are doing, and will continue to do, everything we can."

Footsteps approach the bed and Sharpe feels the pressure of fingertips on his forearm. "Oh, Dad. What have you done to yourself?"

His daughter's touch. His daughter's voice. Finally, her name comes to him like a burst of light. A camera flash in the dark. He calls out to her. "*Emily, it's Emily.*"

She doesn't hear him.

"What's going to happen to him?" she asks. "Is he going to be okay? Is he in pain? Do you think he can hear what we're saying?"

The doctor walks to the foot of the bed and lifts a clip-board off the rail. "It's extremely difficult to predict anything with any accuracy when it comes to coma patients. He's getting the best treatment available and there is always a chance that he'll pull through. If he starts to show any sign of improvement, then there's a chance that we'll be able to take him off the ventilator and let him start breathing for himself. In answer to your question about pain, well, it varies from patient to patient. The deeper the coma, the less likely that they feel anything. It's unlikely that he can hear what's going on around him, but talking to him can't do any harm. If you have no more questions, I'll leave you to it."

As the door closes, the room falls silent, except for the hiss of the ventilator and electronic beeps from the monitor. Sharpe wonders whether Emily left with the doctor until he hears her sobbing softly beside him. In his mind, he pushes himself up into a sitting position, takes her in his arms and hugs her tightly.

Movement near the foot of the bed catches him by surprise. Someone else is in the room. He should have known that Emily wouldn't have come to the hospital without her mother.

"Please don't cry, darling," she says. "We have to be strong and stay positive. Why don't you try talking to him? The doctor said it might help."

Sharpe visualizes his ex-wife standing near the door, straight-backed, not a hair out of place, a frown of concern on her face. The image is strangely comforting. The marriage ended badly, and if anything their relationship deteriorated after the divorce. But Clare always has Emily's best interests at heart and will do anything for her. She's a strong-willed woman and fiercely protective mother, and Sharpe is grateful that she's at their daughter's side.

Emily sniffs. "I'm not sure what to say to him. What should I say? What if he can't hear anything? He probably can't."

"What if he can? Maybe he can't make out what you're saying, but the sound of your voice might trigger something."

Emily reaches for a chair propped against the wall behind her, drags it to the side of the bed and sits down.

"Everything is going great at university," she says, making a big effort to sound cheery. "I was pretty nervous about going, wasn't I? But I've made lots of friends already and I'm loving the course. Psychology is cool. I've taken a few days off to come down to see you and that will mean I'll miss of few lectures, but it's not a problem, I'll soon catch up and I . . ."

Her voice cracks, and she falters. She starts to sniff again and her sniffing swiftly turns to sobbing. Sharpe focuses every ounce of concentration on trying to open his eyes. He's desperate to show Emily that he's still there, trapped inside his body. He wants to tell her not to be upset and that everything is going to be all right, even though he's scared that it won't. His eyes stay closed.

Both her hands grip his arm, and she leans a little closer to his right ear. "I'm so sorry, Dad," she says, speaking so quickly now some of her sentences are garbled. "I'm sorry that I didn't visit when you were in prison. You told me not to, didn't you? I know you did. And I decided, and Mum agreed with me. We decided that it was best to do what you wanted. I thought about you every day you were in that place. I know it must have been horrible and I should have ignored what you said. I'm so sorry."

The agony of not being able to comfort his daughter, not being able to tell her that she didn't let him down, is worse than any other pain Sharpe is feeling.

Emily stops crying, and Sharpe can hear her mother whispering in her ear but he can't make out most of the words.

Warm fingers trace lines gently across his forehead and down his right cheek. "We have to go, Dad. We'll be back as soon as we can. You're not on your own anymore. Hang in there. Please hold on. I really am so sorry."

Sharpe tries to shake his head, open his eyes, clench his left fist, roll on to his back, bare his teeth, scream at the top of his lungs. Nothing happens.

The door clicks shut and he's left alone with his thoughts. They whirl around in his head until, eventually, one dominates. He has to survive and he has to remember. For Emily.

He gathers his fragmented memories and attempts to piece them together. He's about to give up when, somewhere in his brain, a severed circuit reconnects and fresh images shower like shattered glass.

A hesitant knock on his front door. Tears on her cheeks. Boyish hair. Somehow, someone drugged him. He knows exactly who that someone is. She needed to talk, she said.

Sharpe recalls her pale face as she stood on his doorstep. He let her into his home and she slipped something into his coffee. She drugged him.

Because of her he's paralysed, helpless, unable to take a single breath without the help of a machine. She's out there, somewhere, wanting him to die, and the truth to die with him.

CHAPTER 32

Liv

I lift my coat off the kitchen table, stuff it in the black plastic bin liner with the rest of the clothes, and twist the top of the bag into a knot. It feels good to have a clear out, to do something ordinary.

My life has taken a turn I could never have expected. At times, recently, I've felt like a stranger in my body. I try not to think too much about what I have done and what I have to do because it frightens me.

Am I changing, or is this the real me emerging? Maybe Mother was right all along. What if she could see right through me, see what I was hiding from the world?

I always thought I'd done pretty well for myself, considering where I started. I used to believe I deserved credit for carving out a career as a feature writer, making it in the glamorous world of magazine journalism. But did I do it for myself or to prove something to the mother who rejected me, and to the little sister I wanted to look up to me?

I lift up the bag of clothes and head down the hall to the door. Apart from giving me an excuse to treat myself to some new outfits, getting rid of this stuff is going to ease my mind by eliminating the risk of being caught out by stray DNA. A few months ago, I wrote a feature on Scotland Yard's forensic services and it was fascinating to be able to see close up exactly what these crime scene investigators do.

I leave the house and step out on to the busy street, the bag flung over my right shoulder. Weak spring sunlight filters through the layer of cloud above the city but it's a cold afternoon. I pull my woollen hat down over my ears and walk briskly along Byng Street. The nearest recycling centre is a twenty-minute walk away. Once I dump the clothes in the landfill container, I can relax.

I can't help wondering what Lottie would think about the way I'm dealing with her death. I'd like to think she'd approve of me taking positive action to right a wrong. She was like me, in so many ways. Everyone who saw us together commented on how we looked so alike. The eyes, the hair, the pale skin. I lapped it up, even though I knew deep down that she was a prettier, kinder, brighter version of me. She would have taken the world by storm, if she'd been allowed to. I had such big plans for her.

As I pass a convenience store, I'm forced to step onto the road to avoid a woman sitting hunched and shivering on the pavement, her back resting on the shop window. In her late teens, she's wearing a thick woollen sweater several sizes too big for her, dirt-streaked jeans and a pair of battered trainers.

On the ground in front of her lies an upturned baseball cap and a piece of card bearing the words "Please help the homeless" scribbled on it. I stop and smile down at her. She smiles back, with empty eyes.

"Are you hungry?" I ask. She hesitates as if she's struggling to understand the question. While I wait for a reply, I put the bag of clothes down and wonder how she ended up begging on the street. Bad decisions, bad people, or both?

"Money, please help," she says, her words clipped by a strong Eastern European accent.

Dipping into my jacket pocket, I pull out my purse, scoop out all the loose change, and trickle it into the baseball cap. She doesn't look impressed and, for some reason, I feel offended.

With a shrug, I start to turn away but stop when an idea pops into my head. I reach for the bag of clothes, untie the knot, pull out my hooded coat and black ankle boots, and offer them to her.

"You can have these," I say. "The coat will keep you warm at night, and these boots have hardly been worn."

She takes them, puts them down on the pavement beside her and nods towards the baseball cap. "Money, please. I need money."

I squat down and rest my hand gently on her knee. "Put them on now," I say slowly, stressing each word. "I want to help you. Let me help you."

At first, she looks confused, then I see a flash of fear, and that's when I know she's going to do what I say. She kicks her trainers off, slides her feet into the boots and pushes herself up. I hand her the coat and watch, a smile on my face as she slips it on, flipping the hood up.

"There you go," I say. "That's perfect." It's not perfect. I didn't realize how short and stocky she was until she stood up. The coat is much too tight around the shoulders, and the sleeves are so long the fur trims on the cuffs cover her hands. It doesn't look good, but it'll keep her warm and that's what matters.

She sits back down on the pavement and tugs the hood until it covers most of her face, as if she's trying to hide from me. *Rude, ungrateful little bitch*, I think. My Lottie would never have behaved like that.

"No need to thank me or anything, it's my pleasure," I say, as I pick up the bin bag, which now contains only two pairs of jeans and a couple of sweaters, and walk away.

At the end of the road, I spy a charity shop and realize there's no need to tramp all the way to the council dump. I drop the bag on top of a box of books someone has left outside the shop entrance and turn left onto Westferry Road.

After a few minutes, I find myself outside one of my favourite drinking haunts, the Diamond Inn.

Despite the homeless woman's ingratitude, I'm feeling good about my spontaneous acts of kindness and decide it's not too early to spoil myself. I sit at the bar and sip my perfectly chilled wine. The place is quiet, almost empty, but I'm not looking for company.

I've proved to myself that I can still show compassion, and at the same time I've got rid of evidence that could potentially link me to a crime scene.

Doing a good deed makes you feel warm and fuzzy inside. It's a feeling similar to the satisfaction you get when you manipulate someone into doing something they really don't want to do.

CHAPTER 33

Earl

Dusk is falling as Detective Earl pulls up and parks outside his home. He shuns the lift and takes the stairs to the second-floor flat. Exercise for the day ticked off.

Inside, he makes straight for the fridge and helps himself to a cold beer, adjusting the remaining bottles on the shelf into two equally spaced lines.

In a day or so, the full forensic report will be in on Sharpe's drug overdose. If he survives, his family will be advised to arrange help for him: medication or talking therapy. A combination of the two would be the safest bet. If he doesn't pull through, then the evidence gathered at the scene will be passed to the coroner prior to the inquest.

The fake fur fibres found on Sharpe's sofa had piqued Earl's interest but they could have been there for some time. He takes a gulp of beer and shakes his head in frustration. It's not difficult to believe that, after all he's been through, Sharpe descended into a pit of despair and tried to top himself.

Confessing to a cowardly crime, being crucified in the media, going to jail and coming out to find yourself a social pariah would be enough to drive anyone to despair.

Earl is thinking about whether to have another beer or wait until later when the doorbell chimes. He puts the empty bottle onto the table, hurries down the hallway and peers through the security spyhole. The fish-eye lens distorts the face of the woman on his doorstep into a green-eyed, brown-haired caricature.

"My favourite ex-wife," he says, opening the door with a flourish. "What a pleasant surprise."

Detective Sergeant Laura Sands gives him a nod and strides in without waiting for an invitation. He follows her into the kitchen, where she stands, hands on hips, scanning the room with interest.

"I'm glad to see you're keeping our old place tidy," she says.

When they were together, she used to enjoy teasing him about his obsession with neatness and hatred of clutter, but it was always light-hearted. Earl knew she counted herself fortunate to be living with a man addicted to housework.

"I do my best," he says. "It's a lot easier to keep a place exactly as you want it when you live alone."

She's wearing a dark brown, tailored trouser suit that matches her hair, and in her heels she's almost as tall as Earl. She eyes the empty beer bottle and tilts her head.

"Oh dear, drinking on your own? Do you think that's a good idea?"

Earl goes to the fridge, takes out two beers and neatens up the remaining bottles again.

"I more or less do everything on my own nowadays," he says, twisting off the tops and giving her a bottle. "I suppose you want a glass?"

"Of course. You know I never drink out of a bottle. If you don't use a glass, you ain't got no class."

Earl opens one of the wall units, hands her a tall glass and watches her pour the beer slowly to the brim.

"It's always good to see you and you're always welcome, but to what do I owe this honour?" he asks, even though he knows the answer. She's checking up on him, making sure that the threat of redundancy hasn't sent him over the edge.

"Happened to be passing by," she says. "I haven't seen you for a while and thought it'd be nice to call in and say hello."

"East London is a long way from Sussex. I doubt you were just passing."

Sands pulls back a chair and sits down at the kitchen table. "I'm having dinner with a friend later and staying overnight in the city."

Earl is tempted to ask whether the friend is male or female but restrains himself. They are both free and single now. Her personal life is no longer any of his business.

Sands gives him a pointed look, as if she knows exactly what he's thinking and is challenging him to ask.

"I hear that you've been given a stay of execution," she says. "I'm happy for you. You must be relieved. I hope you're not going to put this second chance at risk by continuing to dig around in that old hit-and-run case."

Here then, Earl thinks, is the real reason for the visit. Gossip travels faster than light in the police service.

"Daniel Sharpe is lying in a coma in hospital after overdosing, accidentally or otherwise on GHB. If he dies, and my concerns about him confessing to the Lottie Miller hit-and-run are correct, then every police officer involved in the investigation will be to blame for his death."

Sands shakes her head in frustration. "This is typical you," she says. "Everything is black or white, good or bad, right or wrong, true or false. The world is more complex, more layered than that, and always has been. Why have you never been able to accept that?"

Earl takes a long swig of beer. He knows she isn't being critical. She's simply telling it as it is, with his best interests at heart.

"I know what you're saying, I do. But that's one of the things you loved about me, isn't it? Once upon a time. Long, long, ago. Before it all ended unhappily ever after."

She stands up, leans forward and gives him a light peck on the cheek. "I have to go. I'll let myself out. Please remember what I said and don't do anything stupid. Tanner's given you a chance. Don't ruin it."

When she's gone, Earl sits down and lets out a long sigh. He's let himself believe that all his marriages failed because he's always been too devoted to his job, the noble lawman obsessed with putting bad men and women behind bars. Deep down he knows he's been kidding himself.

He can fall in love. Perhaps too easily. He can be kind, considerate and even romantic when he wants to. What he's never been able to do is develop a deep, special, emotional connection.

Sometimes, lying awake in bed at night, he wonders whether it's because he was the only child of emotionally distant parents, but always dismisses the idea as an excuse rather than an explanation. Maybe the time has come for him to stop looking for answers, to stop looking for approval and accept who and what he is.

He picks his ex-wife's glass of beer off the table and pours it into the sink. He walks into the living room, scoops his laptop off the coffee table and sits on the sofa. He opens up a search engine and types in *Lottie Miller hit-and-run death*. What's the harm in reading through old newspaper reports of the case?

Half an hour later, he's skimming through a tabloid newspaper article on the public's reaction to the length of Sharpe's prison sentence. The judge was heavily criticized for being too soft, but he'd argued that the fact that Sharpe had never been in trouble with the police before, that he had handed himself in, confessed and pleaded guilty to the charge, preventing the need for a drawn-out trial, were all mitigating factors.

The jail term had been fiercely condemned by Lottie Miller's older sister, Liv. The feature writer's media contacts meant that she'd been able to generate widespread coverage for her views.

Earl studies a photograph of her standing on the pavement outside court, talking to a pack of quote-hungry reporters. He's about to close the story and click on another when something makes him hesitate.

He's drawn back to the photograph and this time what he sees makes him catch his breath. It's impossible not to notice the steely determination in Liv Miller's eyes. Her complexion is pale and marble smooth. Her coat is zipped up to her chin, her face framed by the grey-and-black fur trim of her hood.

CHAPTER 34

Liv

I stand on the concrete steps outside the hospital, my hands in the pockets of my coat. Yesterday I donated clothes to a homeless teenager. Today I'm ready for good deed number two. Time to pay a visit to a very sick man.

I climb the steps and walk through the main entrance. The reception area is hectic, with visitors heading to the bed-sides of their sick loved ones, and that morning's out-patients fighting their way through the crowd on their way to the exit.

I avoid the queues at the reception counter and study a large, metallic information board on the wall. The intensive care unit is in Zone A115 on the first floor. On my way to the lift, I pass a café full of people drinking coffee and eating cake, and a small store full of people buying sugary treats for their sick relatives.

I find four people waiting for the lift and decide to take the stairs instead. I exit onto a corridor decorated with ama-teurish watercolours and follow the red arrow painted on the floor.

I pass a couple of female nurses and a porter pushing an empty trolley bed. Nobody gives me a second glance. They have more important things on their minds. The palms of my hands are moist with sweat. I lift them out of my pockets and wipe them on my coat. What if Sharpe is awake, with his memory intact? I'm hoping I'll find his room empty, his body transferred to the hospital morgue.

At the end of the corridor, I turn right and stop outside the locked doors of the intensive care ward. A printed notice on the glass informs me that during visiting times I need to press the green button and wait for a nurse to let me in. I pull out my mobile, pretend to be reading something important and wait.

A couple of minutes pass before a middle-aged couple, holding hands, approach the door. The woman glances at me, her face drawn and tear-stained, while the man presses the button.

I take a small step back, wondering whether this is my chance. The lock mechanism buzzes, the man pushes the door and the couple step inside. I move forward but I'm too late and the door closes with a loud click.

Cursing myself, I go back to staring at the screen of my mobile. I'm wondering whether I've missed my best chance when the door buzzes again before swinging open. A white-coated, pony-tailed young doctor strides out, her head down, eyes fixed on a beeping electronic pager. This time I don't hesitate. Before the door shuts, I slip through.

The corridor is narrow with doors to side rooms on both the right and left. I walk purposefully, as if I'm in a hurry and know exactly where I'm going. As I pass a central desk area where a male nurse sits, a telephone clamped to his ear, I spot a whiteboard with a list of names written in black marker. Halfway down I see it.

Daniel Sharpe. Room five.

CHAPTER 35

Sharpe

Time doesn't exist in a coma. There is someone in the room and he doesn't know who it is, or how long they have been there.

Whoever is there is keeping perfectly still and quiet, but he knows they are watching him. He can feel the weight of their stare.

The silence is menacing. He feels exposed, as helpless as a fresh laboratory specimen pinned to a dissection board. He wills the night-shift nurses to burst into the room, ready to run a damp cloth over his face, empty his bag and move him off his back onto his side.

Footsteps. At last. Soft, tentative, approaching the bed. An intake of breath before speech. When the words come, they are infinitely more frightening than the silence.

"You poor, poor man. I didn't mean for this to happen, but you'd be better off if you'd died. It'd be better for everyone."

CHAPTER 36

Liv

I don't know why I expect him to react in some way, but I do, and it maddens me that he doesn't even blink.

He's lying on his back, his chest rising a fraction every time the ventilator hisses. Apart from that, he's motionless, as close to death as anyone can be. Even closer now that I'm in the room.

I try to guess how long it would take for all brain activity to cease if I unplugged the life support machine. Less than a minute probably, though I suspect an alarm would sound, and doctors and nurses would come running.

I place a thumb on his right eyelid and raise it gently. The eye has rolled high into the right-hand corner of the socket, and the pupil doesn't respond to the light. I'm not a doctor but I'm sure that's a bad sign.

Moving around to the other side of the bed, I examine the intravenous drip inserted into the back of his right hand. I guess it's either keeping him hydrated, or regularly topping up the cocktail of medication that's helping to keep him alive.

I check the room for a security camera, then wrap my fingers around the plastic tube at the point it connects to the bag of clear fluid. It'd be so easy. But I know that somewhere in the hospital, walking through the main reception area, or entering the ward, I would have been captured on film. It'd be stupid to give the police a reason to view the footage.

The patient monitor seems to be beeping louder and faster than before. I cross the room, crouching to check the screen. I'm no expert but I don't think you need a stethoscope and a white coat to work out that a pulse of ninety-eight beats a minute is high, considering he's lying there doing nothing.

Curious, I draw closer to the bed, and run the tip of my forefinger across his neck slowly, in a cut-throat motion. I flinch and step back. Did his right eyelid really twitch, or did I imagine it? Unsure, I repeat the action. There it is again.

He's not as close to death as he looks. He's hiding from me, inside himself. If he can feel, then he can probably hear. I bet he can remember too.

Bending down, I place my mouth close to his left ear. "You don't deserve to be alive. You know that, don't you? You took Lottie from me and it's only right that you pay for that. Who knows if you're going to come out of this? But believe me, it'll be better for everyone if you don't."

I check my watch. I've been in the room for five minutes, and the longer I stay the higher the risk of being discovered. I try to think what Lottie would want me to do. She'd probably tell me to walk away, say that he's suffered enough. She was like that. Kindhearted and wise beyond her years.

I move my mouth closer to his ear and speak slowly and clearly to give him every chance to understand.

"If you do survive this then you'd better hope that your memory is shot to pieces. I believe that's pretty common with people who've come back from a coma. Memories are fragile but they can also be very dangerous. Not just for you but for people who are close to you. Do you understand me?"

I pause to let the message sink in. His eyelid twitches again and I take it as a yes.

It's time to go. I stand up straight and stare down at his face for a few seconds. A wave of frustration washes over me and I bite my lip to stop myself crying.

He looks dead but he's not. It's strange because when I saw Lottie lying in the hospital morgue, she was definitely dead. She didn't look it, though. I swear, if I hadn't known better, I'd have thought she was sleeping, she looked so peaceful.

"Emily is such a lovely young woman," I say. "You're so lucky to have her. I bet she's enjoying life as a student. I know Lottie would have loved the chance to go to university. Especially in such an interesting and lively city."

CHAPTER 37

Earl

The first thing Earl does when he arrives in the squad room the next morning is call Becky Andrews in forensics.

"You must be psychic," she says. "You're on my urgent list today."

Earl feels a familiar buzz. When case breakthroughs come, they often arrive like London buses. All at the same time.

"You've something new for me on the Sharpe inquiry?"

"Impressive deduction. How on earth did you work that out? Ever thought of doing police work?"

Normally, Earl would indulge the crime scene manager's love of verbal sparring but he's eager to get down to business.

"What is it?"

He hears a couple of clicks and assumes Andrews is opening a file on her computer. "The report is complete and the team have come up with a couple of interesting things. On the living room floor, next to the armchair in which Sharpe was slumped, we found a sticky patch of dried saliva, which contained the drug GHB. At some point Sharpe dribbled onto the carpet."

Earl picks up a pen and drums it on the desk. "And that is significant because . . .?"

"Because, embedded on top of the saliva, and I stress *on top*, were a couple of the same fake fur strands that we found on the sofa."

Earl pauses to process this information. "So, if the strands of fur were on top of the saliva stain, then the person wearing the coat, who left traces of fur on the sofa, must have been in the room when Sharpe drank the coffee, not someone who'd visited the house previously."

"Precisely, Detective. Unusually sharp of you, pardon the pun. And there's more. On a mug we found in the kitchen, even though it appeared to have been washed, we found traces of coffee and lipstick."

Earl's mind races. "If Sharpe had company, it's possible that he didn't deliberately take an overdose, or even accidentally overdose. There's a chance that someone spiked his coffee with the GHB."

"I'd say that is a strong possibility."

"Thanks, Becky, excellent work."

"Kind of you to say so but not necessary. Excellence is a minimum standard as far as my department is concerned."

Earl puts the receiver down and moves the telephone back slightly to line it up with his computer monitor.

He looks up to see Akinola crossing the squad room carrying two cardboard cups. As she puts one down on Earl's desk, a drop of coffee spills over the rim.

"Don't say I never give you anything," Akinola says with a smile.

Earl takes a wad of tissue from his jacket pocket, lifts the cup and wipes the table. "Thanks. I need a shot of caffeine. I missed breakfast this morning."

Akinola goes to put her cup on the desk but thinks better of it and takes a sip instead. "What's the latest on Sharpe?" she asks.

"I rang the hospital on the way in and he's still in a bad way."

Akinola shakes her head. "You've got to have some sympathy for the guy, don't you? I don't think he's a bad person. He'd never committed a crime before. He makes a mistake that means he loses everything. Then he takes an overdose."

"He didn't, though," Earl says.

Akinola sighs. "You have to let this obsession with the Lottie girl go."

"No, I mean I'm pretty sure it wasn't a suicide attempt, or even an accidental overdose. According to forensics, it's very possible that Sharpe's coffee was laced with GHB without his knowledge."

"You're joking?"

"Am I laughing?"

"Shit," Akinola says. "What now?"

Earl drains his coffee and drops the empty cup into the waste bin beside his desk. "I need to brief Tanner right now and get the go-ahead to upgrade the investigation to attempted murder. Then we're going to pull the suspect in for questioning and apply for a warrant to search her home."

Akinola splutters into her coffee, and takes a second to wipe her chin with the palm of her hand.

"What did you say? Who is this suspect?"

"Take a guess."

CHAPTER 38

Liv

I stand in front of my bedroom mirror, twisting unsteadily in high heels and looking over my shoulder to check the fit of my new jeans. I'm happy with what I see. They're snug but not too tight.

I slip on a loose, navy-blue sweater, move closer to the mirror, tilt my head and practise putting on a pained expression. I'm aiming to combine sadness with determination, and it takes me several attempts to get the balance right.

I've agreed to join Matt Lamb for an early evening drink at a pub around the corner from my house. He called to ask how my treatment was going, and he was being so sweet to me I didn't have the heart to refuse when he suggested that we meet up.

Besides, I like him a lot. I really do. I haven't dated anyone since Lottie died. It hasn't seemed important. My choice in men has always been terrible. I've always gone for bad guys, and inevitably it always ends badly. I guess Walton would say it's because I associate love with pain. But maybe it's time for things to change. Maybe after I've sorted out the Sharpe situation, I'll find myself a nice guy. Someone like Matt.

I don't want to do anything that might hurt him. He's always been good to me. I know I shouldn't have started the cancer lie, and I regret it, but when it all turns out fine in the end, Matt will be happy. That's a good thing. It was too tempting to resist at the time, and it's impossible for me to back down now. He'd never understand if I tried to explain that I was simply testing my ability to play mind games. It means I've had to keep the make-up to a minimum. It's tricky trying to look good but at the same time not too healthy.

I slip on my new coat before stepping outside. It's a crisp evening, not even a hint of spring in the air, and I hitch the hood up. The coat is bright red, the hood lined with dark red faux fur.

Normally, I wouldn't choose to wear anything that bright but it popped up while I was shopping online, and I figured, why not? I'm such a different person now, a person I never once imagined I could be. Red is the colour of danger, excitement and fire, and I have to confess, I love the *don't mess with me* message it sends to the world.

My Lottie enjoyed wearing bright colours, summer or winter. They suited her bubbly personality. She was an improved, updated, more sophisticated version of me. My mother definitely believed that was the case.

I'm sure Lottie's brain was perfectly formed when she came into the world. She was empathetic, sympathetic, loving and forgiving. She forgave Mum for banishing me, and she forgave me for retaliating by shutting them both out of my life. Until that day.

Thinking about her is physically painful, and I walk faster to try to distract myself from the tightness in the centre of my chest. By the time I reach the Compass pub, I'm desperate for some kind of human contact, and a glass of wine.

Matt is already leaning against the bar when I enter, and he greets me with a broad smile. The pub's ornate ceilings, huge oak wall panels and gleaming brass fixtures are elegantly Victorian and obviously fake.

I walk over to Matt, unzip my coat, flick the hood down and let him kiss me on the cheek.

"Hello again," he says. "It's lovely to see you, it really is. You're looking good, Liv . . . er, I mean, well . . ."

He falters, and I'm sure he has to stop himself adding the words "considering you have cancer". I know it's early but I can't resist playing for sympathy.

"I'm not too bad, trying my best to stay positive," I say. "It's lovely to see you too. It's so good to get out and see a friendly face. I seem to spend all my time moping around at home or in hospital."

He winces at the mention of hospital appointments and takes a hurried gulp of his beer. "What can I get you to drink?" he asks. "I don't suppose you're allowed alcohol while you're being treated, or are you?"

Horrified at the suggestion that I might have to do without wine, I shake my head and laugh softly. "Oh no, thank God. According to my doctors, sensible drinking is permissible. In fact, the occasional dose of chilled Pinot Grigio is compulsory, I think."

Matt grins, clearly impressed at the way I can joke about something so serious, and orders me a large glass of my favourite medicine. When it arrives, we carry our drinks over to a corner booth and sit down.

"How are things going at the magazine?" I ask, although I'm not at all interested. "Are they keeping you busy?"

I'll have to return to work soon. I need the money but I'm dreading it. I don't know why I used to consider that world glamorous and exciting. It seems so mundane and unappealing, as phoney as the pub décor now.

Matt raises a hand to brush a tangle of hair from his forehead. He loves his job and harbours an ambition to occupy the editor's chair one day. He's an excellent journalist but I don't think he'll make it. He's not ruthless enough.

"It's the same as always. You know how it is. Busy becomes hectic as the deadline looms. Then as it nears, everyone starts to panic. We always get the magazine out on time, though, don't we? Naturally, we're missing you. Well, I am anyway. We've not yet found a feature writer anywhere near your standard."

I feel I should be blushing a pale pink with modesty, but it's Matt who reddens. I take a sip of wine and try my hardest not to look too smug.

"Well, you'd be doing me a big favour if you don't take on a replacement on a long-term contract. The doctors are telling me that the treatment is going well, much better than expected actually, and I'm hoping to be back researching and writing fascinating features for you to admire before long."

Matt picks up his beer, holding it up over the table for me to clink with my almost-empty wine glass in celebration.

"That's fantastic news," he says. "I'm so pleased for you. I can't begin to tell you how worried I've been. Rest assured there'll always be work for you. There's no need to rush back. Don't do anything that might put your recovery at risk. Your feature on psychopaths will be in next month's edition, by the way. It's such a brilliant, interesting read, Liv. The editor loves it so much she's told us to make sure you get a picture byline."

I stand up, turning my face away to hide my delight as I take off my coat and drape it over the back of my chair.

"Did she actually say that? That's really encouraging to hear and, not that we need one, a perfect excuse for another drink. Same again?"

I don't wait for an answer and go to the bar, feeling happier than I've been for a long time. All reporters and feature writers love the ego boost that comes with seeing their name in print on top of an article. If it's accompanied by a headshot that's been enhanced to make you look younger and prettier than in real life, it can send your ego into orbit.

While waiting for the drinks, I sneak a sideways look back at Matt, who's engrossed in something on his mobile.

He's undoubtedly an attractive man, and kind with it. An unusual combination, in my experience. If only things were different. If I'd never had the brain scan, never found out what I truly am, maybe I'd have a chance to be happy.

Matt lifts his eyes from his mobile and catches me staring at him. His smile is so cute and genuine, it warms my heart. I turn back to the bar, scolding myself for getting carried away. I know he's too kind, too gentle to deserve to become involved with me.

I take our drinks back to the table and hand him his beer. "Are you trying to get me drunk?" he asks, with a grin.

"Of course not, but if I was, I don't think I'd have to try very hard. You've never been able to hold your drink. Don't you remember the state you were in at the last Christmas party?"

"I remember nothing. Not a thing."

"My point exactly."

We carry on chatting for another twenty minutes, and he offers to buy more drinks. The sensible thing to do is to refuse and go home. I weaken and accept.

When Matt returns from the bar, he drinks his beer slowly but I down most of my wine in a few unladylike gulps.

"Maybe you should slow down a bit," he says, concern creasing his brow. "You've got to take care of yourself."

It's the most irritating thing he's said all night. I knock back the last drop of wine and glare at him defiantly. He looks bemused and the corners of his mouth tighten when I slip my coat off of the back of the chair and get up to put it on.

He stands too, buttoning his jacket. "Well, I've really enjoyed myself," he says. "I tell you what, why don't I walk you home? It's in the same direction as the Underground station, and I'd like to make sure that you get home safely."

I'm tempted to tell him that the most dangerous person walking the streets between the pub and my house will probably be me. I don't, of course.

"It's very thoughtful of you, Matt, but no thanks. It's not necessary. You should stay and finish your drink. I'm not rushing off because I haven't had fun. It's been great, but I've got an appointment at the hospital early tomorrow morning and I need to try to get some sleep."

He moves closer, puts his hands on my shoulders and squeezes them gently. "Listen, if you need me to come to the hospital with you, to give you support, I can easily make arrangements to take a few hours off work."

I'm touched by the offer, even though I know I won't be going anywhere near a cancer treatment room. I smile ruefully. "That's really sweet of you but, honestly, there's no need. I've coped all right on my own up to now, so don't worry, I'll be fine."

He shrugs and leans forward to give me a goodbye peck on the cheek. Inexplicably, I turn my head at the last second and our lips meet. We kiss for several seconds before I pull away.

His face is flushed, his eyes wide, but before he can do or say anything, I twist away and hurry out of the pub. I walk as fast as my high heels will allow, and after a minute or so, I look over my shoulder to check that Matt's not following me.

What the hell was I playing at? Matt would never have tried to kiss me like that, not unless I made it obvious that I wanted him to. And I didn't want him to, then suddenly I did. I've never been that impulsive before.

I know that he's going to call me soon, ask me out again. He'll be convinced that I'm interested in a relationship with him, and who can blame him? I'll have to fob him off, be cruel if necessary. It's the best thing I can do. I have too much to deal with right now.

I wish things were different. I'd love to try being with him. A proper couple. I know he'd never hurt me. I imagine what it would be like to be truly in love and deeply loved, to be content and safe.

Although the thought fills me with a rush of happiness, I fear that if Matt really knew me, knew what I'm capable of, he'd be repulsed. He's caring and generous, but he doesn't know the truth. He can't see the ugly secret hiding inside me.

CHAPTER 39

Sharpe

"I'm going to give you an injection now," the male nurse says. "This has been prescribed by your doctor to help keep your heart rate steady. It'll be all over in a second and you won't feel a thing."

Sharpe appreciates that even though the nurse has no idea whether he can be heard or understood, he always explains what he's about to do before he does it.

Despite the nurse's reassurances, he feels pressure on the right side of his stomach, then the prick of a needle piercing the skin. A strong chemical scent with a trace of lemon and ginger fills his nostrils. It must be the nurse's deodorant, and it's the first time Sharpe has been able to smell it. Hope buzzes his brain. Things are changing fast.

"There you go. All done. Call me if you need anything, or have any questions."

Sharpe is confused. It takes him a moment to work out that the nurse wasn't speaking to him, and that another person must have entered the room.

Fingertips tentatively stroke the back of his right hand. Emily is back. She says nothing, but her breathing is fast and shallow, and he can sense her anxiety, her fear. He's desperate to tell her he's close to breaking through, that she needs to hold on, to be brave.

She edges closer to the bed and he catches her scent. She smells of fresh green apples and antibacterial hand sanitizer. Sharpe wants to hug her, comfort and protect her.

"Mum's going to join me a little later," she says. "She's gone to do some shopping. I told her that I wanted to see you on my own for a while."

Sharpe shakes his head, mentally. The last thing he wants is his daughter wandering around the hospital by herself. It's not safe. Not now. That woman could be watching the main entrance. She could wait for Emily to leave, follow her and find out which hotel she's staying at.

"If you can hear me," Emily says. "I want you to know how incredibly proud I am of you but sorry for everything that's happened. I feel like I've let you down. All these years I've let Mum push you away, keep you away from me. I could have been stronger, should have been. I should have insisted, should have been honest about wanting a proper relationship with you."

Sharpe hates the thought that his daughter has probably been up all night rehearsing this speech. It hurts him to hear her blame herself for something she's not guilty of. He's the one who cheated on his wife when she was pregnant. He couldn't come up with an explanation when it happened, and he's never been able to explain it to himself. He confessed and begged Clare to forgive him. She didn't. She used their child as a weapon of vengeance, and he understands why.

He focuses his mind on lifting his eyelids. He knows he can do it if he tries hard enough. He's done it before, hasn't he? Perhaps he only imagined it. Maybe his brain is playing tricks on him. He pushes the thought away. He needs to give his daughter a sign, let her see that he can hear every word, that after all that has happened, everything is going to be all right.

Emily wraps her warm fingers around his cold hand and squeezes. A single raindrop falls onto Sharpe's forearm, then another, and a third. Before the fourth lands, he realizes they are tears.

"If I'd known how you were suffering, I'd have tried my best to help — really, I would. I don't want you to die. Please don't die."

Sharpe's right eyelid flickers. Emily is still sobbing softly, her head bowed, and she doesn't notice the twitch. He wants to explain to her that the police have made a mistake. He didn't take a drug overdose. No matter how desperate he felt, he'd never do that to her. He'd abandoned her once. It would never happen again.

But he knows that even if, even when, he is able to breathe on his own, move his lips and speak, he won't be able to tell anybody what really happened. He can't afford to get the police involved. He could handle their questions. He's had a lot of practice. But who knows how Emily would react under pressure? What she'd admit to?

She stops crying, wipes her eyes, sniffs and holds his hand in silence until she spots his arm is wet with her tears.

"Wait a second," she says, rummaging in her handbag. "I think I've some tissues somewhere. I definitely put them in here this morning. What the hell have I done with them?"

Her voice cracks with frustration. She needs to take some slow, deep breaths to calm herself down. Sharpe visualizes sitting up, pulling her gently into his arms and telling her not to worry, that everything is going to be all right.

A sudden, stabbing pain shoots from his right shoulder down to the tips of his fingers. He cries out in agony but makes no sound. Is someone attacking him?

Emily is silent, and the silence is frightening. Sharpe can't even hear her breathing. Emily? Where is she? He wills himself to open his eyes, puts everything he can into raising even one. He's dazzled by a white light, and his eyelid clamps shut before he can see what's happened to her.

Footsteps skitter across the room towards the door, there's a crash as something hits the floor. "Help me," Emily yells, her voice choked. "Someone please, help."

Sharpe's head spins, as if he's about to pass out. A fresh pain shoots down his arm. What have they done to Emily? He struggles to open his eyes again but the light forces them closed.

Emily is shouting louder now, almost screaming. "Please, someone, we need help here! I need a doctor!"

Sharpe is dizzy and nauseous. Emily's words fade like distant echoes in his ears. *Is this it?* he wonders. *Is this the end?* He's not ready. He lifts both eyes a fraction but they snap shut.

A flurry of footsteps, a clamour of voices. Everyone seems to be talking at once, at each other and at him. He can't make out what they're saying. Emily is the only person he can understand. She gasps for breath between each sentence as she speaks, repeating the same words over and over again.

"He moved his arm and opened his eyes. His right arm definitely moved. I saw it. I did. And his eyes. Both of his eyes opened a little. He can move. I saw him move. And look, there, on his cheeks. He's crying. See, he's crying."

CHAPTER 40

Liv

I tip my head back and let the hot water rinse the shampoo out of my hair. One of the big advantages of going for the pixie crop is that it's low maintenance.

The water stings my face but I stay where I am and accept my punishment. I still haven't forgiven myself for last night. I keep picturing Matt's face after I pulled away. I don't know what came over me but I can't deny I enjoyed the kiss. It felt good. It made me feel like a normal person. Is there a way back to normality once this is all over? I'd like to think so.

Stepping out of the shower, I pat myself dry with a fluffy towel and cross the hall to my bedroom where I dress quickly. My plan this morning is to head back to the hospital to check on my favourite coma patient. I'm hoping he's been moved to the morgue by now, freeing up the bed for someone who deserves to live. I wait for a tiny stab of guilt. It doesn't come.

Hunger gnaws at my insides. I haven't eaten anything since lunch yesterday. It's not like me to go without food for that long, and I'm definitely feeling lethargic. I go to the kitchen to fix myself brunch. The fridge is empty except for a tub of margarine, two open cartons of pineapple juice and an unripe avocado.

I slam the door shut and pick up a couple of chocolate biscuits someone has left on the worktop next to the sink. It must have been me, though I can't remember. All this stuff going on in my head is playing havoc with my memory.

I eat them quickly and decide I need a strong coffee to kick-start my day. While I'm waiting for the kettle to boil, I fill a glass tumbler with water and drink it down in one. Why am I so thirsty? I fill the glass again, but before I can raise it to my mouth the doorbell rings.

I pour the water into the sink and walk down the hall. I hesitate at the door, worried that it might be Matt eager to discuss the meaning of that kiss. I'm not in the right frame of mind to talk to him, and I consider pretending that no one is in. The bell chimes again and the sound riles me. I don't know why.

I take a deep breath and exhale loudly. What's the point of putting this off? I open the door and am surprised to see it's not Matt. A man in a smart grey suit nods and smiles at me. He looks familiar but I can't put a name to his face. Tall and clean-shaven, his hair is darker than mine and speckled with grey at the temples.

With him is a sterner-looking younger woman. Her dark hair is in a ponytail and she's wearing a navy-blue skirt and matching jacket. At once I know what they are and a shiver slides down my spine.

"Good morning, officers. What can I do for you?"

The man holds up what I assume is a warrant card but I don't bother to look at it.

"Good morning," he says. "I'm Detective Sergeant Earl and this is my colleague Detective Akinola. We'd appreciate it if you'd come down to the station with us to answer a few questions. We'd also like your permission to search your home. We can get a warrant if necessary but that will only drag the process out."

I flash him a smile, to demonstrate that I have absolutely nothing to hide.

"Are you serious?" I ask. "This is some kind of joke, right?"

"This is an extremely serious matter," the woman detective says. "We don't go around knocking on doors for fun."

I ignore her. I don't even look at her because I know she'll hate it, and keep my eyes on Earl. I'm confident that they won't find anything incriminating, but the thought of strangers going through my personal belongings fills me with dread.

Instinctively, I half close the door. I need time to decide on the best course of action. I could refuse them entry until they come back with a search warrant but I don't want to appear obstructive.

"I think it would help if you tell me what this is about."

Earl exchanges a quick glance with his colleague. "We'll explain everything back at the station," he says. "We're not going to conduct an interview on your doorstep."

I continue to smile, despite the questions filling my head. I'm guessing this has to be about Sharpe. Have I slipped up somehow? It's not possible, is it? Intelligent psychopaths are meticulous planners and I've been obsessively careful. Panic flutters in the back of my throat but I swallow it down. *Stay calm*, I tell myself. *There's nothing to worry about. You know you can do this.*

The secret me can do anything.

I hide my thoughts behind wide-eyed astonishment. "Are you actually going to arrest me? But that's ridiculous. I've never been in trouble with the police before."

"If we have to arrest you right here, then we won't hesitate," Akinola says. I still don't acknowledge her presence, and I can tell it's getting to her. "If you make us do that, I'll have to handcuff you, and I'd rather not. It'll be easier for everybody if you come with us voluntarily."

She's lying. I swear she's hoping that I'll refuse to cooperate. I bet she's dying for the chance to slap those cuffs on me and haul me to the car like a common criminal. There's no way I'm going to give her the pleasure.

"All right then, if you think this is really necessary. Shall I leave the door unlocked so your officers can get to work straightaway? I hope they'll be careful with my things. Give me a minute to get my coat, and I'll come with you now."

I know it's silly but I'm actually a little excited by the thought of taking a ride in the back of a police car. Especially if they're going to switch on the siren and blue flashing lights.

A few minutes later, we're heading east in heavy traffic along Marsh Wall. Akinola is behind the wheel, and Earl is in the back with me. We're crawling along behind a red double-decker bus, inhaling diesel fumes. No siren, no flashing lights, and I'm already bored out of my mind.

"How long is this so-called informal interview going to take?" I ask Earl.

Before he can reply, Akinola answers for him. "It'll take as long as it takes. We're investigating a possible serious crime."

I turn to Earl. "Is she like this with everybody?"

He responds with a blank look, and I realize where I've seen him before. He's the detective who led the investigation into Lottie's death. I remember not being all that impressed with the inquiry's lack of urgency, but in the end Sharpe made things easy for everyone when he walked into the police station to give himself up.

I turn to look out of the window. Steel-and-glass towers, concrete office blocks and neon shop signs slide by. We pass a sandwich bar and a fried chicken takeaway and my stomach growls.

"Is there any chance we can pull over so I can get something to eat? I was about to prepare brunch when you guys turned up."

Earl sighs. "I'm sure we'll be able to find you something to keep you going in the station canteen."

I smile my thanks and consider fluttering my eyelashes in an attempt to get him on my side, but judge him unlikely to be influenced by something so superficial.

At the police station, I'm marched along a musty-smell-ing corridor by Detective Akinola, who has obviously decided not to speak to me unless she has to. She takes me into a chilly interview room. The walls are painted pale green, and the only furniture is a grey table and two red plastic chairs.

Akinola stands with her back against the wall, and sig-nals with a wave of a hand for me to take a seat. I do as she suggests.

The door opens and Earl walks in carrying a pre-packed sandwich and a cup of coffee. He puts both down on the table in front of me.

"I hope chicken mayo will do, because it's that or nothing."

I pick the sandwich up and examine it, reading the list of ingredients carefully and peering through the plastic wrapper at the filling. It looks like something a dog would turn down, but I don't want to appear ungrateful.

"Thank you. It'll do, I suppose. I think I'll take it home and eat it later. I seem to have lost my appetite."

Detective Earl sits opposite me, leans back in the chair and folds his arms across his chest.

"I know this must be a painful subject for you, but can you remember the last time you saw Daniel Sharpe?"

I try to imagine how Earl would react if I tell him that I'd been to see Sharpe in hospital a couple of days ago and had come close to yanking the power cable out of his life support machine. A smirk tugs at my lips, but I manage to keep my expression neutral.

I've watched plenty of crime dramas on television and know that offering a bland "no comment" in answer to every question is probably my safest bet. But where's the fun in that? Anyway, I bet the police think only guilty people say no comment, and I want to make it clear I have nothing to hide.

"That coward who calls himself a man killed Lottie," I say. "The last time I saw his pathetic face, I was sitting in the public gallery in court when he was sentenced and the sight of him made me feel physically sick. Why would I ever want to see him again?"

The detective looks straight at me, weighing up my reply. I gaze into his eyes, hiding the untruth behind my boldness.

"Are you aware that Daniel Sharpe is in hospital?"

I don't blink. "Something incurable, I hope."

Earl breaks eye contact, flicking a sideways glance at Detective Akinola. I look down at my hands and examine my nails. I desperately need a manicure.

"He's in a coma after an incident at his home."

"An incident? What sort of incident?"

I'm delighted to hear that Sharpe's still comatose, and at the same time I'm irritated that he hasn't done the world a favour and died.

"You don't read newspapers or watch the news bulletins on TV?" Earl asks.

I shrug and shake my head. "I try to avoid it if I can. It's all so depressing, isn't it?"

I've set myself a challenge of answering every question with a question. I wonder how long it'll be before cracks appear in the detective's composure. I don't think he believes a single word I'm saying, but it doesn't matter. I've been careful.

I pick up the coffee, take a small sip and put the cup back down. A tiny drop flows over the brim and slides onto the table. Earl's eyes are drawn to the spillage. His jaw clenches tight and I realize the man's a neat freak.

"I like your coat," he says. "Is it new? The colour suits you."

"Do you think so?"

I don't know exactly where he's going with this line of questioning, but I think it's unlikely he has a genuine interest in women's fashion.

Earl surprises me again when, without another word, he stands and walks out. I assume that it's part of a prepared interview tactic, because as soon as the door closes Detective Akinola crosses the room and sits on the vacant seat.

I can tell by the way she looks at me that she doesn't like me. I don't take it personally. Sometimes, when you meet someone, you instinctively know that you're not going to be best gal pals, don't you?

"Can you tell me what you did on Saturday, the seventh of March?" she asks.

Of course I can. I remember it like it was yesterday. It was the day I did something the old me would never dare do.

"Isn't it about time you stopped keeping me in the dark and told me what this is about?"

Akinola puts both her hands on the table and entwines her fingers. I notice she's not wearing any rings.

"Can you confirm that you have, or used to have, a dark green coat with grey-and-black fake fur around the hood?"

She asks this with a smirk, and it's then that I realize why I took an instant dislike to her. She's probably only a couple of years older than me, and although she looks nothing like her, she reminds me of my mother. Demanding and impatient.

Mother had a superiority complex too. I was never good enough for her. A big disappointment. A terrible let-down. Everything changed when Lottie arrived. Things became even worse. I felt like an outsider. Excess to requirements. I loved my little sister, though. And she loved me. That was part of the problem, I think.

"Did I have a green coat?" I ask. "Now you mention it, I think I did. A while ago. What has that got to do with anything?"

Akinola lifts a hand to her mouth and yawns loudly. I can tell she's faking it to give the impression that she's not really that interested in anything I'm saying. The poor misguided fool thinks she's in control, and I suspect she believes she's about to spring a surprise on me.

"We are investigating an incident at Daniel Sharpe's home in which he was seriously injured. Although it appeared to be a simple drug overdose, we have reason to believe it's possible he was the victim of a serious crime."

I respond with a puzzled smile. "Are you saying that you think I might have been involved in some way?"

Akinola narrows her eyes and tries to intimidate me with a stare. "Were you?"

I meet her gaze and we have a staring contest across the table. She wins. I crack after about five seconds, shaking my head in disbelief.

"Do you actually think that I'd want to do Sharpe serious harm? That I'd risk everything to make him pay for what he did to my Lottie?"

Akinola pauses, cups her hands and tucks her hair behind her ears. I'm pretty sure she's not having as much fun as I am.

"I think it's a possible scenario," she says. "A grieving older sister plots to murder the man who ran down and killed her younger sibling. That's a pretty strong motive in my book. I don't think a jury would take much persuading that you had good reason to want Sharpe dead. They'd probably even have some sympathy for you."

She's trying to frighten me, and it's working. I tell myself to stay strong, stay in psychopath mode. The police have nothing on me, and as long as I don't sabotage myself everything will be fine.

"I won't lie to you, because I'm actually not very good at lying and an experienced detective like you would see right through it. I wouldn't feel the tiniest bit sorry if Sharpe was to die, and I'd gladly shake the hand of anyone who made that happen. But the sad truth is, no matter how much I want him dead for what he did, I'm simply not capable of harming another human being. It's not in my nature, and we can't change our nature, can we, Detective?"

Before she can reply, the door opens and Earl strides in. He stands to the right of Akinola, facing me, his hands in his pockets. His arrival annoys me. I'm enjoying the sparring match.

"My team have completed the search of your property," he says. "They tell me they couldn't find a computer, or a laptop, which is strange considering what you do for a living."

I raise my eyebrows and shrug, taking encouragement from the fact that he hasn't come straight in with the TV cop show spiel about me not having to say anything but anything

I do say will be *blah, blah, blah*. It suggests that they didn't find anything suspicious.

"I had a big clear out a few days ago. I always do around this time of year, to make room for new spring and summer clothes. Got rid of some jumpers, jeans, boots, an old green coat. Gave them to a well-spoken young man from a charity who knocked on my door. Can't remember what the charity was called, but I think he was collecting unwanted clothes for the homeless. I decided to donate my laptop as well. I'd had it for years and I'm going to treat myself to a new, flashy one. I'd like to leave now. As I'm not under arrest, I can go when I want, can't I?"

Earl walks back to the door, reaches for the handle but hesitates. "Thank you for your cooperation," he says. "You're free to go, but first Detective Akinola is going to organize for a DNA sample to be taken. It's just a quick swab on the inside of your mouth. Don't worry, it's routine."

On the outside I don't react, but my mind is churning. Why would they want to take a sample of my DNA? It can't have anything to do with the search of my home. Naturally, my DNA is going to be all over the place.

The thought calms me down, and I realize that Earl is telling the truth. It's routine. They ask for DNA samples because they can, that's all. They store them on their national database and hope they'll come in useful in the future. It strikes me that DNA sampling could make an interesting subject for a feature article, if I can come up with a good angle.

"If you think that's necessary, it's not a problem for me," I say. "I've got nothing to hide, have I?"

Earl doesn't look convinced. "That's good to hear," he says. "If that's the case then you've nothing to worry about. Oh, and there's one other thing before you go. A few minutes ago, we received a call from the Royal London Hospital. Apparently, Daniel Sharpe has come out of the coma. He's already able to breathe without a ventilator and is making a remarkable recovery. According to the doctors, he's going to be well enough to be interviewed in a day or two."

The news hits me like a slap in the face, but I don't flinch. My heart is pounding so hard I'm sure the detectives can hear it.

"I'm puzzled why you're bothering to tell me this," I say, my voice impressively calm. "I have no interest in that man, and no interest in his medical condition."

My pulse slows as I think the situation through, and realize that I can no longer afford to be passive. I can't sit at home waiting and hoping that I frightened Sharpe enough to make him heed my warning and keep his mouth shut. I have to be proactive. I have to increase the pressure on him, and that means getting closer to his daughter. Close enough to do her harm, if I decide it's necessary.

I am what I am thanks to the way my brain formed as I grew in my mother's womb. There's an argument to say I shouldn't be held responsible for what my brain makes me do.

Anyway, it's nothing personal. I'm sure Emily is a lovely girl, as innocent and blameless as Lottie. But if she's the best way for me to get to Sharpe, to make him weep like I wept, then nothing will stop me, because nothing can. I don't even think I can stop myself.

CHAPTER 41

Liv

Standing on the pavement outside the police station, I use my mobile to order a cab. Estimated pickup time is fifteen minutes.

While waiting, I unwrap the sandwich Detective Earl gave me, take a bite and chew it slowly. The bread has the texture of cardboard and the processed chicken tastes like sawdust. I force myself to swallow it, and put the rest of the sandwich back into my coat pocket. It's destined for the first rubbish bin I see. I'd like to give it to a homeless person but that would be cruel.

There's a constant flow of people walking in and out of the police station entrance, and I watch them with contempt. Men or women, young or old, they all have the look of potential victims to me. I'm a slight woman. Physically, I'm not a threat to anyone, and I've always, in the back of my mind, had to be cautious about becoming a victim of crime. That's changed. I've crossed over.

I replay the interview in my mind, trying to figure out exactly what Earl and Akinola do and don't know about Sharpe's brush with death. It's clear that they suspect that it wasn't a suicide attempt or an accident. They believe that someone did their best to kill him, while trying to make it look self-inflicted.

Having to give a sample of my DNA unnerved me, but I'm confident I left no forensic traces in Sharpe's house. If the police had proof that I was present when he took the GHB, they'd never have let me walk out of the building.

They have nothing. That's why they're putting pressure on me in the hope that I'll crack. They believe I have a motive for wanting Sharpe dead, and they want to pin this on me. If I stay tough mentally, then they will fail. Thankfully, my mind is stronger than it's ever been.

A marked police car screeches to a halt in front of the police station. Two uniformed police constables climb out and drag a shaven-headed man out of the back seat. Despite the chill in the air, he's wearing a tight T-shirt, and his muscular, tattooed arms are handcuffed behind his back.

The officers escort him to the station entrance, and as he passes he turns his head and leers at me like a hungry reptile. I've met bullies like him before. I'd normally avoid eye contact and walk away. He wants to intimidate me with his stare, draw nourishment from my fear. I respond with a stare and give him the finger. The look of surprise on his face makes me chuckle.

The cab arrives and I climb in the back. Inside, the car smells of fresh sweat and stale vomit. The driver is from Poland and chatters like a magpie. He tells me, even though I never at any point express an iota of interest in his personal life, that he has a wife and four children he hardly gets to see because he's always working.

I get the impression that he's actually happy to spend as long as possible away from his family. He agrees to drive me to the nearest hardware store and wait while I do some urgent shopping. I keep my promise to be no longer than fifteen minutes, and for the rest of the journey home I have to listen to the driver explain how living in London is so stressful it's making him ill, how one day he's going to crack and probably end up putting his foot hard down on the accelerator and killing someone. It'll probably be a cyclist, he informs me, because he hates cyclists even more than he hates Romanians.

After paying the fare, and giving the driver a five-pound tip, I take the carrier bag containing the items I bought straight up to Lottie's room. I sit on the bed, placing the bag beside me, and take a long look round.

The bedroom is exactly how it was on the day that Lottie died. On the oak bookshelf next to the window stands her collection of Harry Potter books. She read them all, several times over, and even when she grew out of them, she couldn't let them go. Neither can I. That would feel like a betrayal.

Her clothes still hang in the wardrobe, and her shoes, including her favourite yellow trainers, lie in haphazard rows under the foot of the bed. Beside her fluffy blue pillow sits the tattered panda toy she brought with her when she first moved in. She always claimed that our mother bought it for me and it was passed down to her, but I have no memory of it at all. It's the one thing in the room I probably will get rid of. Its beady eyes creep me out.

I take a long, deep breath. The citrus scent of Lottie's favourite perfume still hangs in the air. To say I miss her doesn't express the depth of the pain I feel about her absence. It would be more accurate to say that it feels like she's missing in me.

There have been times when I've considered clearing out the room, redecorating and turning the space into a study. I'm not ready to do that and it's more than likely I won't ever be. All my memories of Lottie live inside these four walls and we'll never make new ones.

That thought brings with it another headache. I hold my head in my hands and weep. I don't know if it's the pain or my grief that's making me cry, but the tears spur me into action. I tip the carrier bag upside down, spilling the contents onto the bed with a metallic rattle.

I pick up the new screwdriver and two window locks. Time to get to work.

CHAPTER 42

Sharpe

When you've been in a coma for a while, being conscious takes a lot of getting used to. Sharpe can move all his limbs a little but it's painful. His arm and leg muscles seem to have melted away, and he'll need daily physiotherapy to get him back on his feet.

Although his vision is normal, following moving objects and focusing on faces is more tiring than it should be. Every so often, he has to shut his eyes to give them a break.

His daughter sits beside his bed, staring down at him, awe and wonder on her face. It makes him feel like a recently landed alien creature.

"You really are looking so much better," she gushes. "I'd almost given up hope."

It's not a great achievement to look better than you did when you were in a coma, is it? He wants to smile but his lips won't do it. It's strange, because he can talk, kind of, but he can't smile yet.

"I was here, in this room, all the time," he says. "I didn't go anywhere. I was trapped. Deep inside myself. It's hard to explain but it was horrible. Worse than anything you can imagine."

His vocal cords are fragile. It's painful to speak and he sounds like he has a severe case of laryngitis.

Emily shuffles her chair closer to the bed. "The doctors are amazed at your progress but it'll be weeks before you're well enough to go home. They say you need to start eating regular meals, proper, solid food, build up your strength, and start walking first."

Sharpe is only half-listening to his daughter, because he's also trying to concentrate on breathing steadily. He misses the reassuringly monotonous hiss of the ventilator. The job of filling his lungs with air is now his responsibility, and it makes him nervous. It's going to take him a while before he can trust his body again.

"Sorry, darling, what?" he says. "I didn't catch what you said. I'm finding it a bit difficult to stay focused sometimes. It's hard to take everything in."

Emily laughs and shakes her head. "Don't worry. I think you can be forgiven. I was saying you won't be able to go home for a few weeks. But the doctors expect you to make a full recovery. There's no medical reason you can't get back to being your old self."

Although what he's hearing sounds positive, he's hoping for a very different outcome. He doesn't want to be his old self anymore. Look where his old self has ended up. He wants to emerge from this a better man.

Clare did everything she could to cut him out of their daughter's life, but he has to stop using that as an excuse. The truth is, he gave up too quickly. He surrendered because it was the easy thing to do.

Maybe Clare put all those obstacles in his way to see how hard he was prepared to fight for the right to be a father to Emily, to see how committed he really was. If it was a test, then he failed miserably.

Emily puts her hand on the back of his and rubs his knuckles softly with her thumb. "The police have been calling the hospital to check how you're doing. They want to send a couple of detectives to talk to you as soon as you feel up to it."

Sharpe nods slowly as this information sinks in, trying his best to appear unconcerned. He wonders if it's normal for detectives to investigate a drug overdose. The prospect of having to answer their questions makes him feel nauseous. He's not sure he can trust himself not to slip up.

"Have they said exactly what they want to speak to me about?"

Emily shrugs. "I suppose they want to go through what happened to you. They'll want to ask how you got hold of the GHB, but I doubt they'll prosecute. I'm sure it's routine stuff. The police have so many forms to fill in nowadays. If you're not ready, tell the doctors and they'll put them off."

Sharpe wishes he had his daughter's confidence. Would the police waste their valuable time questioning someone who either deliberately or accidentally took an overdose? He doubted it. Maybe they want to know who supplied him with the drug. He's not going to be able to help them with that line of inquiry.

"While we're on the subject," Emily says. "There is one other thing we need to talk about."

She pauses and looks away. Sharpe wonders what's coming. He's pretty sure he's not going to like it.

"Go on."

"Well, er, I've asked the doctors to arrange for someone to speak to you about what you did — you know, a counsellor or therapist. You need professional help to sort yourself out. Mental health is as important as physical health, right?"

Sharpe studies every inch of her unblemished, youthful face. His beautiful daughter is worried about his state of mind, and that makes him angry. It's all wrong. He hates that he has to lie to her, and to the police, but not enough to risk incurring the wrath of Liv Miller. There's something about her that chills his blood.

"I can't really explain what happened that day, my memory is still not working properly. I want you to understand, though, that it wasn't an attempt at suicide. It was stupid to take that drug, I know. I've never taken drugs before and

I didn't know what I was doing. I'd recently come out of prison, my head was messed up, that's all there was to it. You've nothing to worry about, and that's the truth."

Emily's bottom lip quivers. "After what happened, after what you did, it's impossible not to worry. At least promise me you'll think about talking to somebody who can help."

Sharpe clenches his fists to control his frustration. The instinct to protect his child from harm burns in his gut, but he's bedbound, weak and helpless, with nobody to turn to.

"If it means that much to you, I'll think about it," he says. "You're probably right, but give me a bit of time to get used to the idea."

A male nurse enters the room, takes the clipboard off the end of the bed and reads through the medical notes.

"What's it like to be back in the land of the living?" he asks.

Sharpe recognizes the voice. It's the nurse who always took the trouble to talk to him, to explain every procedure. He looks older, greyer and slimmer than Sharpe had envisioned.

"I feel lucky, but living can be pretty tiring," he says with a sigh, letting his impossibly heavy eyelids drop shut. When he opens them, the nurse is no longer in the room. Emily is still sitting by the bed, holding his hand.

"Did I fall asleep?"

"You did. Not for long. Five minutes or so, that's all."

Sharpe hasn't a clue what time of day it is. The corridor is quiet, so he guesses it's late in the evening. He doesn't want Emily walking back to her hotel on her own.

"Where's your mum?" he asks.

"She's had to go back home. She had a call last night about an emergency at the office. I think someone has called in sick and they're short-staffed. She caught an early train, and asked me to explain and say sorry she didn't have time to say goodbye."

Sharpe is a little disappointed but not at all surprised. Clare has constantly juggled full-time jobs with being a mother, and he's always admired her for that. There's no doubt she's set Emily a good example. For the past two years she's been working as a legal clerk, and she loves it. Anyway, it's probably better that she stays away.

"She's left you in the hotel on your own?"

Emily rolls her eyes. "I'm nineteen years old, Dad. I'm not a child. The hotel's only round the corner. You do remember that I go to university, that I live away from home now, don't you?"

Sharpe's mouth is suddenly dry, and the patient monitor in the corner beeps faster as his heart rate jumps.

"Yes, I do, darling, but maybe it'd be a good idea if you caught a train back to university tonight. I don't want you missing too many lectures and falling behind with your studies after all the hard work you put in to get there. I'm definitely on the mend now, and we can speak on the phone every day."

Emily screws up her face. "I've been given permission to stay away as long as I need to. I don't want to leave you on your own. It doesn't feel right. Not after everything you've been through. After everything you've done for me."

Sharpe fights a strong urge to tell his daughter not to be silly, to pack her bags and catch the next train to Leeds. She'd be far safer, far harder to find, as an anonymous student on a bustling university campus. He wishes he could report Liv Miller to the police. Have her locked up for what she did. But he doesn't want them asking awkward questions. He especially doesn't want them talking to Emily. There is far too much at stake to risk that.

"Don't think I'm being ungrateful, but to be honest I'd prefer it if you went back now, and came down to see me when I'm feeling stronger. It's lovely to have you here, of course it is, darling, but you can see I'm tiring easily at the moment. I'm even finding lying here talking to you exhausting. I need to preserve energy for my physiotherapy, to get stronger as quickly as possible. Distractions won't help me do that."

Emily drops her gaze to the floor and chews her bottom lip. Being described as a distraction hasn't gone down well, and Sharpe immediately regrets his choice of words. Still, his priority is keeping her out of danger. If he has to hurt her feelings to get her to leave London as soon as possible, then so be it.

He tries again, this time choosing his words more carefully. "As much as I love that you're here, I'd be happier if you were to return to your studies right now. You've worked so hard and I'm so proud of you. I don't want you to miss out on lectures and study time. I'd be able to concentrate on getting better, and by the time you come back I'll probably be sprinting up and down the corridor. What do you think?"

Emily shrugs sulkily, pulls her mobile from her bag and taps furiously on the screen.

"If you think it's best, then I'll go. There are plenty of trains tonight, but I'd rather check out of the hotel after breakfast tomorrow and catch one that will get me back on campus by lunchtime."

Sharpe decides not to nag her further, even though he'd feel happier if she left the city within the hour. He doesn't want to make her suspicious, or upset her any more than he has already.

"That's a good idea," he says. "When did you become so sensible and grown-up? You're on your own tonight, so watch yourself. Even grown-ups have to be careful. You get a lot of strange people lurking around hotels in this city."

Emily gives him a wry smile. "I'll be fine. I'm quite capable of looking after myself. The only person you need to worry about is yourself, and how you're going to get yourself better."

Sharpe wishes that were true. Liv Miller is capable of anything. The woman has been deranged by grief. That's the only logical explanation he can come up with, and despite everything he has a tiny bit of sympathy for her.

He can't imagine how he'd react if their roles were reversed. If Emily, not Lottie, had been killed that morning.

Would he seek revenge for the loss of his child? He'd like to think not, but who knows?

Emily checks her mobile and jumps out of her seat. "Hell, I didn't realize it was that late. Visiting time ended fifteen minutes ago. The nurse will be coming to throw me out soon."

She leans over the bed to plant a gentle kiss on Sharpe's forehead. "Take care, then, Dad," she says. "If you change your mind about me leaving tomorrow, then call or text me. I can definitely stay for at least another week if you want me to."

Sharpe tries to smile. This time the right side of his mouth obeys, creating a crooked smirk that makes Emily chuckle.

"I'd feel happier if you went back to your studies for now," he says. "Call me every day, though, so I can update you on my progress. I'm planning to wow these doctors by getting back on my feet and fit enough to go home in record time. I'm a physiotherapist, remember. I know exactly what's required."

Before Emily reaches the door, Sharpe calls her name. She turns to face him and takes a step back towards the bed.

"Remember: be careful," he says. "Promise me that you'll be careful."

CHAPTER 43

Liv

I'd forgotten how therapeutic a good cry can be. The pain in my head has gone. I'm emotionally cleansed and fully focused on the task ahead.

I see her the moment she walks out of the hospital, stops on the pavement and glances nervously around. Everything about her, even the way she stands and tilts her head, reminds me of Lottie.

She turns left and walks along Whitechapel Road. I'm hoping that means her hotel is nearby, because the nearest Underground station is in the other direction.

I hitch my hood over my head and follow her, keeping close but not too close. This part of East London is lively, day and night, and I have to dart around pedestrians to keep eyes on her.

Dusk has fallen and the traffic is still heavy. A seemingly never-ending stream of headlights flowing east out of the city.

As we pass the dome and minarets of the East London Mosque, Emily stops and stares at her phone. I hang back and pretend to peer through the window of a curry house already packed with diners.

After a few moments, she's on the move again. She walks with a new sense of urgency and I'm forced to increase my pace to keep up. For a brief moment, I consider abandoning my plan. But I dismiss the thought. There is no going back. Letting this girl go would be betraying Lottie. Hurting her all over again.

She catches me by surprise when she turns left into a dimly lit narrow street. Desperate not to be left behind, I run around the corner just in time to see her disappear through a revolving door. I slow down to a brisk walk, slip the hood back off my head and follow her into the New London Hotel.

I stop just inside the entrance and pretend to read one of the tourism brochures arranged neatly on a small oak table, waiting for the right opportunity.

Out of the corner of my eye I see her talking to a smartly dressed young man behind the hotel's reception desk. My heart sinks. She's making straight for the lift. I watch her raise a hand to press the lift button, change her mind, walk across the lobby and enter the hotel bar.

This is my chance. I linger outside for a moment, pretending to send a text. By the time I go in, Emily is already sitting on a bar stool sipping a drink, her back to me.

The place is deathly quiet. The only other customers are two middle-aged men sitting silently at a chrome-topped table in the centre of the room, nursing their beers.

Any nerves I had have disappeared. An almost unnatural confidence flows through me. Nothing can stop me. I am unstoppable, invincible.

I order two large white wines and carry them along the bar. I put one down in front of the girl.

She looks up and gives me a quizzical stare. I respond with a smile, raise my eyebrows, and my glass. She's slightly built and, just like Lottie, she has a thin strip of freckles running across her nose and cheeks that makes her look younger than she is.

"I don't think I know you, do I?" she says.

"No, you don't, but I know who you are, Emily."

CHAPTER 44

Sharpe

"So, exactly what do you remember?" Detective Sergeant Earl asks. "I understand that your memory might be hazy right now, that there are going to be gaps, but take your time. I'm not in a hurry."

Sharpe is sitting in bed, propped up on his pillow, his leg muscles aching from his last physiotherapy session. He recognized the detective the moment he walked into the room, and knows that this is going to be more difficult than he had hoped. Earl is no fool.

"One thing I do remember is that I was making myself a coffee, and lacing it with the drug."

"With GHB?"

Sharpe nods. Says nothing more. He has to be careful. He can't afford to slip up. This detective is a details man.

Earl paces over to the patient monitor and checks the screen. "I wish my blood pressure was as good as yours," he says. "My doctor tells me I need to lose a few pounds to get mine down to where it should be. He even suggested I change to a less stressful job, would you believe?"

Sharpe doesn't comment. He doesn't want to lose focus by being drawn into casual conversation. Telling outright lies, while trying to appear honest, takes a lot of concentration, especially when it doesn't come naturally.

"I understand that depression is complex but I don't understand what you were doing taking a drug like this. You have no record of drug misuse. The worst was behind you. You survived the prison sentence. We know you were putting the house up for sale, so you had the chance of making a fresh start somewhere. It doesn't make sense to me."

Sharpe thinks about feigning a dizzy spell. He wants the questions to stop.

"None of this makes sense to me either. I can't explain what I did. I take it you've never suffered depression, Detective?"

Earl shrugs. "I know mental health isn't black or white, all or nothing, but I'm trying to put myself in your place."

Sharpe glances at his mobile lying on the bedside table. He and Emily had agreed to make contact every day. He's not heard from her yet but this would be her first day back attending lectures, and she had a lot of catching up to do.

"I can tell you that the overdose was accidental," he says. "I had no intention of harming myself. I wanted to blot everything out, at least for a while. I heard about the drug in prison. Someone told me it makes you feel elated, zones you out, wipes out your worries. I know it was a stupid thing to do."

Earl pulls up a chair and sits down. He looks tired, his expression suggesting he doesn't believe a word. Sharpe wonders whether he always gives that impression, whoever he's talking to and whatever he's talking about.

"What was the name of the prisoner who told you about GHB?"

"I can't remember."

"Who supplied you with the drug?"

"I bought it off some guy in a bar."

"Which bar?"

"I can't remember."

"What did the man you bought it off look like?"

"I don't remember."

"Did someone call around to your house that morning?"

The speed of the questions and their direction make Sharpe even more nervous. He slides down the bed onto his back and shuts his eyes, hoping that Earl will get the hint and leave.

"Did you have a visitor who was wearing a coat with a hood lined with fake fur?"

"I'm getting tired, Detective, and the more tired I am the worse my memory is. I'm pretty sure nobody called around that day. What's this about?"

"Our forensic team found fake fur fibres on your sofa, and a trace of lipstick on one of the cups in the kitchen."

Sharpe opens his eyes. The patient monitor is beeping rapidly, and Earl gets up and studies the screen again.

"Your heart rate appears to be increasing, your blood pressure is up. Are you feeling all right?"

"I don't remember anything else about that morning. I definitely don't recall anyone calling at the house. Why all these questions anyway? I'm sorry for the trouble I caused you and your colleagues. I know you've plenty to do, real crimes to investigate. I've promised my daughter that I'll never do anything like this again, and I mean it."

Earl walks slowly back to the chair and sits down. "We have a duty to investigate incidents like this, to make sure they are what they appear to be, that nobody else was involved. We need to be one-hundred-per-cent sure that you've not been the victim of a crime."

Sharpe laughs. He knows it sounds hollow. "That's admirable. I wish I could blame all this on someone else, I really do. The truth is, after the accident — you know, what happened to the girl — my life has gone down the pan. I always seem to be making stupid decisions. That's all there is to it."

The detective's eyes soften, and for a moment Sharpe thinks he's finally got through to him.

"So, you're admitting that you lied?" Earl asks.

"What do you mean? Lied about what?"

"You said you couldn't remember exactly what happened, now you say you know for sure that nobody else was involved."

Sharpe rolls his head from side to side on the pillow. "I'm confused. I told you everything is still a blur. If and when I recall more details, I'll let you know. Could you call for a nurse? I'm feeling dizzy. I think I'm going to throw up."

CHAPTER 45

Earl

Earl turns into the police station car park, pulls to a stop and kills the engine. The Sharpe interview raised more questions than it answered and he's more convinced than ever that the man is hiding something.

It wasn't simply that he was deliberately evasive and vague. Interviewing hundreds of people over the years, both suspects and victims, has sharpened Earl's ability to tune into negative character traits and emotions, such as hatred, fear, greed and anger.

Sharpe's time in jail is bound to have changed him. Even a short spell behind bars can harden a person, make them distrustful of authority, make them paranoid. Overall, he still comes across as a decent human being. But it's clear he's scared of something, and that fear is clouding his judgement.

As Earl climbs out of the car, his mobile rings. The name Becky Andrews flashes up on the screen.

"Hi, Becky. Two calls in the space of a week. I'm honoured."

"Well, don't expect another one for a while. I know you might be surprised but I'm not ringing just for the pleasure of hearing your voice."

Earl grins. "Go on, then. Get on with it."

"It's about the DNA sample from Liv Miller. We've found something I think you'll be interested in."

Earl starts walking towards the station entrance, excitement rising in his chest. "You've found a match in Sharpe's home?"

"No, it's not that straightforward. There's been an interesting development in the Lottie Miller case."

Earl stops dead. It's not like Andrews to waste his time. "Excuse me for stating the obvious," he says, "but we're not investigating the Lottie Miller case. This is about her sister."

"No, it's not."

"What do you mean?"

"I mean what I say. They're not sisters, not biologically. The DNA samples show they're not related at all. Not sisters, not cousins. Nothing."

CHAPTER 46

Liv

I spread margarine thinly on the toast, add a liberal helping of peanut butter and lay the plate on the tray next to the carton of orange juice.

As I climb the stairs, I recall taking Lottie breakfast in bed the first morning after she moved in and the memory makes me smile. She was still suffering from the shock of losing our mother but the gesture cheered her up a little.

"I could get used to being spoiled," she told me, with a thin smile.

"You could but you won't because I can guarantee I'm not going to make a habit of spoiling you," I replied, and she giggled. I hadn't heard her laugh for a long time and it was the loveliest sound.

I couldn't believe that my little sister was with me. Living under my roof. Mine to take care of. After everything that had happened, after the way our mother had cast me out, my dreams had come true.

I slide the bolt back, step inside and quickly shut the door behind me. Emily is sitting on the floor leaning against the side of the bed, her legs stretched out, head bowed, her tangled hair hanging down, hiding her face.

She looks up, turning to me in slow motion, as if every muscle in her body hurts when she moves. Unsurprisingly, she doesn't look well. Her complexion is sickly, her eyes trance-like and red-rimmed. I glance at the bedside table. The glass of water I left her is half empty. Perhaps that should be half full. I'm a lot more positive these days.

"Where am I?" she asks, her voice croaky. "Why are you doing this?"

I drop onto one knee, put the tray on the carpet and slide it until it nudges the top of her left thigh.

"You're staying with me for a while. There's nothing to worry about. You're my guest and it's lovely to have you here. I hope you like peanut butter. It was Lottie's favourite toast topping."

She doesn't answer but something flickers in her eyes at the mention of Lottie. Things are clicking into place.

"I want to go now, please. I won't say anything to anybody. I'm supposed to be back at university. They'll be wondering where I am."

I stand up, walk over to the bookshelf and run my fingertips along the spines of Lottie's Harry Potter novels.

"I've already explained that you're here as my guest. A special guest. You know, you remind me so much of her. I'm going to love taking care of you for a few days, whether you like it or not. You might as well make the most of it. Rest, relax, read some of these books if you want. I promise everything will be fine."

She gives me a blank look, raises a hand to her face, shuts her eyes and massages her eyelids with her forefinger and thumb.

"I really don't feel fine. My head is thumping so hard I can't think straight. My arms and legs are so weak I can hardly move them. I really think I need to see a doctor."

I'm happy that the GHB in her system is doing exactly what it's supposed to. Work its magic, keep her passive, pliable, easy to handle. It certainly made it easy to get her out of the hotel and into a cab.

"I'm not surprised you're feeling a bit delicate, the amount of wine you got through last night would give anyone a mega hangover," I say. "It was a struggle to get you back here in one piece. You could hardly put one foot in front of the other. I don't suppose you remember. You were so out of it."

Emily raises her chin and looks directly at me. I have a feeling that she knows I'm telling her a barefaced lie. I don't care if she does. There's nothing she can do about it, especially if she keeps sipping the magic potion. A raging thirst must be quenched. That's why I put salty peanut butter on the toast instead of jam. I lied about Lottie loving it. In my mind she always was and forever will be a jam person. She had a sweet tooth like me.

Emily puts her hands on the floor and tries to push herself up. The effort makes her grunt as she struggles up onto her knees, but after a few seconds she slumps back down. Tears stream down her face, dripping onto the carpet as she curls into the foetal position, sobbing so hard her body shudders. She even weeps like Lottie wept. Like a spoiled brat.

I return to the kitchen and pour myself a strong coffee. Sitting at the pine table, I switch on my new laptop and scroll through the news websites, looking for reports suggesting the police have suspicions about Sharpe's overdose. There aren't any, but I do find something that makes me want to scream.

Two of the national tabloid newspapers have published articles about his supposedly miraculous recovery from a coma. Somebody working at the hospital, or a police officer, must have leaked the story. Reporters have contacts everywhere, especially when they're willing to pay for information.

The articles read as if they've been written by the same person. Identical piles of crap. They make Sharpe out to be some kind of hero. A man of good character who commits a crime, confesses and does his time. This poor soul is still so eaten up by guilt at what he did, he turns to drugs and overdoses. Instead of dying, he astounds his doctors by emerging from a deep coma, ready to make the most of his second chance. He has done his penance. He has suffered enough.

I want to hurl my cup of coffee at the screen. Only the fact that I paid a lot of money for the new laptop stops me. A man wakes up from a coma. So what? That's not an achievement. That's not being brave. It doesn't involve any conscious or unconscious decision on his part. Good for him. Bad for me. As for him being determined to make the most of a second chance at life, that disgusts me. My Lottie didn't even get her one chance. He took that away from her.

My mobile rings and I'm so glad of the distraction I don't look at the screen to check the ID of the caller. Big mistake.

"Hi there, Liv. How are you?"

I say nothing. I don't know how to answer that question without lying.

"Liv? Are you there? It's me."

Me is Matt. I'm guessing he wants to meet up to discuss the significance of what happened between us the other night. The kiss. I'm tempted. It would be so good to forget everything for a while, to be my old self for a few hours.

"Oh, hello, Matt," I say. "I'm feeling good, considering, er, everything. How are you?"

I sound pathetic. He probably thinks the hesitation in my voice is embarrassment because of what happened. I want to tell him how much I enjoyed the other evening but I can't think straight. I have genuine feelings for him, I do, and that's the reason I hold back.

"I'm great, thanks. Really great," he says. "Actually, would you mind coming to the door and letting me in because I'm on your doorstep. I enjoyed the other night so much I've brought something for you."

Surely he's kidding me. I walk quickly down the hall and peer through the spyhole. Oh shit. He's not joking. He's standing there, a big grin on his face, holding a large bunch of white roses.

It's the sort of cheesy, romantic gesture that would have impressed me if life hadn't become so complicated, if I didn't have to stay focused on the task ahead. I take a deep breath and open the door.

"You really are a total idiot," I say, laughing. "What are you doing? They are so beautiful. Thank you."

Matt hands the flowers to me, a faint blush on his cheeks. "They're nothing much. The thing is, I had such a great time the other night I was wondering whether we can . . . well, I think we should do it again. You know, go out for a drink, and stuff."

"What stuff?" I ask with a smile, knowing full well what he means.

"Well, the usual, I suppose. Wine, or beer, and a chat. That sort of thing."

He edges closer, eager to be invited in but I stand my ground. I don't want him inside. Not now.

"That's a lovely thought," I say. "To be honest with you, although my course of treatment has ended, I'm still feeling the effects, the fatigue, you know? Maybe, you could give me a call in a couple of weeks? I'm bound to be feeling stronger, and I'll be so much better company. That is, if you think a night out with me is worth waiting for?"

Matt can't hide his disappointment but manages to put on a resigned smile. "Of course, that's not a problem. I should have thought. I suppose there's always some kind of delayed reaction to that type of treatment. It's going to take a toll on anybody. I'll call you in a week or two, then, shall I?"

I want him gone, in case my guest stops sobbing and starts screaming. I'm already closing the door as I speak. "The flowers are so gorgeous. I love roses. They're my favourite flower. Thank you so much, give me a call in a couple of weeks. Yes, please do. See you then. Bye, bye."

I catch the surprise on his face as the door slams shut and feel a twinge of sympathy. But I'm still seething inside about the way the media has chosen to give Sharpe some sort of credit for his recovery.

Back in the kitchen, I sit down at the table, snap the heads off all the roses, one by one, gather them up and drop them into the waste bin.

I pick up one of the discarded stalks and press the pad of my right thumb on the point of the largest thorn. It pierces the skin and a drop of blood wells up, like a ruby tear. I suck the blood off and press my forefinger against the tiny wound until the bleeding stops.

If only I could stop everything else so easily. Part of me fears the path I've chosen, but the other part, the secret part, relishes the danger ahead and won't let me turn back.

I go to Lottie's bedroom and stand outside the door for a few seconds before unbolting it and stepping inside. Emily has levered herself up off the floor and is sitting on the edge of the bed. She hasn't eaten any of her toast, or drunk any more of the water.

I look down at her and imagine how her father, the so-called hero who beat the odds to survive a coma, would feel if his precious little girl died today. It doesn't take much to guess. I have felt that agony first-hand.

Emily has tidied her hair as best she can without a brush, and is clearly feeling less dazed. "Can I go to the bathroom?" she asks. "I need to use the toilet and have a wash. I stink."

She does smell a bit ripe, but she can put up with it if I can. "I'll bring you a bucket and some toilet paper. That'll have to do you for now. It can't be helped."

"I can't, that's not right, that's disgusting," she stutters.

Her whining puts me on edge. I have to quieten an urge to scream at her to shut up.

"It's the bucket or nothing," I say, picking the glass of water off the bedside table. "I'll get you a fresh one of these, maybe even more orange juice. You must be thirsty." She can refuse food as much as she wants but I know she'll have to drink something soon.

She looks at me, a frown on her tear-stained face. "I think I've lost my mobile phone," she says. "I can't remember what I did with it. I'm worried I might have dropped it on the way here last night. Have you seen it? I have to make an urgent call."

I take a side step closer to the door. "Don't worry yourself, calm down," I say. "I have your phone. You dropped it and would have lost it if I hadn't been looking out for you. Trust me and I'll take care of you."

She puts out a hand, her fingers curled and shaking, like a child begging for sweets. "Please can I have my phone back? Please? My dad will be worried sick about me. I promised him I'd ring when I got back to Leeds."

The more he worries about the safety of his daughter the better, as far as I'm concerned. Worry will keep his mouth closed, stop him thinking about going to the police.

I smile and shake my head. "I'll keep the phone for now. I'll look after it for you. All you have to do is relax. You need to eat and drink to get your strength back before I can even consider letting you out of my sight. If you do as you're told, and your father does as he's told, then everything will be fine."

Emily narrows her eyes and gives me a hard stare. Her senses may be dulled but her brain is still ticking over.

"It's you. Yes, that's it," she says. "Your hair's different but I remember you now, from the court hearing. You were there, watching, staring. Oh my God. You're Lottie Miller's sister, aren't you? The girl who . . ."

I don't answer her. I turn away because I don't even want to look at her. Something deep inside me, something darkly fearful, is trying to claw its way out. I need to leave the room before it escapes.

CHAPTER 47

Earl

Tanner may have made it to the dizzy heights of detective inspector but his office is small and smells of melted cheese.

Earl is seated across the desk from his boss, and Akinola stands, her back resting against the door.

"Tell me what's so interesting about this jailbird taking too much GHB," Tanner growls. "If the idiot wants to put himself into a coma then I'm all right with that. I'm puzzled why two of my best detectives are devoting so much of their valuable time to this incident when there's so much serious crime going on in this part of the city. Multiple street stabbings, moped gang robberies, not to mention two separate serious sexual assaults on our patch last night."

Earl is jumpy. On edge. Not because Tanner is being his usual sarcastic self. It's because the desk between them is covered with clutter. He desperately wants to collect up the pens and paperclips, put them neatly in a box or hide them away in a drawer. The yellow Post-it notes stuck around the screen of the computer need to be binned, and the large red mug needs washing with hot water and soap to remove the coffee stains. Worst of all is the empty takeaway pizza box lying at an angle on the in-tray.

"I'm working on the theory that far from being a simple drug mishap, this could be a case of deliberate drugging, maybe even attempted murder," he says.

Tanner looks across at Akinola and grins. "The man's got a theory. A proper theory, no less. I thought he might have. I hope it's better than the one about Sharpe not being guilty of the crime he confessed to."

"For what it's worth, I think there's something in this one," Akinola says.

It's not a shining recommendation, but Earl is relieved that she's been brave enough to voice her support. He shouldn't have doubted that she'd have his back.

"The forensic evidence suggests Sharpe had company when he overdosed," he says. "He has no history of drug misuse, not before his time in prison or during it. It's possible that someone wanted him dead, spiked his coffee and left him to die when he fell into a coma."

Tanner grunts, snatches one of the Post-it notes off the computer screen, reads it, folds it in half and slips it into his jacket pocket.

"Forensic evidence is always good," he says. "I like that a lot. What I don't like about this theory of yours is the insertion of words such as *possible* and *someone*. In my book, possible and someone don't make a case. I much prefer words like *motive* and *suspect*."

Earl sighs. How does the saying go? Untidy desk, untidy mind. Tanner's brain may well be cluttered but he's sharp enough when he needs to be.

"It's early in the investigation, but right now the one suspect we have is Liv Miller. Unfortunately, the forensics on her are weak. The only evidence the scene-of-crime team found at Sharpe's house were a few fake fur fibres, and we know she owned a coat with a hood lined with similar fake fur. The search of Miller's home drew a complete blank. But the motive is there. Revenge. Punishment. She made it clear at the time, in several interviews she gave to newspapers, that she thought the jail sentence was too short, that Sharpe was getting off lightly."

Tanner shakes his head dismissively. "Without her coat to examine, the fake fur found in Sharpe's house is worthless. The avenging sister thing, I don't buy it. If I remember correctly, the sisters hadn't seen each other for years, had no contact until their mother died. That suggests to me that they weren't particularly close."

Earl pauses, and allows himself a small smile. "There's more to this than we knew. A lot more unanswered questions. The DNA sample we took from Miller shows that she isn't Lottie's older sister. Not biologically, in any case. We need to find out what's been going on and why Liv Miller's been lying to us. Detective Akinola's been busy talking to our counterparts in Manchester, to get some background on the Millers."

For the first time since the meeting started, Tanner is looking interested. He shifts his heavy frame forward and nods at Akinola to fill him in.

The detective constable pulls a tablet from her pocket and takes a few seconds to skim through her notes.

"Liv Miller's mother, Jane, was a single parent. Well-educated and ambitious. Manchester police have a record of being called out to the family home several times for what they described as domestic incidents. It seems that the teenage Liv Miller and her mother didn't get on at all. Nothing violent, but loud shouting matches and some damage to windows and furniture. We know that social services became involved after Jane Miller complained that Liv was possibly a danger to her younger sister. We don't know exactly what went on, but when Liv Miller finished school at eighteen, she left home to study journalism in London. As far as we can tell she had no contact with her mother or Lottie for years. Not until the mother's death in a road accident."

Tanner interrupts with a wave of a hand. "Let's get this straight," he says. "A stroppy teenage girl falls out with her mother, goes off to London to start a new life and they never speak again. Well, that's sad, but it's not totally unheard of, is it? Unfortunately, we all know there are worse things than that happening in the homes of messed-up families all over the country."

Earl has heard enough and steps in. "The DNA shows that Liv Miller is not biologically related to her younger sister. Maybe she doesn't know, or doesn't think it's worth mentioning. But the woman's hiding something. I'm sure of it."

Tanner drums his pudgy fingers on the desk, glances at Akinola, then back at Earl. "How would you move on from here? You've already searched the woman's home and found nothing."

"We question her again. Hit her with the DNA result. Then we press all her buttons until she cracks."

The detective inspector sits back in his chair, his hands clasped over his stomach. Earls knows he's weighing up the case, assessing the media attention it would attract if a prosecution was brought against Liv Miller for attempting to murder Sharpe. Tanner would take a lead role in any post-conviction press conferences, and he's a man who loves the flash of a camera, and the sound of his own voice.

"All right, then," he says. "You might be on to something. I still have my doubts, though. Go prove me wrong."

CHAPTER 48

Sharpe

He opens the door and steps into the corridor, one hand on the wall to steady himself. Even though his legs feel like they're full of sand, and his hips and lower back still ache from his last physiotherapy session, he's determined to do everything he can to speed up his recovery.

He takes his hand off the wall to shuffle around an abandoned trolley loaded with dirty breakfast plates and cups. A harassed-looking nurse hurries by without giving him a glance. Her arm brushes his elbow and the glancing blow sends him staggering like a drunk to the other side of the corridor. He rights himself, concentrating on lifting one foot at a time. Picking up momentum, he gains confidence and starts swinging his arms.

Up ahead, about twenty metres away, is the door visitors use to enter and exit the ward. If he can reach it and still have the strength to make it back to his room, he'll be satisfied.

Another nurse, a man he knows as Harry, sticks his head out of a side room. "What the hell are you doing?" he says. "I don't think it's a good idea for you to be walking around on your own."

Sharpe turns his head. He's already exhausted and is tempted to lean against the wall and slide down into a heap on the floor. Instead, he gives Harry a cheery thumbs up.

"I'm absolutely fine, but thanks for caring," he says. "My physio says the sooner I'm up and walking around the sooner I'll be out of this place. Nothing personal. It won't do me any harm. Trust me, I know what I'm doing."

Harry gives him a doubtful look, shrugs and returns to treating his patient. Once he's out of view, Sharpe rests his shoulder on the wall to take a breather, grateful that the medical staff are too busy to guess what he's up to.

After a few deep breaths, he's walking again, his eyes fixed firmly on the blue door at the end of the corridor. It's been two days and he hasn't heard anything from Emily. He's called her a dozen times and left several text messages.

For what seems like the hundredth time, he reasons that she's still a teenager, she's probably forgotten her promise, having thrown herself back into the hectic life of a student, attending lectures during the day and getting drunk at night. Maybe she's simply lost her mobile phone.

No matter how hard he tries, he can't convince himself that any of these explanations are likely. He can't shake off the hollow sickness in the pit of his stomach that's telling him something is wrong.

He reaches the door, grabbing hold of the brass handle to support himself as he turns around, and takes a few deep, slow breaths. Why is there never a nurse in sight when you really want one? He'd gladly hitch a wheelchair ride back to his room if he was offered one.

He pushes hard against the door to propel himself back down the corridor. If he doesn't hear from Emily soon, he's going to have to call the police and tell them everything. Well, almost everything.

It would be better for everyone if he didn't have to get the police involved. There'd be too many questions, too much pressure on Emily to lie. He couldn't trust her not to let the truth slip. Everything he'd done, everything he'd suffered up to now would be for nothing.

He grits his teeth and strides out, ignoring the excruciating pain in his thighs and hamstrings. On reaching his room, he spreads his arms to clutch the doorframe, his breathing loud and rapid.

It takes him five stuttering steps to get to the bed. He rolls onto his back with a groan. After staring at the ceiling for a few seconds, he reaches across to his bedside table and picks up his mobile phone.

He scrolls through his contacts until he finds Emily's mother. Clare won't like him telephoning her when she's at work. She says it's unprofessional to take personal calls in an office environment. In fact, she doesn't like him calling her even when she's not at work.

She answers after four rings. Her voice is clipped and businesslike. "Can this wait, Daniel? I'm snowed under right now."

"No, sorry, it can't."

"What the hell is so important?"

She doesn't sound a happy woman. Sharpe suspects she's sitting with her back to her desk, facing the wall, and speaking through clenched teeth.

"It's Emily," he says. "Have you heard from her recently? She's been back at university for two days and she promised to call me every day."

The line falls silent. Sharpe pictures Clare rolling her eyes in frustration.

"She's not a child, she's a young adult studying for her future and learning to be independent. She's got better things, more important things, to do than call you every day. Let's face it, you didn't have much to do with her when she was a young girl, you can't suddenly start acting like you're a doting parent and demand that she treats you like one."

One of the things that first attracted him to Clare was her openness and honesty. He still finds it appealing, but these particular words slice deep. The truth is always sharper than a lie.

"I'm worried about her, that's all. I had to work hard to persuade her to leave London, and she only agreed to go because we arranged to keep in touch."

"I'm sure she'll call you soon," Clare says, her tone softer, more sympathetic. "You know what that first year in university is like. A little bit of studying and a lot of partying." Sharpe guesses she's probably feeling guilty about her earlier outburst but not enough to take any of it back.

"Maybe you're right," he says, even though he doesn't believe it. "If you do hear anything from her, can you—"

"Sorry, I've got to go," Clare whispers, before terminating the call.

Sharpe places the phone back down on the table, puts his hands behind his head and closes his eyes. A wave of tiredness flows through him but he resists it. Since he came out of the coma, he's been sleeping a lot during the day. It's natural that he needs to rest, but that twilight moment between being awake and falling asleep terrifies him. What if he slips from sleep back into the darkness of a coma?

He opens his eyes, but after a few seconds his eyelids droop. He starts to feel himself drift away, when his mobile pings. He picks it up to check the screen, and instantly he's wide awake. It's a message from Emily. At last.

He opens it and reads quickly.

Hi. Thought I'd let you know that everything is fine. Sorry I haven't called but I've been distracted. There's no need to worry. I'm being looked after. I'm well and will stay well as long as you're careful. XXX.

Sharpe sits up with a jolt and reads the message again. It's hard because his hand is shaking. He reads it for a third time to make sure he understands.

A bead of sweat runs down the hollow of his back. The message, with its barely concealed threat, wasn't written by his daughter, even though it was definitely sent from her mobile. The woman who tried to kill him has his daughter's phone. If she has Emily's phone, then she almost certainly has Emily too.

CHAPTER 49

Liv

It takes ten minutes to walk from my house to the corner shop. The morning air is damp, the sky a threatening grey. In the near distance, I can make out the glass towers of Canary Wharf looming over low-rise apartment blocks.

I'm happy to get out. When I last checked on Emily she was in a deep sleep. She refused to speak to me when I brought her breakfast this morning, but when I returned to empty her bucket, she'd eaten the two bags of salt-and-vinegar crisps and drunk a whole tumbler of my special orange juice.

She's getting a lot more rest than I am, that's for sure. Last night a throbbing headache kept me awake for hours. Even when I finally managed to drift off, the sleep was fitful, my mind haunted by a dark presence and shadowy childhood memories.

I can't say I had a tough time growing up, but my mother was a difficult woman. Anyway, that's what our neighbours whispered to me when she was out of earshot. She wanted me to be forceful too, pushed me to grow up quickly and make my own decisions. But only if they were decisions she approved of. The older I got the less interest she took in me. Lottie became her priority. I understood why, but that didn't mean I had to accept it.

I stop outside the shop, pull Emily's phone out of my pocket and re-read the text messages from Sharpe. Twelve of them. We're fast becoming texting buddies. They all assure me that he's said nothing to the police. They all beg me not to do anything reckless.

Everything I've done in the past few weeks has been reckless, and it's not going to change. My life has become a strange mixture of exhilaration and dread. Sometimes it feels like I'm speeding downhill in a car without brakes.

In the store I fill a plastic shopping basket with bags of crisps, biscuits and cartons of orange juice. A pretty young Asian girl at the counter packs them in a carrier bag and smiles when I give her cash and tell her to keep the change.

On the walk back home, the idea that I've been carrying with me crystallizes. A shiver slides down my spine. I halt and lean against a shop window, breathing slowly until I stop trembling. I feel strangely galvanized. I know what I have to do now.

I've often thought that I'd be happy, that I'd finally find some relief, if he was dead. But is that the best way to punish him? There are other ways to make him pay, other ways to turn guilt into gut-wrenching agony.

CHAPTER 50

Sharpe

He is sitting up in bed trying to argue that he's well enough to be discharged from hospital. The consultant neurologist folds her arms across her chest and shakes her head.

"It's totally out of the question," she says. "It's going to be at least three weeks before we can even consider letting you leave." Doctor Anand is a tall, elegant Indian woman. Her dark ponytail is flecked with grey.

Sharpe lifts his mobile off the bedside table, glances briefly at the screen and puts it back down. There's been no response to his texts, and he's desperate for reassurance that Emily hasn't been harmed. He's tried calling her phone, and left several garbled, panicky voicemail messages.

"I'm feeling stronger every day. My physiotherapy has been going great and I'm walking pretty well now. No offence, doctor, but I've always hated hospitals and I'm going crazy in this place. It's as bad as being in prison. Worse even. The food is better in prison."

Sharpe's lying. He hated every minute he spent in jail. Violence and intimidation cast a shadow over each mind-numbing day, and the place smelled of fear, testosterone and sweat. But he needs to escape from this hospital more than he needed to break out of prison.

Dr Anand takes the clipboard off the end of the bed and reads his medical notes in silence. Sharpe guesses that she is going through the motions, pretending that she's seriously considering his request. After a while, she looks up, her lips set tight.

"It would be foolish to discharge you, and I'm not a fool," she says. "Your vital signs are good and your mobility is improving fast, but we do need to keep a close eye on you for a while yet. Your body and brain suffered a terrible trauma. To be honest, it's astonishing that you seem to have come out of it without any permanent damage. But in cases like yours there is always a danger you could relapse at any time, which is why we have to keep you under close observation."

"Are you saying there's a chance I could fall back into a coma?"

"It's a possibility. Recovery from the type of deep coma you were in is almost never straightforward."

Sharpe doesn't like what he's hearing. Not one bit. He slides off the bed, walks briskly over to the door and back again, as if proving a point. Sending a message. *Look at me doctor. I'm up, moving around and thinking clearly. I'm never going back to coma land. It's not going to happen. I won't let it.*

"I appreciate your concern and take your expert advice on board. I know I've been incredibly lucky but I'm feeling well. I want to leave today. I need to leave today."

Dr Anand pulls a pen from the breast pocket of her green scrubs, writes a brief note and hangs the clipboard back on the end of the bed.

"I strongly advise against it. This close to coming out of a coma you'd be at serious risk outside a hospital environment."

Sharpe has a lot of sympathy for her. He knows she's trying to prevent him making a mistake. She's giving him the best advice she can, and it's clear he's going to ignore it no matter what. He glances again at the screen of his phone. Still no messages.

"As I understand it," he says, "legally, there's nothing to stop me getting dressed and walking out if that's what I want to do. That's right, isn't it?"

Doctor Anand sighs. "That is the legal position. We can't stop you leaving unless we have reason to believe you're not of sound mind, that you're incapable of understanding the danger you'd be putting yourself in."

Sharpe knows the risk he'd be taking and it scares him. Calling the police and what that could lead to scares him even more. He has to find Emily himself, no matter what it takes.

"My mind is in good working order. I know what I'm doing."

The doctor gives him a long, troubled look. "If you do decide to ignore my medical advice, then make sure you sign a discharge form at the nurses' station before you go. If you don't, we will have to report you to the police as a patient who's gone missing from the hospital."

As soon as she leaves the room, Sharpe opens the cupboard under the bedside table and pulls out the clothes he was wearing when they brought him in. He takes off the crumpled hospital gown and dresses quickly.

He walks to the nurses' station and scribbles his signature on a discharge form without bothering to read the disclaimer. The two female nurses on duty make no attempt to dissuade him but exchange concerned glances.

Sharpe suspects Dr Anand has warned them that he's determined to check out. He feels their gaze on his back as he walks to the lift. His heart is racing, his breathing ragged. As soon as the doors slide shut, his shoulders slump, and he falls heavily against the back wall, grabbing the steel hand rail for support.

Stepping outside the hospital, onto the bustling Whitechapel Road, he pulls out his mobile, searches his contacts and taps out a text message. The reply comes almost immediately. Sharpe flags down a black cab heading east, and climbs into the back.

"The Bow Bells pub, please. Bow Road," he says.

The driver, a shaven-headed man who looks like he spends most of his leisure time in the gym, grunts and pulls off into the heavy traffic. Sharpe leans back and closes his eyes. His leg muscles are throbbing. He desperately needs sleep to recharge both his body and his brain.

He stares at the stubble on the back of the driver's head, wondering whether he's doing the right thing. If asked to give advice to someone else in his situation, he'd tell them to go straight to the police.

Yet somehow, it's different when you're the one at the centre of the storm. There's no escaping its power. You can't fight it. Involving the police could easily lead to him being back behind bars. He could probably handle it. If he had to. If he could be sure that only he would be punished.

The taxi's heater is pumping out hot air, feeding Sharpe's fatigue. As he starts to drift off, he recalls Dr Anand's words of warning about slipping back into a coma. Fear jolts him out of his torpor. His heart is still hammering when the taxi pulls up.

The driver swivels his head. "This is it, mate. You getting out or what? I haven't got all day."

Sharpe opens the door, scrambles onto the pavement, tosses a twenty-pound note through the driver's window and hurries into the pub. The bar is warm and busy, the walls adorned with dark wood and tarnished brass.

As promised, Jack Grace is sitting in a four-seat booth near the pool table. The last time Sharpe saw him, he was lying on his back on the top bunk in their prison cell.

Grace takes a swig of his beer and beckons him over. "Hell, mate, you don't half look rough," he says. "What have you been doing to yourself?"

Sharpe sits down with a shrug. "I'm okay, Jack. A little tired, that's all. Nothing a good kip won't fix. You're looking good, though."

A malicious grin splits Grace's pockmarked face. "Of course I am," he says. "Know how to look after myself, on the inside and on the outside, don't I? You'd never have lasted a week in prison if I hadn't taken pity on you."

He's embroidering the truth a little but Sharpe's not going to correct him. Grace is surprisingly sensitive to criticism for a man who has been in and out of jail since he was seventeen.

"I want you to know how much I appreciate what you did for me," Sharpe says. "You helped me survive in there, showed me the ropes. I'm grateful."

Grace nods and takes another gulp of his pint. "You off the booze, then? I reckon that's why you're looking so sickly. You need to get a couple of pints down you. Perk you up nicely, it would."

Sharpe licks his lips. He's sorely tempted. His mouth is dry and a cold beer would go down a treat, but he daren't risk it. Too much medication flowing around his system.

"It's best I don't touch the stuff right now," he says. "I need to keep a clear head."

Grace wipes his mouth with the back of his hand. "Now, tell me, what's this all about? I know you're not here because you're missing your good-looking cellmate. What is it you want?"

Sharpe looks over his shoulder at a couple of drinkers standing close to the pool table, and lowers his voice.

"In prison you always boasted that you knew certain people, dangerous people, had underworld contacts. You said if I ever needed anything I should get in touch."

Grace sits up and squares his shoulders. "Don't give me that boasted shit. I'm bloody well connected around here. Ask anybody. I'm well respected, I am. People come to me if they want problems sorted out, if they need something done. I told you, didn't I? I'm a fixer."

The pub is filling up fast, with a mix of dishevelled students and expensively suited office workers. Someone turns up the volume on the bar's big screen as Bruce Springsteen belts out 'Born to Run'.

Sharpe puts his elbows on the table and leans across. He doesn't want to have to raise his voice to be heard.

"I'm desperate, Jack," he says. "I'm in a lot of trouble and I need your help."

Grace smirks. Sharpe remembers how he loved playing the big man when they shared a cell, doling out advice on how to behave at mealtimes, who to talk to, who not to make eye contact with, and how to avoid getting beaten to a pulp in the communal showers.

He lays on the flattery. "I thought of you straightaway, Jack. I knew if anyone could sort it for me, you could. You did a great job of watching out for me when we were inside. I don't know how I'd have coped without you as a cellmate."

Grace preens himself, puffing out his chest. "I'll do what I can for you. What is it you need? It's not drugs, is it? You know I don't do drugs now, don't you? Well, I smoke a bit of pot every now and then, but that's personal use. I don't deal anymore."

Sharpe loosens a button on his shirt. He's burning up. Beads of sweat trickle down the back of his neck. He hasn't felt this bad for days. Maybe Dr Anand was right.

"It's nothing to do with drugs."

"A job, then? I might be able to fix you up with a nice earner. I know someone who'll need a getaway driver in a couple of weeks." Grace smirks again. "You got experience at driving fast, ain't you?"

Sharpe doesn't laugh. "It's nothing like that," he says. "I need something special and I'm hoping you can get it for me, and quickly."

"What, then? Come on, don't be shy. Is it a woman? If you have enough money, I can get you a woman, no problem, or a man if you prefer."

Sharpe leans even closer and opens his mouth to speak. The words stick in his throat. He can't believe what he's about to do but can't see any other way. He has no choice.

"What I want . . ." he says, turning his head quickly to make sure nobody is listening. "What I need is a gun."

CHAPTER 51

Liv

I feel a buzz of childish excitement when I see the slim, cardboard package on the floor beneath the letterbox. I pick up my internet purchase and walk quickly to Lottie's room.

Before I unbolt the door, I tear the package open and practise locking and unlocking the handcuffs until I'm confident I can do it without thinking. I open the door slightly and peer into the room. Emily is lying on her stomach on the bed, fast asleep.

I step inside, closing the door quietly behind me. She doesn't stir. I stand still and watch her for a while, fascinated by her vulnerability, her childlike innocence. A wave of tenderness reminds me of the times I watched Lottie sleeping in the same bed, and it occurs to me that Emily doesn't deserve any of this. We rarely get the parents we deserve.

I slip a hand under her shoulder and roll her onto her back. She groans, opens her eyes and stares at me unseeing, before falling back asleep. As gently as I can, I put her left hand on the pillow above her head, lock one of the handcuffs around her slim wrist and the other around the outside bar of the metal headboard.

Keeping her in a slightly drugged state has worked perfectly up to now, but I'm fast running out of magic potion. There's probably no point in venturing out to buy more. A corpse is unlikely to give me any trouble.

I carry the bucket from the corner of the room and place it beside the bed, close enough for Emily to get to when she wakes. I have no desire to be cruel for cruelty's sake.

I return to the kitchen to make myself a hot drink but change my mind and decide to visit my favourite coffee shop instead. If I'm lucky, the good-looking barista will treat me to a cake again. I put on my red coat, hitch up the hood and open the door.

As I step onto the pavement, a black, slightly battered car pulls up at the kerb. The woman behind the wheel is Detective Akinola, her passenger Detective Earl. For a moment, I wonder whether Sharpe has called the police and told them everything. I'm seized by an urge to run, but where would I go?

Earl gets out of the car and approaches me. "We'd like to ask you a few more questions. There are some loose ends we'd like to tie up. If you'd rather not go to the station again, we can do this here, at your place. It shouldn't take too long."

I smile, on the inside. It doesn't sound like Sharpe has taken a gamble on his daughter's life after all. It's empowering to know he fears me, and what I might do.

"This is becoming incredibly tedious," I say. "When are you going to leave me alone? I'm trying to move on with my life."

The detective's eyes bore into mine, searching for the truth. I know he doesn't believe a word I say. He's convinced I'm guilty of something. He's just not sure what.

"Let's not waste any more time," he says. "One way or the other, this has to be done."

I shrug, exasperated, and walk to the car. "The police station it is, then. To be honest, the house is in a terrible state. I haven't had the time or energy to tidy up since your search team ransacked the place."

Twenty minutes later, I'm sitting in the same sparsely furnished interview room as before. This time, Detective Akinola takes the seat opposite me and Earl stands with his back to the wall, observing.

"Why am I here?" I ask, glancing across the room at Earl. "I told you before that I had nothing to do with Sharpe's drug overdose."

Earl doesn't respond. I look across the table at Akinola and don't like what I see. There's a glint in her eye that suggests she knows something that I don't want her to know, and she can't wait to drop it on me.

She gets straight to the point. "Our forensics team says your DNA doesn't match Lottie's. If you've not been honest with us about that we're wondering what else you haven't told us."

A dizzying burst of white light distorts my vision, and I grip the edge of the table to steady myself. They've stolen my secret. Akinola's eyes are on me, hungry for a reaction. I want to whiplash a slap across her face. Instead, I do my best to look unperturbed, give her nothing back.

There's no need to ask how they found out. DNA doesn't lie. Families do. What I don't know is exactly how much they've found out. If they've been asking around in Manchester, they'll know most of the story.

"I don't understand what you're trying to suggest. It's not a secret and there's no reason for me to tell everybody I talk to that I was adopted, even if they're police officers. I'm not biologically related to Lottie but she's still my little sister and she always will be."

Akinola's eyes soften and she tilts her head. "Did Lottie know? Having such a big age gap must have made it difficult for you to develop a relationship."

I guess she's trying her best to be sympathetic, but she's really not cut out to play the compassionate female cop. If she's expecting me to break down and sob my heart out, then she's going to be disappointed.

"Lottie had no idea I was adopted. Not until later. Not until she moved in with me."

I smile philosophically, even though the new me believes that philosophy is unscientific bullshit. My mind flips back to the day my mother told me the truth. My throat tightens and my stomach twists. For a brief moment, I'm a frightened, confused and lost little girl again.

"My mother waited until I was eleven before telling me. I think she thought she could soften the blow by announcing that against all the odds she'd fallen pregnant and was going to have her own baby, which meant I'd have a sister. Can you imagine how I felt?"

Earl steps away from the wall and stands behind Akinola. "So, until you told her, Lottie had no idea you weren't her biological sister?"

His bluntness is disconcerting. I am Lottie's sister, whatever anyone says. DNA doesn't lie, but sometimes it doesn't tell the whole truth. When Lottie arrived, I loved her from the start. But once she was past the baby stage, I began to feel frozen out. Whenever she could find an excuse, Mother stopped me spending time with Lottie. I think she was jealous of our special bond. I was downgraded. I wasn't her biological child. I was an outsider, an interloper.

I try to hide my unease by going on the offensive. "We weren't related by blood but we were, and always will be, sisters. I don't see what the hell my private life, my personal relationships, have to do with anything that should involve the police. Why am I here?"

"We're investigating the possibility that someone deliberately drugged Daniel Sharpe with the intention of making it look like an accident, or even a suicide attempt."

I laugh loudly. Earl and Akinola exchange curious glances. "I have to admit I wouldn't be sorry to hear that Sharpe is dead. If someone has really tried to kill him, I'd shake their hand and encourage them to have another try. If you have evidence that proves it was me, then charge me. I'm confident that you don't because I didn't do it."

"Sharpe ran down your sister and left her to die," Akinola says. "That's a pretty strong motive, isn't it?"

The detective constable deserves top marks for persistence, but this line of questioning only confirms that they have no solid evidence to back up their suspicions. She's goading me, hoping that I'll break down and confess.

I decide to give them something, to confess to something I'd never told anyone before. If I am going to convince them that I have nothing to hide, I have to be more open, tell them something they don't know. Even if it's only a partial truth.

"I told her everything, just before she died. I wish I'd kept my mouth shut, but we were having an argument. It was our first big row, and our last. She said she was going clubbing with friends and would be home by one o'clock at the latest, but she didn't come back until five, and I'd been worried sick. From the state of her, she'd been drinking heavily, and I lost my temper."

I remember the look of contempt on her face when I called her a spoiled brat, and tears spill down my cheeks. It wasn't what she said, more the way she said it. Mocking me. Sneering at me. *What makes you think you can tell me what to do? Who the hell do you think you are? Go back to bed, big sister, you're a joke.* Akinola's eyes widen at my unexpected show of emotion, and Earl gives me a nod of encouragement.

"I shouted again, and she yelled back. That's when I did it. I wish I hadn't but I was so furious. I told her about the adoption. I told her she should be grateful that I took her in because she wasn't really my sister. I shouldn't have said it. I didn't mean it."

Akinola takes a tissue from her jacket pocket and hands it to me. I bow my head and dab at my tears before going on.

"I regretted it as soon as the words were out of my mouth. Lottie didn't say a thing. She just stood there, looking as if I'd slapped her. Then she turned and ran out of the house. I never saw her alive again and I can't help blaming myself for what happened. She was angry and upset. She probably wasn't paying attention when she stepped off the pavement."

The detectives exchange surprised glances. "Why haven't you said any of this before now?" Earl asks. "If I remember right, in your original statement you said Lottie had gone out with friends that night and you had no idea why she'd be roaming the streets on her own in the early hours."

I sniff loudly and shrug. "I didn't say because I was embarrassed, feeling guilty, I suppose. It doesn't take away from what Sharpe did. He ran her down and didn't stop."

Earl steps closer, bends down and puts both hands flat on the table. "While you're getting things off your chest, maybe there's something else you want to tell us."

"I'm telling you the truth," I say. "I had nothing to do with whatever happened to Daniel Sharpe but I do hope that he gets what he deserves. Now, unless you're going to arrest me and lock me up, I'd like to go home, please."

Earl walks slowly to the door and opens it. "For now," he says.

A uniformed police constable leads me along the corridor, through two security doors and out of the building. I'm grateful that he doesn't attempt small talk because I need all my powers of concentration to work out what has just happened.

Those detectives ambushed me. They're out to get me. They took my DNA, my very essence, and used it against me. That can't be right, can it? They tried to break me. They failed. I'm stronger than ever.

The moment Sharpe put his foot on the accelerator, he gave me the absolute right to judge. I sentence him to a lifetime of grief. The dizziness I felt during the interview has turned into another vicious headache, and each step I take causes pain to shoot across my skull.

There is no need for Emily to suffer. Her blood won't spill, her body won't be mutilated. She deserves a painless death.

Beneath the throbbing in my head, a tiny voice whispers a plea for me to stop, to go back to being the ordinary me. But I'm not walking this path for myself. I'm doing it for Lottie. I will do anything for her. Anything.

CHAPTER 52

Sharpe

He'd never imagined that one day he'd feel the weight of a gun in his hand. Sharpe sits on his sofa and stares at the weapon, heavy in his palm, his fingers wrapped tightly around the textured handle.

An hour ago, his old cellmate had knocked on his door, grinning like a crazed pizza delivery guy, and handed him a plastic supermarket carrier bag containing a loaded Glock 19 semi-automatic pistol in exchange for £400 in cash.

Aware that Sharpe hadn't a clue how to use a gun, Grace took the time, free of charge, to run through his beginner's guide to shooting someone.

"Point it at your target's head or chest and when you're ready pull the trigger."

Sharpe places his forefinger alongside the barrel. It feels cool to the touch. This thing has been made for one purpose only, he tells himself. To end a life. The thought chills his bones.

He puts the gun on the floor between his feet and covers his face with his hands. Who's he trying to fool? He's not capable of shooting anybody. He could be putting Emily's life in more danger if he charges in waving a loaded gun around.

Everybody involved will be safer if he informs the police, he reasons. He's not a hero, definitely not a Hollywood action man. He's a father who doesn't want his daughter harmed in any way, that's all. He drops his right hand to his trouser pocket and taps his mobile as he wrestles with the idea of calling the police right now. After a few seconds, he pushes the thought away. He has to deal with this himself. It's the only way. He daren't give the police reason to question Emily again. One slip, one careless word would bring everything tumbling down around them.

Maybe Liv Miller's threats are empty. Once she knows the police are on to her, she'll crumble, won't she? Sharpe recalls how harmless she appeared when she came knocking on his door, begging for help in her battle to come to terms with her grief. She played the weak, helpless woman. Then she nearly killed him.

He stands up, exhaustion flooding over him. Every muscle in his body protests as he moves to the window, his weight dragging him down like quicksand. Darkness has fallen across the city, the street lights staining the pavements yellow.

Emily is out there, he thinks, at the mercy of a cold-hearted, unhinged woman. He imagines his daughter lying on a cold floor, crying her heart out, confused and terrified.

He takes his mobile from his pocket and types a text message to Emily's phone. He knows she won't be reading it.

Please don't hurt her. She doesn't deserve any of this. I haven't said anything to the police about you, and I never will. Please, tell me what it is you want me to do and I'll do it.

He walks to the sofa, sits back and closes his eyes. He's on the edge of sleep when his mobile pings. The reply to his message is short and to the point.

I want you to suffer.

There is no chance of reasoning with this woman. She appears innocent enough, even harmless. But she's deceptively dangerous.

He bends forward, picks the gun up and slips it into his jacket pocket. He intended his text message to give her the impression that he's been cowed into submission. It's close to the truth, but he knows the time has come for him to stop thinking and start acting. If she's confident that he poses no threat, then maybe he can catch her off guard.

If he doesn't get some sleep soon, he's going to crash and burn, but he has homework to do before he can rest. He goes into the kitchen, sits at the pine table and powers up his laptop.

It takes him a couple of minutes to find Liv Miller's Facebook page. Most of the posts and photographs on it are connected to her work as a feature writer. There are several links to magazines and newspapers she's written for. He reads a couple of her articles and is impressed by their quality. The dates on the latest posts show the last time she put anything new on her page was the day before her sister died.

A more general search produces a long list of news stories about Lottie Miller's death, and almost all of them feature a quote from her sister accusing the police of inefficiency, and the judicial system of incompetence.

Sharpe had made a conscious decision not to read any of the media reports about the case in the build-up to his court appearance and during his time in jail. He scrolls through the list, skim-reading every one he finds, slowing down to concentrate on the references to Liv Miller.

All of the internet news reports feature the same large photograph of Lottie Miller. No matter how hard Sharpe tries to focus on the text, his eyes are constantly drawn to her smile, the freckly stripe across her nose, her shining eyes. The picture is a shocking contrast to the image of her lying face down, bleeding and broken on the side of the road.

Yawning, he lifts his arms and stretches, then checks the time on his mobile. It's past midnight. He takes the gun from his pocket and puts it on the table beside his laptop. After a few seconds he picks it up again, gripping the handle as tight as he can to reassure himself that it's real, that he's not dreaming. How the fuck has he ended up with a gun?

He extends his arm, aiming at a coffee mug stacked on an upturned plate beside the sink. Could he point the gun at Liv Miller if it meant he could put an end to this madness and save Emily? Probably. Would he be able to stop his hand from shaking? Probably not. It's trembling now, and the only thing he's threatening is a pile of unwashed crockery.

CHAPTER 53

Earl

Earl is led along a narrow corridor to a meeting room furnished with an oval glass conference table surrounded by six grey plastic chairs.

"If you'd like to take a seat, Matt will be with you as soon as he can."

It's eight o'clock in the morning and the dreadlocked receptionist, dressed casually in black jeans and a white T-shirt bearing the magazine's masthead, sounds as if he's already bored out of his mind.

Earl chooses not to sit down. "Can you inform Mr Lamb that I'm here on urgent police business and I'd appreciate it if he made it a priority."

The receptionist rolls his eyes and walks lethargically back down the corridor to the front desk.

The offices of *Our Time* magazine are on the ground floor of a squat steel-and-glass building in the heart of Canary Wharf. The strong chemical scent of a citrus air freshener hangs heavy in the air, and like most modern office blocks, coffee machines, water coolers and artificial potted plants lurk around every corner.

Quickly scanning his surroundings, Earl is gratified to see that the wooden flooring is spotlessly clean, and the waste bin recently emptied. He checks that nobody is watching before shuffling quickly around the table to straighten up a couple of wayward chairs.

The decision to call in to the magazine on his drive to work had been made on the spur of the moment. Akinola's enquiries into Liv Miller's work history had shown that in the past few months she'd written almost exclusively for *Our Time*.

A tall, lean figure appears at the end of the corridor, striding briskly towards the meeting room. Like the receptionist, he's informally dressed. No jacket, a shirt with a collar but no tie, the sleeves rolled to the elbows. Matt Lamb enters the room, lifting a hand to sweep his unruly hair off his forehead.

"Sorry to keep you waiting, Detective. Deadline day today. You've no idea how hectic it can be."

He's right about that. Earl has no idea. He guesses that it's probably a walk in the park compared with a police constable's night shift on the streets of East London.

"Good morning, Mr Lamb. I understand you're the features editor. Is that right?"

"That's correct," he answers with a grin. "Please, I'd prefer it if you'd call me Matt, though. Mr Lamb makes me feel ancient. What can I do for you? I'm intrigued. We've had a few TV crime drama actors in for interviews over the years but never a real detective."

His boyish enthusiasm is delivered with a generous helping of charm, though Earl suspects that it might wear thin after a while.

"I want to ask you a few questions about Liv Miller, one of your freelance feature writers."

Panic spasms across Matt's face. "Oh shit, no. What's happened to her? Is she all right?"

Earl frowns. The blood has drained from the journalist's face. He looks as if he's about to faint.

"As far as I know, she's fine. All I want is information about her work record. I understand she works for you regularly?"

Matt pulls back a chair and sits down. "Thank God. For a minute there, I thought something terrible had happened." He pauses, taking a second to compose himself. "Yes, I'd say Liv is one of the best, maybe even the best, feature writer we have on our books at the moment. She has a real talent for making complicated topics easy to understand."

Earl isn't interested in the woman's journalistic skills. "How would you describe her as a work colleague?"

"Liv is great to work with," Matt says with a shrug. "A delight, actually. Extremely professional but warm, and good fun at the same time. Is she in trouble?"

"She may be connected to a case we're investigating. That's all I can tell you. When was the last time she worked for your magazine?"

Matt shakes his head. "I've known Liv for a while now. She'd never do anything illegal. She's really not that type of person. She's always been a stickler for rules."

Earl says nothing, in the hope that he can encourage Matt to fill the silence by answering the actual question. It works.

"She handed in the last feature she wrote for us about four weeks ago, I think. Great stuff about how the brains of psychopaths are structured differently to the rest of us, how being a psychopath isn't a choice anyone makes because the biology is pre-set in the womb. Our readers loved it. We've had fantastic feedback."

Earl checks his watch. He's starting to regret his decision to visit Miller's workplace. He has better things to do than listen to her boss sing her praises.

"But she hasn't she written anything for you since then?"

Matt grimaces. "Needed time off for her treatment," he says. "It was such a shock when she told me. I'm amazed how well she's coping. She's been so brave. I think I'd have fallen apart. Fortunately, the treatment's gone really well.

Better than even the doctors had expected, apparently. She's tougher than she looks, and is hoping to back with us pretty soon."

Unsure if he heard right, Earl leans forward. "Did you say, 'time off for her treatment'?"

"Yes. For her cancer. A brain tumour. That's why I panicked when you said you'd come about Liv. For a second, I thought you were here to tell me she'd died."

CHAPTER 54

Liv

I break the chocolate bar up into squares and spread them evenly around the plate. It's not exactly a hearty breakfast, but everyone is entitled to something special for their last meal.

I fill a glass with chilled orange juice and pour in the last of the magic potion, shaking the bottle to make sure that not even the tiniest drop is wasted. It's at least a double dose. She needs to be in a deep sleep, totally oblivious to what is happening. I'd like her final moments on this earth to be as peaceful as possible.

Despite knowing what today was to bring, I slept extremely well. Better than I have for a long time. Maybe I relaxed because I'd made a decision, but as I place the chocolate and juice on the tray and head for Lottie's bedroom, doubts start to creep into my mind.

Psychopaths in TV dramas and Hollywood movies never have doubts. They're programmed to relish finishing off their prey. I don't believe that's how it happens in real life. You have to work up to it. Get yourself into the right mood. I've been trying my best and now I know I have to stop delaying. I need to grit my teeth and go for it, or risk it never getting done.

I balance the tray on one hand while using the other to slide the bolt and open the door. The smell of sweat and fear hits me, and I instinctively hold my breath. Emily is sitting cross-legged on the bed, dishevelled and bleary-eyed. Her cheekbones are more prominent than when I first took her, her bare arms pale and thin.

She glances hungrily at the chocolate but says nothing. I put the tray down in front of her and she dives in, using her free hand to shove four squares into her mouth at once. I pick the plate up quickly before she can grab more.

"You need to drink the orange juice first," I say. "All of it, please, then you'll get the chocolate back."

She looks up at me accusingly. It's obvious she's figured out that I've been drugging her drinks. Holding my gaze, she lifts the glass and downs the juice in two large gulps. Some of it trickles from the corners of her mouth, running down her chin, but I'm satisfied that she's swallowed enough.

I watch her devour the rest of the chocolate. Her face is gaunt, her skin pale, almost translucent, and I'm reminded of the moment I stared down at Lottie as she lay in the hospital morgue.

Emily shakes her left hand, rattling the handcuffs against the metal bed post. "Please can you take these off? They're rubbing my wrists raw. It's unnecessary. I'm not going any-where, am I?"

I shake my head sadly. Was that a simple figure of speech, or does she somehow know what's about to happen to her?

"I'm sorry you've been caught up in this. Truly sorry. But it's the only way I can make your father atone for what he did. If you want to blame anybody for what's happening to you, blame him."

She wipes her chin and giggles into her hand. I guess the drug is already racing through her bloodstream, infiltrating her brain.

"You're wrong," she says. "This is all wrong."

I sit on the edge of the bed, suppressing an urge to stroke her hair, even though it's lank and greasy. If it was possible, I'd consider keeping her here, feeding her up, taking care of her. I'd be able to give her all the things I couldn't give Lottie. I'd buy her pretty clothes, read to her if she wanted me to, do everything necessary to make sure she was content and happy.

"What's right and wrong is not as clear cut as people think," I say. "Your father ran down my little girl and left her to die. That wasn't wrong, it was downright evil. The judge was too soft when he sentenced your father. That was wrong. I believe that the right thing would have been for your father to have succumbed to the coma. Instead, he came back to life, and now the newspapers are making him out to be some kind of hero. That's wrong. I want — no, I need him to experience what I experienced. I'm going to make sure he does."

Emily tilts her head and squints up at me, her eyes wild with fear and fury. "You've no idea, have you? You're obsessed. What's the matter with you? His life is ruined, his reputation destroyed. He was broken when he came out of prison. What more do you want?"

Her loyalty is almost touching. It's natural to defend those close to you, but why isn't she capable of acknowledging wickedness? Her eyes close and her head flops forward, but she immediately sits up straight, determined to stay awake.

"You need to sleep now," I say. "There's no point fighting it. Why don't you lie down and rest? I promise this will all be over soon. Everything will be over."

She shakes her right hand, rattling the handcuffs loudly in a childish act of defiance. "You don't understand at all," she slurs. "You haven't a clue what kind of man my dad is, have you?"

I'm quicker to anger than I used to be but it's easy to stay calm because she doesn't understand that she's talking nonsense. The drug is dulling the part of her brain responsible for logical thinking.

I edge closer to her side, placing a hand gently on her elbow. Her skin is cold and clammy.

"Lie down, Emily. Rest your head on the pillow and close your eyes. Everything is going to be all right, you'll see. Sleep now and you won't have to worry about your father ever again."

She shrugs me off. The effort she's making to stay conscious is surprising. I wonder whether, like livestock on the way to the slaughterhouse, she knows instinctively what's about to happen.

"You have it totally wrong. So wrong," she says, her eyes filling with tears. "He didn't. He wasn't."

She's babbling now and I'm losing patience. I decide to go downstairs and come back in five minutes. There's no way she'll be able to stay awake for that long.

I stand and pick up the tray. "I'm going to leave you to rest. Lie down and close your eyes. Let sleep bring you the peace you deserve."

Emily's eyes widen. "No, don't go," she begs. "I need to tell you. My dad wasn't driving. We didn't see her until it was too late. She came out of nowhere. Too fast. I'm sorry. We were frightened. So scared. We didn't know what else to do."

I drop the tray. It clatters to the floor. The plate spins across the room. The glass shatters. I tell myself not to take any notice of what she's saying because it's drug-induced nonsense, but a queasy hollowness rises from my stomach to my chest.

"You're lying," I hiss. "He gave the police a detailed confession. They carried out a full investigation. I don't believe you."

Emily uncrosses her legs and topples over onto her side. She's turned to the wall and I can no longer see her face. She keeps talking, her voice soft but insistent.

"I'd started travelling down to London from Leeds to visit Dad. Mum wasn't supposed to know, I didn't want to hurt her. I'm so sorry about your sister. Dad said he'd take care of it and he did. I should never have let him take the blame."

A numbing coldness flows through my body. I'm desperate to believe the story is a fantasy concocted by her drug-addled brain.

Emily's eyes close. She's sinking fast. Grabbing her shoulders, I shake her hard. I'm desperate to keep her conscious a little longer. She grunts, lifts her eyelids a fraction and tries to focus.

"You don't understand," she slurs. "Dad didn't do it. I didn't. There was nothing she could have done. Mum didn't have a chance. The girl wasn't looking, wasn't paying attention."

I'm struggling to make sense of what I'm hearing. The man confessed. He went to prison. I grab her shoulder and pull her onto her back. Her body is limp, her eyes closed and her breathing shallow.

I could end this now. Once and for all. She's so drugged up she won't realize what's happening. It doesn't matter to me whether she's telling the truth or lying. All I can be sure about is my truth.

I yank the pillow out from beneath her head. I hold it taut and stare at her. A few hours ago, I was willing to snuff out her life to spite her father. Now I'm hesitating.

This has to end now because I don't have the energy to go on. My heart races wildly in my chest. I breathe deeply to try to calm myself. I can do this if I shut everything else out. My brain is wired for it. Once it's done, I can rest, and God knows I need to rest.

Gripping the pillow tightly, I move closer.

CHAPTER 55

Sharpe

Standing at his favourite spot on the Thames Path, he gazes across the river towards the bleak tower blocks of Deptford. The late morning sun slices through the cloud, rippling gold on the mud-brown water.

He'd skipped breakfast and gone for a walk with the intention of clearing his mind, to think carefully and draw up a plan of action. It isn't working. Doubt, fear, uncertainty and anger swirl around his brain.

He slips his hand into his jacket pocket and runs his fingers over the cold metal of the gun barrel. A feeling deep in his gut urges him to hurl the pistol into the water. Instead, he takes his mobile out of his other pocket and sends a message to Emily's phone.

We need to meet. We have to talk. This can't go on. I don't want to go to the police, but what else can I do if you won't meet me? The fact is, I'm panicking now.

He turns around and, with his back to the water, walks slowly along Cuba Street. Every muscle in his body aches, each breath he takes a struggle. He knows Liv Miller lives less than ten minutes away. He finds comfort in the thought that Emily could be there. His worst fear is that she's been taken out of the city, locked up in a cabin in the woods in the middle of nowhere. His mobile pings.

Our favourite coffee shop. Wait for me there. An espresso and a slice of chocolate cake, please. Don't do anything stupid or you'll never find her. Never.

He remembers Miller following him into a coffee shop a few days after he'd been released from prison and speeds up, lengthening his stride and swinging his arms. After a few strides he's out of breath and has to stop to rest.

What does she mean, *You'll never find her*? His chest is heaving and sweat drips from his forehead into his eyes. *Calm down*, he tells himself, takes a couple of long, deep breaths and sets off again.

He drops a hand to his pocket and taps the handle of the gun for reassurance. It doesn't make him feel any better. Perhaps, he thinks suddenly, he'll only have to wave it in her face, let her see it, see what he's prepared to do if pushed.

At the end of Cuba Street, he rounds the corner and finds himself outside the café. He walks in, glad to see the breakfast rush has ended and only two of the tables are occupied. He buys an espresso and a slice of cake, and takes them to a leather sofa littered with copies of that day's newspapers and partially screened off by a row of plastic pot plants.

He collects up the newspapers, placing them in a pile on the wooden floor, and sits down. His view of the door is obscured by the fake greenery and he flinches when Miller appears beside him.

Smiling like an old friend, she sits down, picks up the cake and takes a small bite.

"Perfect," she says. "My favourite."

Sharpe studies the woman who drugged him. Radiating an eerie confidence, she's thinner than he remembers, her frame wrapped in a red, hooded coat that looks a size too big for her.

"Where's Emily? If you've harmed her, I swear I'll . . ." He falters mid-sentence, thrown by the fact that her smile widens at his attempt at a threat.

"First things first," she says, picking up her coffee and taking a sip. "I'd like you to hand over your phone, please. It's not that I don't trust you. I don't trust anybody. You might be tempted to record our conversation. That wouldn't do. Anyway, there are texts I sent you that could be considered incriminating."

Sharpe opens his mouth to protest but says nothing. He wants Emily back and he'll do anything to make that happen. He takes his phone from his jacket and places it on the coffee table in front of him. Miller picks it up and examines it for a few seconds before tucking it into her coat pocket.

"You're looking a little pale," she says. "Are you sure you should be up and about so soon? I hear you came very close to dying."

Sharpe stays silent. He can feel the weight of the gun swinging against his waist. If he can avoid using it, he will, but Miller seems set on pushing him to his limits.

She gives him a curious smile. "Congratulations on your amazing recovery, by the way. You've surprised everyone, especially me. I have to admit, I was more than a little disappointed."

Sharpe has a sudden vision of Emily's body hidden in a shallow grave, and an unfamiliar fury rises inside him.

"Where is she? What have you done with my daughter?"

Miller smirks, nibbles the cake again and offers him a taste. "Go on, try it. It's really good."

Sharpe slips his hand in his pocket, gripping the handle of the gun. He remembers reading a book in the prison library in which a criminal psychologist claimed that everybody is capable of murder if the circumstances are right. He'd decided the theory was flawed and had returned the book without finishing it. Resting his forefinger gently on the trigger of the gun, he concedes that the psychologist may have been right after all.

"What the fuck have you done with her? I won't allow this to go on any longer. If I can't know for sure that she's safe then I've nothing to lose by reporting you to the police."

Miller puts the last piece of cake in her mouth and washes it down with the dregs of her coffee. "Sorry," she says. "I skipped breakfast this morning."

Sharpe watches her dab her mouth with a paper napkin, taking care not to smudge her lipstick. When she's finished, she looks straight at him and shakes her head slowly.

"I know what really happened that day," she says. "The day Lottie died. I know the truth and the truth changes everything."

Sharpe feels dizzy, faint. He takes his hand out of his pocket and grabs the back of the sofa to steady himself.

"I've no idea what you're talking about. Just tell me where Emily is, for God's sake."

"You lied about being behind the wheel when your car hit Lottie, didn't you? You falsified a confession, went to court and spent time in prison, and you did all of that to stop the real criminal being punished."

Sharpe stays silent. He's trying to figure out what to say to give him the best chance of protecting Emily from this woman.

He takes a deep breath. There's no point lying now. "No one asked me to do what I did. It was my choice. I wanted to do it. I'm sorry for what happened. I truly am."

Miller is staring at him, her expression blank, a distant look in her eyes. He can't tell what's running through her mind but assumes she's thinking about her sister. He recalls reading in the newspapers how she and Lottie had been estranged for years, reuniting only after their mother died.

"I was hardly there for Emily when she was a child," he says. "Her mother didn't make it easy but it was my fault. I suppose I wanted to make up for being such a terrible dad. Can you understand that?"

"If the driver had stopped and called the police immediately, Lottie might still be alive, still be with me. That will always haunt me. Can you understand that?"

Sharpe nods. Of course he can. He can understand and he can sympathize. But the woman sitting beside him put him in a coma, and is holding his daughter hostage. He asks himself why Emily would tell her the truth. Had she been threatened? Tortured, even?

Miller is right. The truth has changed everything.

"Surely now you know what I did, the last thing I'm going to do is go to the police? You can tell them what you know about Lottie's death, and everything I've put myself through will have been for nothing. We can end this once and for all if we agree to keep each other's secrets. Emily can return to university, and we can go our separate ways."

Miller stands slowly.

"You think you know my secrets? Come with me," she says.

CHAPTER 56

Earl

A cup of steaming hot coffee in each hand, Earl walks across the squad room towards Akinola's desk. A sense of anticipation underlies the chatter and trilling phones.

Akinola looks up from her computer screen. She stands, takes her drink and, with a nod of thanks, leads him back the way he came to the corridor. They pass Tanner's office, and slip into a recess housing the coffee machine and a water cooler.

"You can't hear yourself think in there at the moment," Akinola says, blowing on her drink. "You must be psychic, though. I'm gasping for a brew."

Earl pulls a tissue from his jacket pocket and wipes the coffee-spattered worktop. Akinola groans.

"Why don't you leave the cleaning to the cleaners? They won't thank you for doing them out of a job."

Earl drops the tissue into the waste bin. "I applied for a disclosure order and we've been granted access to Liv Miller's medical records."

"And?"

"And they show she's never been diagnosed with cancer. She's never been treated for cancer. In fact, it seems that she's disgustingly healthy and hasn't visited a GP for years. The woman's a pathological liar. She hid the fact that she was adopted and that she and Lottie had a furious argument shortly before the hit-and-run."

Akinola blows on her coffee again and takes an experimental sip. "So, she lied to Matt Lamb about having a brain tumour. It's a strange and horrible thing to do, but as far as I know it's not a crime. There's no fraud, no scam involved. All she's gained from it is a few weeks off work unpaid, and a lot of sympathy from a caring boss. You can let Lamb know that he was lied to. He'll make sure she never works for the magazine again. Done."

Earl isn't sure it's that simple. A few days after Miller lies about being seriously ill, an attempt is made to kill the man who confessed to being responsible for the death of her daughter. Although they prove nothing, the fake fur fibres found on Sharpe's sofa still bug him.

He gulps down his coffee. It burns the roof of his mouth. "I still think we're missing something," he says. "Something significant. She's an accomplished manipulator."

"You need to let this go," Akinola says. "I've had an armed robbery and a fatal stabbing outside a school added to my caseload today. I'm sure Tanner's going to assign new cases to you too. Don't piss him off. You need to keep him sweet."

Earl knows she's right but he's not going to take her advice. Not yet. "I need one more day, that's all. There's a couple of questions I want answers to before I can let this go. I want to call Matt and then pay a visit to the neuroscientist Miller worked with on her last magazine feature. If Tanner comes looking for me, I need you to stall him."

"What the hell am I supposed to tell him if he asks where you are?"

"You'll think of something. Use your imagination."

CHAPTER 57

Liv

Sharpe follows me out of the coffee shop, sticking close as if he suspects I'm going to make a run for it. We dash across the road, forcing a black cab to brake and triggering a chorus of car horns. I turn to look through the windscreen at the snarling cab driver and give him a cheesy smile.

My place is no more than a two-minute walk away, but by the time we reach the entrance Sharpe is sweating profusely, his chest heaving. Either his body is still too weak to cope with even mild exertion, or he's extremely nervous. I guess it's a mixture of both.

In contrast, I'm feeling surprisingly relaxed, even a little elated. I have a strong sense that things are coming to a head, and even though I'm certain there's not going to be a happy ending, I don't care too much. I need this to be over.

I lead Sharpe to my front door, and we stop while I fumble in my coat pocket for the key. Sharpe grips my elbow tightly and I turn to face him.

"Is she in there?" he asks. "If you've hurt her, I swear I'll . . ."

I shake him off, open the door and gesture for him to enter. I follow him into the hall and guide him into the kitchen.

"Can I make you a cup of tea?" I say, casually unzipping my coat. "I have a good selection of biscuits." He stares at me in disbelief. He thinks he's dealing with a crazy woman, and maybe he's right.

I've brought him into my home because I want him to walk, full of hope, into a room and find his daughter lying motionless on a bed. I want to savour the agony he feels in that moment, to hear his howl of anguish. But not yet. He can wait. He can wonder. He can hope a little longer.

"Where is she? What have you done with her?" His voice is hoarse, straining with desperation. I slip my coat off and fold it over the back of a chair.

"We'll get to that, don't worry," I say, as cheerily as I can. "I've been thinking about what you said earlier about why you did what you did. About wanting to make up for being an absent father, and you know, despite everything, I have to admire you a little bit for that. I'd like to think that it's possible I'd have done the same. I'm not sure, though. You deceived everybody. The media. The police. The public."

Sharpe says nothing. He looks at me like I'm crazy, wipes the sweat from his forehead with the back of his hand and stalks out of the kitchen. I follow him along the hall and into the living room.

He scans the room quickly before turning to confront me. "Where is she?" he demands. "I swear I'll rip the whole place apart if I have to."

I cross my arms and laugh at him. He should have stayed in hospital. He looks as if he hasn't the strength to rip apart a paper bag.

"Is there anything funnier than a grown man having a temper tantrum? I don't think so."

Sharpe jams his right hand hard into his jacket pocket. For a fraction of a second doubt flickers across his face. His eyes narrow as he pulls out a gun and points it at my chest.

"Take me to my daughter," he says. "Right now."

CHAPTER 58

Liv

I've never looked down the barrel of a loaded pistol before. I don't like the feeling at all. This turn of events is completely unexpected and Sharpe appears to be as surprised as I am. His breath is ragged, the gun shaking in his trembling hand.

My stomach churns and for a moment I'm lost for words. I can see his finger curved around the trigger and I'm desperately hoping that it doesn't slip.

"For God's sake, why don't you just tell me where she is? Don't make me do this. I don't want to hurt you but I will if I have to."

He lifts the gun and jabs it at my face. While my eyes are fixed on the hole at the end of the barrel, all my thoughts are focused on the trigger. One slight increase of pressure, one tiny squeeze and I'm dead. I wonder how much dying hurts if you're shot in the head.

Perhaps I'd be better off taking a bullet in the brain. All my troubles would vanish in an instant. Death could be a blessing. I'd never have to think about Lottie ever again. I'd never have to remember, never have to regret doing what I did. A shiver runs down my back and I push these thoughts away. The instinct to survive is our most powerful drive. No matter how hard I try, I can't fool myself. I want to live.

"Please calm down. There's no need for any of this." I'm impressed by how composed I sound. "I want you to see Emily. I brought you here so you can be reunited. Why don't you stop pointing that at me and put it down? It's dangerous."

"Emily's here? She's here?"

I nod and take a couple of steps to the side. Sharpe swivels to keep the gun aimed at my head.

"She's here, yes. She's in the bedroom upstairs on the right. She's been waiting for you."

He lowers the gun, rushes past me and climbs the steps. I turn and follow him, slowly. I know what he's going to see and I'm not sure how he'll react. He wrenches the door handle before he spots the bolt and slides the bar across. I watch him burst into the room and hear him cry out. The sound echoes along the hallway.

I stand in the doorway. Sharpe is on his knees beside the bed, cradling his daughter in his arms. The gun is on the bedside table next to the empty glass. It looks less lethal than it did in Sharpe's hand. More like a toy pistol. I step in and pick it up.

Sharpe has a hand on the side of his daughter's neck, searching for a pulse. "No, no, please no," he babbles. "Come on Emily, no, no."

I back out of the room, shut the door and yank the bolt across. Running downstairs and into the kitchen, I take a cedarwood-scented candle from the cupboard under the sink, light it and carry it into the living room.

Lottie bought the candle for me a few days after she moved in. I was so moved that she'd bought me a gift I couldn't speak. I swore I'd never use it, which was just as well because I've always hated scented candles. They make me sneeze.

I place it on the window sill and pull the curtains across until the edge of the material is touching the flame. Then I run.

CHAPTER 59

Sharpe

Sharpe leans forward and places his right cheek close to his daughter's blood-drained lips. He can't hear her breathing but the faintest hint of an exhalation brushes his skin. Hope flares in his chest. He puts a trembling hand on her neck below the jaw in search of a pulse. Nothing.

"She's not dead, she can't be dead." He says the words out loud to give them a better chance of being true. He rolls her off her back onto her side.

The movement rattles the handcuffs, and his eyes fall on the ring of sores where the metal has rubbed the skin off her wrist. A shudder of revulsion contorts his face. All this time, she's been chained up like a captive animal.

His brain screams instructions. *Call an ambulance. Call the police. Take Emily to the nearest hospital. Don't let her die. Get your phone back from Miller and make her hand over the key to the handcuffs.*

Sharpe reaches for the gun. It's not there. Confused, he scans the room, but there's no sign of the pistol. Or Miller. He gets to his feet and turns to open the door. It won't budge. Twisting the handle again, he shoves harder. He remembers the bolt, and realizes they're locked in. Rage rises inside his chest. Its power makes him understand that he's never hated anyone before.

He grabs the handle, stands sideways on and prepares to slam his body against the door.

The metal handle feels warm against the skin of his palm. A cautionary voice in his head tells him to hold back. He stands still and listens. A menacing crackle comes from the hall. Despite the stench in the room, he detects a new odour and his heart jackhammers. The smell of burning.

Wisps of smoke slide out from under the door, writhing across the carpet like silvery snakes. Sharpe releases his hold on the handle and steps back. Instinctively, he knows the last thing he should do is open the door.

He rushes to the single, small window, tearing at the curtains. His head drops when he sees the locks screwed into the frame. Slumping against the wall, he closes his eyes in despair. The scream of a siren somewhere in the distance jolts him back to life. He picks up the bedside table and hurls it against the window pane. The glass shatters and Sharpe sucks hungrily at the blast of fresh air.

Turning back to the bed, he grabs hold of the handcuffs and, although he knows he's wasting his energy, he yanks hard. The metal headboard clangs but the cuffs hold firm.

The room is filling with smoke. Red-hot flames crackle and hiss as they lick at the door. Seized by a fit of coughing, Sharpe sinks to his knees. Even if Emily is still clinging on to life, the smoke will kill them both long before the fire consumes their bodies. He picks the large, fluffy pillow up off the bed, shuffles on his knees to the door and jams it against the bottom in an attempt to seal the gap.

Another fit of coughing grips him, his throat burning from the acrid smoke. He wipes his lips with his sleeve and lowers himself onto the bed, wrapping his arms around his daughter.

The sirens are close but he's struggling to stay conscious. He shuts his eyes and starts to drift away. The feeling of drowning in darkness is horribly familiar. He hears a distant voice calling him back. The sound is muffled and he can't make out the words.

Summoning up his last ounce of strength, he raises his eyelids. At the window, through the choking, swirling blackness, he sees the yellow flash of a firefighter's helmet.

CHAPTER 60

Earl

Earl takes his jacket off the back of his chair, slips it on and straightens the knot of his tie. The drive across the city will take him at least half an hour and he's eager to get going. The thought of arriving late for a meeting fills him with dread. He hates being late almost as much as he hates being wrong.

Professor Noble ran the study of the brains of psychopaths that Miller wrote about in her magazine feature. He's the expert she used to validate her lies about having a brain tumour. Earl isn't expecting any significant revelations but he's interested in finding out exactly what they did discuss during their last conversation.

Walking quickly across the squad room, he sees Akinola talking animatedly on the phone and gives her a nod. She slams the receiver down and beckons him over. He doesn't stop but slows a little.

"In a hurry," he says. "I've an important appointment up west."

Akinola is out of her seat and clutching at his arm. "Not now, you haven't. You'll have to cancel. We're needed at the

Royal London Hospital, and trust me, you're not going to want to miss this."

During the drive to Whitechapel, Earl listens carefully as Akinola fills him in about the fire at Miller's home. He keeps silent, even when she tells him how the firefighters needed metal cutters to slice through the handcuffs chaining the girl to the bed.

When she finishes, he exchanges a sideways glance with her but says nothing. If Sharpe and his daughter are well enough and willing to talk, they'll soon know everything they need to.

On the hospital ward, the detectives are shown into a side room. Sharpe is sitting with his back to the door on a chair next to an empty bed, his head in his hands. He's wearing a pale-blue hospital gown.

He turns, looks up and starts to rise, but Earl waves a hand, signalling for him to stay where he is.

"The doctors say you're well enough to talk to us, but you must be exhausted."

Sharpe covers his mouth with a hand and coughs painfully. "Inhaling smoke hasn't done my lungs a lot of good, but I'm told they'll clear in a couple of weeks." His voice is hoarse, his eyes bloodshot.

Akinola crosses the room and leans against the bed. "And Emily is going to be okay."

Sharpe manages a half smile. "Thank God, yes. When I first saw her lying in that room, I thought she was dead. I couldn't wake her, couldn't feel a pulse. She'd been drugged, according to the doctors. She came to when the firefighters were cutting her free. She's sleeping in a room down the corridor."

"We know," Earl says. "We've already been fully briefed by the medical staff."

Sharpe nods slowly, screws up his face and starts shaking his head. "I know I should have called you. I should have told you what was happening straightaway. I'm an idiot. She could have died. We'd probably both be dead if we'd been in that room any longer." He doubles over in the chair, coughing and wheezing in spasms.

Earl reaches for the jug of water on the bedside table and fills a glass. When the coughing stops, he hands it to Sharpe, who takes a sip.

"How long had Miller been holding your daughter?"

"Three, maybe four days."

"And you knew she had taken her?"

"She sent me a text from Emily's mobile. She warned me not to call the police. Told me to keep my mouth shut. I know it was stupid but I was frightened about what she'd do."

Earl knew the answer to his next question but he needed to hear Sharpe say the words. "What were you supposed to be keeping your mouth shut about?"

Sharpe lets out a long sigh of resignation. "It was her. She came to my house begging to talk. I felt sorry for her, she seemed so distraught. She spiked my coffee with that drug. I don't know if she meant to kill me but she almost did. I knew what she was capable of. That's why I was terrified she'd hurt Emily if she suspected I'd called the police. In the end I arranged to meet her and begged her to take me to my daughter."

Earl looks across at Akinola, who responds with an almost imperceptible nod. "We believe she did try to kill her," he says. "Apart from the drug in her system, we've been told that she has slight bruising around her lips and nose consistent with being smothered with something like a pillow. It's possible that Miller thought she'd succeeded and stopped too soon, or her conscience got the better of her and she couldn't go through with it."

Sharpe buries his face in his hands. At that moment, the door opens and a grey-haired nurse pops her head in, a wide smile on her face. "Emily's wide awake and she's asking for her father," she says.

Sharpe jumps up and runs down the corridor, followed closely by the two detectives. They find Emily sitting up, holding a cup of tea.

Sharpe moves quickly to the bed. "Hi, darling," he says. "It's great to see you looking so well." Emily sips her drink, looking warily at the two police officers.

"I've been telling these detectives what happened. They're going to catch her. You have nothing to worry about."

Emily doesn't look convinced. "You have no idea where she is, though, do you?" she asks, turning to Earl.

"After starting the fire, she fled. She could be anywhere in the city by now but I'm confident we'll find her. She's out of control, not thinking straight."

"What if she comes here, to the hospital?" Emily says, reaching for her dad's hand.

Earl shakes his head. "Don't worry. We'll have officers guarding both your rooms twenty-four-seven. We'll make sure you're safe."

Sharpe leans over and kisses his daughter gently on the forehead. "Your mum's on her way down to London," he says. "She'll be here in a couple of hours and she's going to have a lot of questions."

"We'll leave you now," Earl says. "When you're both feeling stronger, we're going to need to take full statements off you."

He steps towards the door and gestures with a nod of his head for Akinola to follow. As she moves, Emily calls out for them to wait.

"Don't go. There's something else I want to tell you," she says, flicking a worried glance at her dad. "Something important."

"Earl waves a dismissive hand. "It can wait. You need to rest. We've all we need for now."

"No, you don't understand," Emily says, her voice cracking as a single tear spills down her face. "I want to talk about the hit-and-run. I want to tell you what really happened."

* * *

Neither detective speaks as they ride the lift to the hospital's ground floor. Nor as they walk side by side to the exit, their steps echoing down the tiled corridor.

"You were right all along," Akinola says at last. "Tanner's going to have a coronary when you tell him."

Earl doesn't say anything. He's still trying to digest Emily's account of the accident and its aftermath. His initial exhilaration has evaporated. He's been proved right, and that's satisfying. But more than anything, it's a relief.

Akinola stops suddenly and turns to Earl. "What about Sam Carter's helmet-cam footage? It clearly shows Sharpe at the wheel."

The video had thrown Earl off track. It had been too easy to accept as incontrovertible evidence.

"He did drive his car that morning. There's no doubt about that. But he didn't run down Lottie Miller."

Akinola raises a hand and clicks her fingers. "It was after he got the call from Emily telling him what had happened. That's when he almost knocked Sam Carter off her bicycle, wasn't it?"

CHAPTER 61

Earl

Clare Sharpe props her elbows on the table and rests her head in her hands. Her shoulder-length hair swings forward, hiding her face. Sitting opposite her, Earl switches on the recorder and gives his rank and name.

"This interview is being recorded and filmed," he says. "Can you confirm that you have declined your right to legal representation?"

Clare sits up, smoothing her hair behind her ears. She takes a deep breath and straightens her shoulders. Her eyes are red but there is no sign of tears.

"Yes, I want to get this over with," she says. "It's all true. I was behind the wheel when the car hit the girl. I was frightened. Panicking. Probably in shock. Emily was crying hysterically. I didn't have time to think. He didn't do it for me, you know. He did it for our daughter."

Earl holds up a hand. "Please slow down a second. I need you to tell us exactly what happened, in chronological order. From the start. Can you do that?"

"I think I can," she says, her voice cracking. "All this time I've pushed the memory away, done my best to wipe it, but something as horrible as that never really leaves you. The evening before I drove to Leeds to pay Emily a surprise visit and buy her dinner. There was no sign of her at her digs and she wasn't answering her phone. A roommate said she'd gone to London for the weekend. I started driving home, disappointed that she hadn't told me and puzzled why she'd go to London and not back home if she had the weekend free. I knew she must have gone to visit Daniel."

She pauses to clear her throat, lifts a shaky hand to cover her eyes and massages her temples with her thumb and forefinger.

Earl has checked her background and has to give her some credit. Considering she's never been in trouble, never had reason to step inside a police station before, she's doing a good job of holding herself together.

"Is that such a bad thing?" he asks. "He is her father."

Clare lifts her head and straightens her back. "I was furious. I won't deny it. We'd decided a few years before that she'd cut all contact with him. He'd let her down so many times. What hurt more than anything was the secrecy, the deceit. If she'd told me she wanted to see him, then we could have talked and sorted something out. She's old enough to make her own choices. But I was angry, hurt. I telephoned Daniel and accused him of trying to turn Emily against me. He denied it, of course. Claimed he had no idea what I was talking about. It might surprise you, considering how he managed to fool everybody else, but I've always been able to tell when he's lying. I turned around and drove down to London, to Daniel's house. I didn't get there until 4 a.m. That's when it all went wrong."

* * *

She presses the doorbell, holding her finger down for a good five seconds. It's 4 a.m. and the house is in darkness. She doesn't care. The long drive south hasn't calmed her at all.

One of the first-floor windows lights up as she rings the bell again. She hears the distinct sound of footsteps descending the staircase. Daniel

254

opens the door. He's wearing a black dressing gown, nothing on his feet and a look of disbelief.

"What the hell are you doing here?" he says, his voice an incredulous whisper.

"I'm taking Emily home. Right now."

"Don't be ridiculous. Do you know what time it is? She's in bed."

"Then get her up — now. I want to leave before the traffic starts getting heavy."

Daniel steps forward, pokes his head over the threshold and checks the street. It's deserted. Every house dark and silent.

"Keep your voice down, please. People are sleeping."

"I don't care what people are doing," she says. "The sooner Emily is ready the sooner we can go."

Daniel sighs and steps back.

"Come on, Clare. This is silly. Come inside and we can have a coffee and talk about this. Sort everything out. You don't want to drive back now. You must be tired and it's freezing out there."

The invitation is tempting. But she stands her ground. She's too hurt to be capable of having a considered, grown-up discussion.

"I'm going back now and Emily is coming with me. There is nothing to discuss."

Daniel pulls at his dressing gown and tightens the belt.

"I didn't want her to keep this from you but she was scared you'd react badly. You're proving her right."

He turns at the sound of footsteps. Emily, her hair dishevelled, her backpack slung over one shoulder, stands by the staircase. She's wearing her coat over her pyjamas.

"It's all right," she says. "I'm ready to go. Please, I don't want you two to argue. I'll call you when we get back."

She walks past him and Clare without looking at either of them and climbs into the front passenger seat of the car.

"This is bloody ridiculous," Daniel says. "It doesn't make any sense to drive back now. We can sort this out. The three of us."

Clare storms to the car and gets behind the wheel. In the rear-view mirror she sees Daniel on the doorstep, watching the car pull away.

She glances sideways at Emily. Her head is bowed, her arms wrapped around the backpack on her lap.

Clare reaches out and sets the satnav for home. It gives the journey time as four hours. The roads are empty, but by the time they get to the motorway the traffic will be building up.

Emily still hasn't said a word. Clare knows she must be angry with her, embarrassed at being dragged out of bed like a naughty child.

"You know, the worst thing is being lied to. It's not something I'd expect of you. Not in a million years. If you'd told me you wanted to start seeing your father again, we could have arranged something together."

For a few moments, Emily says nothing. Then she explodes.

"That's what you say now. But if I'd said anything, you'd have tried to change my mind. I know you would. I'm eighteen, I'm at university, I can make my own decisions. I don't need you to make them for me. I would have said something when I was good and ready. But sometimes, you're impossible to talk to."

Clare slows as they approach a T-junction but her heart is racing. Emily has never spoken to her like that before. She turns right onto another deserted street and speeds up.

"How can you say that? It's always been me and you. I can't believe you——"

Emily screams. Too late. The thud is wet, sickening. The girl flies into the air, her body spinning over the bonnet. Clare freezes, her foot still hard on the accelerator. She can hear Emily shouting at her to stop, but she can't. Not yet. She has to get away. She can't see. Can't look.

"Oh God. Oh my God. What have I done?"

* * *

Clare covers her mouth with a hand and shuts her eyes. Earl thinks she might vomit.

"Maybe this is a good time to take a break," Earl says. "Get you some water, if you need it, or a hot drink."

"No, I'm all right. I need to get this over with."

"If you're sure, then please go on."

"Well, I turned left down the next side street, drove to the end and pulled over. Emily was crying. I was crying. She said we should call an ambulance. I stopped her. I knew the girl was already dead. She had to be. I wasn't thinking straight. Panic and fear take over, don't they? Instead, she called Daniel."

"And he came?"

"Straightaway. He was still wearing his dressing gown. It probably took him no more than ten minutes but it felt an age."

Earl imagines Sharpe pulling up behind their car, comforting his sobbing daughter — listening, horrified, as his near-hysterical ex-wife fills him in.

"Whose idea was it that he should take the blame?" Earl asks.

Clare grimaces. "His, of course. He took control of the situation. Didn't hesitate. I know I should have resisted. Should have called an ambulance and the police there and then. But I was in pieces. Can you understand that?"

Earl doesn't answer. He would love to tell her his thoughts about what they'd done. But the interview is being recorded.

"Can you remember exactly what Daniel did?"

"Not everything. I was in a terrible state and it was a long time ago. The first thing he did was check my car. I remember that. There was damage to the bumper, a dent in the bodywork and some blood. He found an old piece of cloth in the boot of his car and used that to clean the blood off. I remember you found similar damage to his car. He must have caused that himself to make sure you believed him."

Clare pauses and shakes her head. "Daniel said I had to calm down and drive us back to Manchester as planned, and that he'd call me later to explain everything. He made me promise, then drove off."

"In which direction?"

Clare looks right at Earl and blinks hard. But she can't stop the tears rolling down her face.

"He went back the way I'd come. He was going . . . I think he was . . . He wanted to check on the girl, and then call an ambulance. Can we finish now?"

Earl nods and switches the recorder off. Clare covers her face with her hands and sobs. After a moment, she lifts her head and wipes her eyes with the back of her hands.

"He did it all for Emily, you know. He said she'd fall to pieces if I went to prison. I think he was right, and that's partly why I went along with it. We'll find out soon if we were right, won't we?"

CHAPTER 62

Liv

Hunched against the cold, I gaze across the Thames at Limehouse, as the last rays of sunlight bleed on the city's skyline. I'm always staggered by how beautiful this part of the river is at sunset.

I need a plan of action but I'm struggling to think straight after all that's happened. I have no home. The police will be after me. I'm a fugitive with nowhere to run to.

I believed I was up to it. I was sure I could get away with it. I failed spectacularly, letting my rage get the better of me. I've tried my best to be ruthless and calculating but I have to face facts. When it comes to being a psychopath, I'm still a beginner.

The temperature has fallen with the darkness, and my frosted breath curls in front of my face. I'm facing a night on the streets, and the prospect is scary.

By now the police will have worked it out. They'll be preparing to splash my face all over the newspapers and on every TV channel. *Have you seen this woman?* Members of the public will be warned not to approach me. I'm too dangerous. An attempted murder suspect. A deranged arsonist.

I hear something scrambling towards me to my left. It's a crooked-nosed bull terrier, it's slit eyes glinting in the dark. It's not on a lead but its owner is ambling a few feet behind. I press up close to the railing to leave room for them. The man, short and wiry, puffing on a cigarette, winks lasciviously as he passes.

I breathe a sigh of relief when they've gone, feeling more desperate than ever to find somewhere safe to spend the night. An idea comes to me and I wonder why I hadn't thought of it before.

I leave the Thames Path and head into Narrow Street, pulling my hood down as far as I can over my face and staring at the pavement when passing anything resembling a CCTV camera.

Last Christmas, Matt held a party at his home for the magazine's freelance writers. The whole thing was probably a ruse to corner me and ask me out. I decided to give it a miss but I remember the address on the invitation.

I pass the Grapes, one of the oldest pubs in London, and turn right. I'm feeling better now that I've come up with a plan.

Five minutes later, I'm standing on the doorstep of a terraced house and ring the bell. The door opens before I've had a chance to consider my strategy. Matt stares at me open-mouthed, and for a horrible moment I think he's going to slam the door in my face.

"Surprise," I say, slipping my hood down and smiling up at him. "I know it's a bit late but I'd love a cup of tea or even something stronger."

Matt stumbles back, dumbstruck, and I walk inside, doing my best to look more confident than I feel. The narrow hall leads straight into an open-plan living room and kitchen. The house must be at least one hundred years old but everything in it is shiny and modern.

"Lovely place," I say. "I didn't know features editors were so highly paid."

Matt shrugs. "They're not. I got lucky. A timely inheritance from an auntie."

I grin, trying to appear genuinely delighted for him, but probably end up looking like a crazy woman.

"What do you want from me, Liv? Why are you here?"

Matt is even less pleased to see me than I thought he'd be. My charm offensive isn't working. I switch tactics, scrunch up my face and let the tears flow.

"I need somewhere to sleep," I say. "One night. That's all. I need somewhere safe and warm. One night and I'll be gone in the morning. I promise."

He hesitates, chewing his bottom lip. It's not a good sign. "I don't understand. You're not making sense. We can call a taxi to take you back to your place. That's not a problem, is it?"

At least I know the fire hasn't made the news bulletins yet. Despite that, there's something about Matt's manner that suggests he's angry with me.

"I can't explain right now but I'd rather not go back home tonight. Please, Matt. Trust me."

"But I can't, can I?" he snaps, his face flushing red. "I know about the cancer. I mean, I know you haven't got it, that you've never had it. You lied to me, Liv. A horrible, cruel lie."

I walk slowly over to the sofa in the middle of the room and sit down. My mind is whirring, searching for a way out of this mess. I decide the best way to get out of trouble for lying is to tell more lies.

"I'm so sorry, Matt. There's no excuse for what I told you, and I can't give you a good reason other than I'm still struggling to come to terms with Lottie's death. I've been pretending to cope but I'm seeing a psychologist now, trying to sort my head out. She believes that I'm suffering from post-traumatic stress disorder. It'll take while but it can be treated."

I bow my head and sniff loudly. Matt is ominously silent and still. I have the feeling there's something he's not telling me.

"How did you find out?" I ask. "I was going to tell you anyway. I'd already discussed it with my therapist. She said

261

you'd understand. PTSD can make people do inexplicable things."

Matt shrugs unsympathetically. "That detective. Earl. He called me. He came to see me at work, asking about you. It scared the life out of me. I thought he'd come to tell me you'd died."

I sniff again, and murmur, "Sorry, so sorry," into my cupped hands, over and over again. "I don't blame you for hating me."

Matt walks over to the sofa. I expect him to sit down next to me and put his arm around my shoulders but he stays where he is.

"I don't hate you," he says. "Earl called me a couple of hours ago. Told me he needs to speak to you urgently, but you'd gone missing. Said if you tried to contact me, I should call him."

I stand up, sobbing now. "Oh God, Matt. I didn't want to involve you, but they want to question me about Daniel Sharpe's drug overdose. I don't know why. Honestly, I don't. They've got it all wrong. I'm going to the police station in the morning to answer their questions but I need to sleep first. I want to gather my thoughts, get my head together. The state I'm in at the moment, I'm scared I'm going to fall apart."

Matt steps closer, puts his arm around me and hugs me. I rest my head on his shoulder and nuzzle his neck.

"You'll have a lawyer sitting with you, advising you," he says. "That's your legal right. You've nothing to be scared of. You need to tell them the truth."

I step back, wiping my eyes with my hand. "You're right. I know you are. But I'll wait until the morning. Call the taxi for me, would you, please? I'll go back home, if that's what you want. It's just that, sometimes, the memories in that place, of Lottie, are too hard to bear."

Matt's expression softens. He's wavering.

"You're the sweetest, kindest person I've ever met and I regret, with all my heart, telling you such a disgusting lie. I hope that one day you'll be able to forgive me."

He takes a deep breath and his shoulders sag. That's the moment I know I've won.

"I don't suppose it's going to make any difference whether you go to the police now or first thing in the morning. You can stay in the spare room. Take your coat off and I'll fix you a drink."

I struggle to suppress a smile of triumph, and wipe my eyes to cover it up. "Thank you so much," I say, sounding as grateful and as feeble as I can. "You really are an amazing person. But it's late and I'm exhausted. I'd rather go straight to bed."

Matt nods. "Okay, follow me."

He leads me up the narrow staircase and into a recently painted box room. "The bed is already made up, and the bathroom is next door. If there's anything you need, give me a shout."

I wait for him to leave before kicking off my shoes and sitting on the end of the bed. I don't understand how Matt can bear my presence, let alone show me kindness. Maybe he truly cares for me. I'd like to believe that.

The mattress feels soft, and I flop onto my back and close my eyes. I desperately need some sleep but my mind keeps flipping back to that morning. If only I'd stayed in bed.

* * *

I hear the key turn in the lock and breathe a sigh of relief. She's home. She's safe. She's not lying dead in a dark East London alley.

She climbs the stairs, her footsteps clumsy, uncoordinated. I know I should turn over and try to go back to sleep but I don't. I get out of bed, slip my dressing gown on and step out onto the landing.

Lottie stops and glares. "What?"

She looks tired. Mascara smudged, dress creased, and I can smell the alcohol on her breath.

"Where the hell have you been?"

She rolls her eyes and sighs. "I told you. Clubbing with friends."

"Until now? I don't believe you. I've been worried sick. You could at least have sent me a text or something to let me know you were all right."

She only has to say sorry and I'll let it go, but she lifts her chin in defiance. The gesture reminds me of our mother. Eyes full of contempt for my needs, my feelings. Lottie takes a step towards her bedroom door.

I reach out and grab her arm, accidentally pinching her skin. She shakes free of my grip and spins to face me, her eyes wide, teeth clenched.

"Get away. Don't you dare touch me. Not ever."

She spits the words like hate-filled bullets. I'm wounded. We were growing close. How can she speak to me like this? After all I've done for her.

"I'm sorry. I didn't mean to hurt you. I haven't been able to sleep at all waiting for you to come in. You're my little sister. I was scared that something bad had happened."

I'm trying to calm her but I can see that I'm wasting my time. She's shaking with fury, relishing the prospect of a row. It must be the drink.

"Who do you think you are?" she sneers. "What makes you think you have the right to tell me what to do? We hardly know each other. I don't need another mother, so you can stop worrying about me, what I do and who I do it with."

Her voice breaks and tears stream down her cheeks. "She's dead. Do you understand? I'd give anything to have her back. I know you don't care, you never cared, but I do. She loved me. What we had was special."

I should walk away but I don't. My anger won't let me. My cheeks are burning and I want to fly at her, slap her hard. I can't do it, but you don't need to hit someone to hurt them.

"There was nothing special about our mother. She was selfish and cruel. She didn't want us to be close. Not like proper sisters. She pushed me away so she could have you to herself."

Lottie wipes her tears with her sleeve and steps closer, right into my face.

"You bitch," she hisses. "Don't you dare. She warned me about you and she was right. She said you hated it when I came along. Hated that you weren't the centre of attention anymore. You were so consumed by jealousy she couldn't trust you not to hurt me. She was a kind and gentle person. The bond we had was special."

I move back, shaking my head. When I speak, I make sure my voice is calm. I want to change this fight into a serious discussion.

"You're fooling yourself. There was no special bond. She should have told you the truth years ago but that's her all over. You have a right to know the truth. You were adopted. She adopted you. She did. I think she wanted another child because I was such a disappointment. She had no partner and was probably too old anyway. I know you don't want to hear this but she wasn't your biological mother."

Lottie blinks hard. Her chest is heaving and for a moment I think she's going to slap my face.

"You liar," she snarls. "You're lying. What the hell is wrong with you? Why would you even say something like that? It's total bullshit."

I sigh softly. "I'm sorry Lottie, but it's true. You have a right to know and I'm not telling you this out of anger. I'm telling you because I love you. We can probably get copies of the adoption papers if you want. The fact that you're adopted makes no difference to me. I swear. You are my little sister. My family. You always will be."

I move to her and open my arms for a hug. She pushes me aside and runs down the stairs. I hear her sobbing loudly, then the front door slams. I walk back into my room and sit on the bed. I'm already regretting what I've done. It was cruel and childish but I couldn't help myself. I slip back under the duvet and lie awake, my heart trembling as I try to work out how I can put this right.

* * *

I sit up with a start, my face clammy with sweat, remembering that the next time I saw Lottie she was cold and still, pale and lifeless. Not there anymore.

I haul my mind back to the present. London is a vast, sprawling city and I'm sure I can live under the radar for a few weeks. It'd be better, though, if I could hole up in some out-of-the-way place.

To do that I'm going to need money. A lot of money. Something Matt said comes back to me. *An inheritance from a distant aunt.*

I'm wondering where he'd keep his wallet and bank cards, and whether I could search the house once he's asleep, when I hear someone murmuring downstairs. I open the door and walk out onto the landing.

The voice is louder but I still can't make out the conversation. As I rest a hand on the varnished banister, two words freeze my blood. *Detective Earl.*

I descend the stairs silently. Halfway down I see Matt standing with his back to me in the centre of the living room, talking on his mobile. I'm slammed by a feeling I haven't felt for a long time. Betrayal.

It comes back to me then, the moment I learned that I was adopted and that I would soon have a baby sister. The moment I knew I was surplus to requirements.

As I reach the bottom step, Matt turns. His head jerks up. His eyes widen. He's shocked because he's been caught out, and because I'm pointing a semi-automatic pistol right at him.

I feel the heat of rage but the blood in my veins is ice cold. The one person I thought I could depend on has let me down. Kind, caring, sympathetic Matt has abandoned me. Everyone abandons me.

He's still holding the phone and trying to speak but his mouth isn't working. His expression reminds me of my mother. I feel judged and found wanting. Again. Not good enough. A disappointment.

I lift the gun a little higher and pull the trigger. Matt's body jerks and crumples to the floor.

The explosion of gunfire has temporarily deafened me. I can't hear myself scream as I run across the room and kneel beside his body. An obscene amount of blood is pooling beside him, slick and shiny on the wooden floor.

Looking into his unseeing eyes, I mouth the word *sorry* and I mean it. I slip an arm behind his head, raise his body and hold him tight.

I can't explain how it's come to this. How I've killed a man who cared for me, who showed me kindness when I didn't deserve it. My brain screams get up and run. But running is futile.

The wailing of sirens cuts through my thoughts. I rise, slowly, walk down the hall and open the front door. I lift a hand to shield my eyes from the flashing blue lights.

Three armed police officers wearing full body armour point their weapons at me. "Armed police! Armed police! Raise your hands!"

CHAPTER 63

Earl

He enters the interview room with a glance at Akinola, who's sitting opposite the duty lawyer, a bespectacled man wearing a crumpled grey suit that matches his crumpled hair.

Miller doesn't acknowledge Earl, even when he sits down and looks directly at her across the table.

Most suspects look a little worse for wear after a night in a holding cell, but Miller is alarmingly pale and fragile.

Earl waits patiently. He's not going to speak until she looks at him. It's always a mistake to rush in. The lawyer squirms uncomfortably in his chair. In the end it's him who breaks the silence.

"I'd like to request a bit more time alone with my client," he says. "She appears to be a little distracted."

Miller straightens up quickly. "Sorry, I was miles away. I'm finding it hard to stay focused on anything nowadays."

Earl sits back and gives her an easy smile. He's confident they'll be able to get convictions for the kidnapping of the girl, the killing of Matt Lamb, arson and attempted murder. The evidence is plentiful and solid. He's less sure about the drugging of Daniel Sharpe because of the lack of forensic evidence. They have only his word for it, and the word of a man who's already been in jail, and may be going back there for lying to the police, can be all too easily challenged by an experienced defence barrister. He doesn't want the interview delayed if it can be avoided.

"What do you think?" he asks. "Are you ready to press on with the interview, or do you need more legal advice?"

Miller gives the lawyer a contemptuous sideways glance. "No, I'm fine. I'm not sure my legal expert here would approve if he knew what I'm about to say, so I don't believe there's much point in us having a conversation. Where would you like me to start?"

"What about the beginning?"

Miller smiles. "What a good idea. But first I'd like to state for the record that I admit it all."

The lawyer splutters and holds up a hand to prevent her saying more. "My client needs a break. She's clearly confused."

Miller turns to him. "Be silent, please," she says. "Let me have my say."

He stiffens, scowling hard as red blotches appear on his cheeks.

"I admit it all," Miller repeats. "I drugged Sharpe. I drugged his daughter and held her against her will. I shot Matt Lamb dead. I admit it all, but I also believe that I'm not guilty of anything. Not a single thing. Let me explain."

CHAPTER 64

Liv

I pause for a second. The air thickens with anticipation. Everyone is eager to hear what I have to say.

We're in an interview room I've never been in before. This one is slightly bigger than the others, the walls painted a darker blue. At ceiling level in one of the corners is a camera recording everything.

What I'm about to say could have a significant effect on the length of my prison sentence. I've had a lot of time to consider what my defence would be if I ended up being caught. From the moment I chose to hunt down Emily I knew that this is how it would end.

I spoke to the duty lawyer for half an hour, but it took me five minutes to work out that he, like Winnie the Pooh, is a person of very little brain. As soon as I can, I'll hire myself a high-powered barrister.

Earl opens his mouth to either prompt me or ask a question. I shut him down.

"Please wait. I need to say this without interruption. I want to be completely honest and tell you what happened to me, how my world changed for ever."

Earl clamps his mouth shut and lets his hands drop onto his lap. I take his silence as a sign that he's going to let me speak.

"It all started with the brain scan I had done for a feature on a study of the brains of psychopaths. Most neuroscientists agree that the structure of their brains differs from non-psychopaths and is determined in the womb. To make the feature less scientific and more accessible to the magazine's readership, I came up with the idea of getting the researchers to scan my brain to show readers how a 'normal' brain looks. Professor Noble, the scientist running the study, called me to his office to explain that far from being 'normal', my scan showed all the characteristics typically seen in brains of diagnosed, violent psychopaths."

I pause for effect again. Earl is frowning sceptically and itching to interrupt, so I move on quickly.

"As you might imagine, this news came as a shock. I'd never considered myself to be a violent person. Not then. Naturally, I panicked, but I was assured that my non-violent, law-abiding past showed that my propensity to psychopathic behaviour had never been triggered by environmental factors, that it was unlikely to ever be triggered and that nothing would change."

Earl is shaking his head slowly and I realize that I'm not going to be able to stop him interrupting this time. I pause and raise my eyebrows, inviting him to say what he's thinking.

"What has this to do with the charges you're facing? Whether you have the brain of a psychopath or not, it's irrelevant. Most people who end up in prison convicted of violent crime are not psychopaths. They're simply nasty, violent people."

It irks me that he hasn't the patience to let me explain a complicated issue. Before I can point that out to him, he asks, "And if this was what you were told about your brain scan, why tell Matt Lamb that you had cancer, and carry on the lie by pretending to be having treatment for a brain tumour?"

I drop my gaze to the table. Matt betrayed me but he didn't deserve to die. He probably thought he was doing the right thing. I don't believe it was me who fired the gun. I held it in my hand. I pointed it at his chest. Someone, or something, else pulled the trigger. This is why I need Earl to shut up and listen to what I have to say.

"I didn't want to lie to Matt but I was ashamed. That's why I never mentioned my brain scan in the finished article. Who would want everyone to know that they have the brain of a psycho? Matt was the person who sent me an email telling me Professor Noble wanted to speak to me. I had to tell him something. I can't explain why I came up with cancer. It was stupid of me."

Earl exchanges a look with Akinola, and I sense that he believes that I genuinely regret it. I really do. I stare thoughtfully up at the camera lens for a few seconds. I need to get my story told early, and I want to look convincing on the video.

"It's hard to explain but I'll do my best," I say. "I tried to forget what I'd learned about my brain, but it was impossible. I had to stop working because I couldn't think of anything else. I couldn't get a night's sleep because of worry. Crazy thoughts started whirring around in my brain. My psychopathic brain. In the end I thought maybe, instead of trying to push the knowledge away, I should embrace it, find the positive. I started going online to read about psychopaths and their traits. The result was I began to believe I had a whole new range of abilities at my disposal. But then I learned that Sharpe was about to be released from prison. Something flipped inside my head. I started having thoughts that weren't my own. Instead of getting angry, instead of complaining to the newspapers again and achieving nothing, why not use these newly discovered traits? Why not punish the bastard?"

Earl crosses his arms and sits back in his chair. His expression is thoughtful but not unhappy. He thinks I'm doing his work for him. Spilling my guts and convicting myself. He shouldn't make the mistake of underestimating me.

"To be absolutely clear," he says, "are you claiming voices in your head told you to kill Sharpe, to hold his daughter hostage and to shoot Matt Lamb?"

I laugh shakily. "I'm saying nothing of the sort. Please pay attention, Detective. I'm saying that those thoughts were coming from the psychopathic part of my brain, a secret part I had no knowledge of until I was told it was there. It started taking over, telling me to take risks, do things the old me would never even contemplate. I committed those crimes but I don't believe I'm guilty of them. I wasn't in control of my brain. My brain was controlling me."

I spread my hands and shrug, feeling proud of the way I've managed to explain why I shouldn't be held responsible for what I've done. I'm not sure whether it was the old me talking, or the secret me.

Earl stands up. It's clear he has something on his mind but he's not going to share it with us.

"I need to leave you in the capable hands of Detective Akinola for a few moments," he says.

Once he's gone, Akinola shifts across into his chair. Earl's departure makes me nervous. He's up to something and, although it's not saying much, I think he's definitely smarter than the average detective. Speaking of average detectives, Akinola is eyeing me like I'm her next meal.

"That all sounds very interesting," she says. "But didn't you say that Professor Noble told you not to worry, that nothing would change because your so-called psychopathic traits had never been triggered?"

I shake my head nonchalantly and smile. "You know, Detective, I live in hope that you're going to surprise me with an intelligent question, or a significant insight, but you always let me down. I don't suppose it's occurred to you that simply being told you have the brain of a psychopath can be a trigger?"

Akinola is still trying to make sense of my suggestion, when the door opens and Earl returns, his face flushed, a fresh urgency in his stride. He sits in the chair opposite the duty lawyer and fiddles nervously with the knot of his tie.

"How are you feeling?" he asks me. The question is both confusing and unnerving. I don't reply. My heart is thudding in my ears because it doesn't want me to hear what Earl is about to tell me.

"I've been speaking on the telephone with Professor Noble," he says, a softness in his voice I'd never heard before. "His version of your conversation is very different to yours. He says he called you to his office to tell you that your brain scan showed evidence of a tumour, and to advise you to seek medical help as soon as possible."

CHAPTER 65

Liv

I finally get my wish to ride in the back of a police car with the blue lights flashing and the siren screaming. It's not as much fun as I expected because I'm being rushed to hospital.

I've been told I have something in my brain that's not supposed to be there. Did it, I wonder, turn me into something I'm not supposed to be? If this is true, I've been living a lie. Feeling sorry for myself, I slump forward and cover my face with my hands. I want to cry but the tears won't come.

The way the uniformed police constable behind the wheel weaves through the traffic makes my stomach flip. At least, I think it's his driving. I suppose it could be shock that's causing this sick feeling.

I've hardly said a word since Earl announced I have a brain tumour. I've been trying hard to recall the details of the discussion I had with Professor Noble. The harder I try, the hazier the memory becomes.

Have I deceived myself? Did my brain conjure up this psychopath delusion as an act of self-protection? I thought I'd told the cruellest lie to the only person I trusted with the truth.

The car pulls up outside the Royal London Hospital's accident and emergency department and the stocky police constable in the passenger seat climbs out. She helps me slide along the seat to the door and step onto the pavement. While we wait for the driver to join us, she lifts my hands to check the handcuffs are still secure. I may be seriously ill and in urgent need of medical treatment, but I'm still a prisoner.

A police officer either side of me, I'm escorted into the hospital, where a weary-looking, overweight porter is already waiting with a wheelchair.

I want to insist on walking, but my legs are so shaky I don't trust them to hold me up. When the porter nudges the chair towards me, I give him a grateful nod.

Ten minutes later, I'm sitting on a bed in a ward side room, being questioned by a young doctor with glasses and a goatee. The police constable has removed the handcuffs and is sitting in the corner, trying her best not to nod off.

"So, how have you been feeling recently?" the doctor asks. "Any limb weakness, or speech difficulties?"

I want to tell him that there have been days when I've felt euphoric, even invincible. That sometimes I've been confused about exactly who and what I am. I'm tempted to explain that I've been reckless, aggressive, even murderous, and it's given me a sense of freedom I've never experienced before.

"I've not been too bad," I say. "I've noticed a loss of appetite, which has meant my weight has dropped a little. Sometimes I feel really tired and then I have unexplained bursts of energy."

The doctor frowns, lifts his clipboard and scribbles a note. "Have you been experiencing prolonged, severe head-aches, and maybe hallucinations?"

He's enjoying his work so much I feel a need to disap-point him. I shrug. "Nothing out of the ordinary."

"What about confusion and memory problems? Have you ever forgotten what day it is, where you are or where you're meant to be going?"

"I can't remember," I say, with a grin.

The doctor gives me a puzzled look and slips his pen into the breast pocket of his checked shirt.

"Right, good," he stutters. "We'll let you settle in, then. There's a clean hospital gown on the table there, and once you're in bed we'll take a blood sample. We'll give you a sedative so you can get a good night's sleep, and we'll arrange for a brain scan first thing in the morning. Once that's done, we'll get a consultant to take a look and he'll pop in to let you know the result. How does that sound to you?"

It sounds horrific, but I keep my opinion to myself. As soon as the doctor leaves the room, I pick up the pale-blue hospital gown, unfold it and lay it on the bed. The police constable is looking at me expectantly. I jab a finger at her, shaking my head.

"There's no way I'm stripping off while you're in the room. It's not happening."

She throws me a glare, stands up and picks up the chair. "I'll be right outside the door," she says. "I'll be there all night, and in the morning another officer will take my place. You're still officially under arrest and in police custody."

Once she's gone, I undress quickly, slip into the gown and climb into the bed. The mattress is thin and hard, the sheets crisp. Sitting up, I raise my knees and rest my forehead on them.

Despair is knocking on my door, but I won't let it in. I still harbour hope that the detective and the professor got their wires crossed. But if I had the choice between having a potentially fatal brain tumour, or the brain structure of a violent psychopath, I'd choose being a psycho every time.

* * *

The sedative injection worked a treat. I slept the sleep of the innocent. Still drowsy when they wheeled me out in the morning, I drifted off while lying in the scanning machine, despite the rhythmic clanging of the magnetic coils.

I'm back in my room in time for breakfast but turn down the opportunity to feast on cereal, yoghurt or porridge, settling instead for a cup of tea. As I swallow the last mouthful, the doctor with the goatee enters the room accompanied by a short Asian woman.

"This is Ms Chang," he says. "She's a consultant neurosurgeon and she's come to tell you what she's found on your scan."

I wasn't expecting to be told the results so quickly, and wonder whether this means the news is bad. I put the empty cup down on the bedside table and turn my attention to the consultant. She's standing straight-backed, in dark trousers and a white blouse, her delicate hands clasped at her waist.

I want her to like me, to do her best for me, and offer her a tight but genuine smile. She smiles back and steps closer to the bed.

"You do have a tumour in the prefrontal cortex of your brain," she says, her voice reassuringly matter-of-fact. "We don't know yet whether it's benign or malignant, but either way we are going to have to remove it surgically as soon as possible."

I let her words sink in and wait for fear to flood my veins, but it doesn't come. I've read psychopaths don't fear death, but that shouldn't apply to me. I'm not the psychopath I thought I was. I'm sick.

"Why do you need to operate so quickly? Surely medication would be safer?"

"The tumour is pressing on your amygdala, the region of the brain crucial for emotion and behavioural control. It has already damaged some tissue and we want to prevent more permanent damage being done."

I lie back on my pillow and take a deep breath. The beast in my head is not what I thought it was. I wasn't born with it. It's not part of me, it's an invader.

I look up at Ms Chang and ask the question. "Am I going to die?"

Now she smiles. "We're all going to die eventually, aren't we?"

278

She thinks she's being clever but she's not. She's being irritating. I say nothing and shut my eyes, hoping that when I open them Ms Chang and her bearded friend will have disappeared. I don't want to die, but if I survive this, I'm facing the prospect of a long prison sentence. Sometimes death can be a mercy.

CHAPTER 66

Four weeks later . . .

Sharpe

The visitors' centre has more natural light than any other room in the prison. The tables are evenly spaced. Five rows of four. Sharpe's eyes are drawn to the large windows, where he catches a glimpse a hazy spring sky.

He heads for a table in the far corner, wipes his hands on his yellow tabard and sits with his back to the wall. The other inmates take their places in silence, watched by four prison guards.

The atmosphere in the room is tense. A mixture of excitement and dread. Nobody can be sure their visitor hasn't had second thoughts and decided to stay at home. Sharpe knows from experience that even some of the toughest prisoners can be brought close to tears by a no-show.

All eyes turn at the sound of a door being unlocked, and the visitors stream in. Men and woman wave frantically across the room, and overexcited children shout at the top of their voices.

Sharpe spots Emily and beckons her over. She sits opposite him and clutches his hand.

"Thanks for coming," he says.

He's glad to see she's looking stronger than when he last saw her. The black circles under her eyes have faded. He's smiling at her, but her lips stay drawn tight.

"It's not right, you being in here. You've already served a prison sentence, for something you didn't even do. It's crazy."

Sharpe squeezes her hand and sits back in his chair. "I was released early on licence. My arrest on a charge of perverting the course of justice meant I'd breached the terms of that licence and had to be returned to jail immediately. I'm back in court in a couple of weeks and there's a good chance I'll be released. My lawyer says the time I've already served and the circumstances of my false confession will count for a lot."

Emily lifts her hands to her face and rubs her eyes. "That's great, but Mum's going to prison, isn't she? She's frightened, and I'm scared for her."

Sharpe leans forward and clasps both her hands in his. "She's stronger than you think. She's never been in trouble before and she's pleading guilty, which will go in her favour. There is a chance that she'll get a suspended prison sentence. If the worst happens, then we'll help her get through it. You're stronger than you think too."

A shaven-headed prison guard appears beside the table, glaring down at Sharpe. "That's enough," he snaps. "Hands."

Sharpe lets go of his daughter and turns his palms up for inspection. The guard grunts and turns away disappointed.

"He thought you were passing me drugs, or a mobile phone. There's a big problem with smuggling in this prison."

Emily ignores him. She doesn't want to change the subject. "She's putting on a brave face, but she's terrified of going to jail."

Sharpe resists the urge to stand up and hug her. "I persuaded her to go along with it, and everyone will see that she's genuinely remorseful. Don't forget her defence team will be able to use what happened to you. They will argue that you need your mother's support to recover from your ordeal. She has a chance. It may be slim, but it's there."

Emily shrugs and chews her bottom lip. "No matter what she did, I can't help feeling a little sorry for Liv Miller. She's ill. She's probably dying. I don't think she really knew what she was doing."

Sharpe nods. He agrees that, despite everything, Miller is a victim too.

Emily scans the room to check that all the guards are busy, reaches across the table and takes her father's hand again.

"When you're out, whatever happens to Mum, things are going to be different," she says. "I want to see you regularly, and there'll be no need to keep it secret. What you did for me, well, that proves something, doesn't it? Whatever happens, I'll never forget it."

Sharpe looks at his daughter and squeezes her hand.

"I'd do it all again, if I had to," he says.

CHAPTER 67

Earl

She looks better than Earl had expected. Wrapped in a light-blue dressing gown and perched on the edge of the hospital bed, she's even thinner than when he last saw her, waif-like. Her head is shaved and luridly scarred but her eyes are bright.

"Good morning, Detective," she says. "How kind of you to drop in. You have the dubious honour of being my first and probably last visitor."

Earl responds with a taut smile. He glances at the chair beside the bed but decides to stay standing. He's never felt sorry for a suspect facing attempted murder, kidnap and murder charges before.

"I'm told the surgery went well."

"Yes, they managed to get most of the Beast out," Miller says, grinning at Earl's frown. "Beast is my pet name for the tumour. As you can tell, I didn't die on the operating table, which is a result. For me, anyway. The surgeon was happy with the outcome. I'm sure you've seen all the medical reports and know that Beast was benign, so there's a good chance it won't grow back."

"I'm glad to hear it."

Miller crosses her arms and gives Earl a curious look. "Are you being completely honest, Detective? I guess you were rather hoping that I wouldn't make it, that the Beast would do your job for you. Any trial now is going to be far from straightforward, don't you think?"

Earl's eyes are drawn to the fresh scar running like a train track across the top of her forehead, curving back to the top of her ears. He imagines the surgeon peeling back the skin, removing a section of the skull, and cutting into her brain.

Miller lifts a hand and runs her fingers over her scalp. "I know I'm not looking my best at the moment, but, you know what, simply being alive makes me feel beautiful. As long as I choose the right hairstyle to hide this scar, I'll be as good as new in no time."

Earl has to admire the woman's resilience. She's a lot tougher than she looks. "I'd never wish you or anyone else dead," he says. "All I want is to do my job to the best of my ability, and that means putting criminals behind bars."

Miller tilts her head to one side and flashes him a grin. "That's the point, though, isn't it? Am I criminally responsible for what I did? If you've read the medical reports then you will have seen that the tumour altered my personality, changed my behaviour. The effect it had on the prefrontal cortex of my brain not only made me think I was a psychopath, it actually made me behave like one. There has to be a strong argument that I was in no way responsible for my actions, and I'm sure I can find several experts in the field to testify to that in court. The days drag in this place. I've had plenty of time to do my research. I think the best plea for me is temporary insanity caused by my illness."

Earl has read the medical reports. Several times. He knows the argument she makes is a powerful one. The Crown Prosecution Service has already suggested to Tanner that it may not be in the public interest to prosecute, that even if the case goes to trial it will be difficult to convince a jury that she knew what she was doing.

"How much longer do you expect to be in hospital?"

Miller shrugs cheerfully. "I'm getting stronger every day. In fact, they said they'd be happy to discharge me a week ago. The problem is, I have nowhere to go, and no one to go to. My sister was killed by a hit-and-run driver, some lunatic burned down my home and a delusional psychopath shot dead my boyfriend."

Earl can't tell whether she's joking or not. Either way, her attitude is a little disturbing.

"I'm here to officially inform you that you're no longer considered likely to abscond and have been granted police bail. You must let us know of any change of address and we will inform you as soon as any decision has been made on prosecution."

"Don't you worry," Miller says. "The Beast has gone and I'm a peace-loving, non-violent, law-abiding citizen again. A very lovely social worker is doing her best to find me somewhere to live, and as soon as she does, I'll let you know my new address."

Her cheery manner is starting to grate. She's unsettled Earl more than any other suspect he's dealt with. He's always believed in right and wrong, law and order, crime and punishment, good and evil. No grey areas.

Miller is making him reassess his beliefs. The ground beneath his feet is shifting. If a brain tumour transformed her into an out-of-control criminal, should she be held responsible?

If a person is born with a brain structure that means he or she will probably grow up to become a violent psychopath, then should they be demonized and punished when the inevitable happens? Miller is smiling sweetly at him, and he's not sure of anything anymore.

CHAPTER 68

Liv

I see doubt in the detective's eyes, but he keeps his thoughts to himself and leaves the room. He doesn't want to believe me because it means changing the way he thinks about the people he puts behind bars.

If biology is destiny, should psychopaths be blamed for who they are? I don't know the answer to that and neither does Earl. He's clearly struggling with the question. I don't care.

I lie back on the bed and put my hands behind my head. From the moment I opened my eyes in the recovery room after the operation, I've been buzzing. After everything that's happened to me, I'm ecstatic to still be here. To exist.

A few weeks ago, it would have been simple to convince myself that life without Lottie wasn't worth living. I take a long, deep breath and welcome the distinctive aroma of a hospital. The stench of sweat, disinfectant, blood and decay. If you can smell death, you're alive.

I fetch my mobile phone from the bedside table and skim through a selection of news websites. They all feature stories about Daniel Sharpe being sent back to prison after falsely confessing to mowing down Lottie.

Both the media and the public acknowledge that what he did was wrong, but clearly admire him for it all the same. They're calling for his release, and it looks as if they'll get what they want pretty soon.

I suppose I'm glad that he and the girl didn't perish in the fire. I never wanted that. Not really. I was angry and I wasn't in control. Not completely. Not like now.

The worst thing about the fire, apart from losing my home, is that all my clothes, my casual gear, my smart work outfits were destroyed. Hospital gowns definitely don't suit me at all.

One of the first things I'm going to do when I leave this place is get myself a whole new wardrobe. I fancy a completely fresh look. A style to suit the life I'm going to live when I finally get out of here.

Everything is going to be different. There's no getting away from that — Ms Chang, the consultant neurosurgeon, explained it all to me this morning. She kept it simple so I would understand.

The tumour affected the chemistry and connections in the prefrontal cortex of my brain. It caused the splitting headaches, but the other symptoms were more sinister. I didn't process what Professor Noble was actually telling me about my scan because I didn't want to hear it. The tumour was already making me delusional. Instead, I created a different crisis. I believed something else, imagined a false reality that explained the changes in my personality.

The surgery couldn't have gone better, Ms Chang said. Most of the tumour was successfully removed with minimal disturbance to the surrounding tissue. I will need regular checkups for a long time, but there is a good chance the problem will never return.

Then she hit me with the big *but*. Naturally, as it grew, the tumour damaged the amygdala and brain tissue around it. The damage is irreversible. That means the changes to my personality are irreversible.

The tumour made me behave like a psychopath. The surgery I had to remove it means there's no way back. Even so, I thanked Ms Chang for everything she and her team had done. They saved my life, after all.

She told me I can arrange sessions with a psychotherapist to help come to terms with what has happened. I agreed to give the offer of therapy serious consideration, but I was lying.

I put my phone back on the table, slide off the bed and walk across to the window. I am a changed woman. I may appear the same to the world, but the world looks very different to me now. It's there for the taking.

I know exactly who I am, what I am, what I'm capable of. It no longer frightens me. But I've a list of people who should be frightened. I can't wait to tick their names off, one by one.

THE END

Thank you for reading this book.

If you enjoyed it please leave feedback on Amazon or Goodreads, and if there is anything we missed or you have a question about, then please get in touch. We appreciate you choosing our book.

Founded in 2014 in Shoreditch, London, we at Joffe Books pride ourselves on our history of innovative publishing. We were thrilled to be shortlisted for Independent Publisher of the Year at the British Book Awards.

www.joffebooks.com

We're very grateful to eagle-eyed readers who take the time to contact us. Please send any errors you find to corrections@joffebooks.com. We'll get them fixed ASAP.